Loving the Marquess

Suzanna Medeiros

OTHER BOOKS BY SUZANNA

Dear Stranger

Landing a Lord series
Dancing with the Duke
Loving the Marquess
Beguiling the Earl—summer 2013

Hathaway Heirs
Lady Hathaway's Indecent Proposal—spring 2013

DEDICATION

To Neil, with all my love.

CONTENTS

ACKNOWLEDGMENTS

I want to say a great big thank you to Aida Amaral, Maureen Frew and Maria Medeiros for all your input on this book. A special thank you goes out to Maaike van der Leeden for encouraging me when self-doubt threatened to take hold.

And thank you to my family for your continued love and support.

CHAPTER ONE

Kent
1806

A knock at the door in the middle of the night never brought good news. Casting a longing glance at the welcoming bed she'd been about to sink into, Louisa Evans tied the sash of her dressing gown. Pushing aside the weariness that dragged at her, she hurried downstairs.

She expected to find one of her neighbors when she opened the door and was surprised to find, instead, a stranger. A very tall man with dark hair who sagged against the door frame, his eyes closed. She shivered as the cool autumn air cut through her nightgown and dressing gown.

"Can I help you?" she asked.

When he didn't reply, she wondered if he were foxed and had somehow stumbled across their cottage. She placed a hand on his arm to gain his attention and repeated her question.

His eyes opened and he pinned her with a gaze that was dark and penetrating.

"I require assistance..." he managed to say before closing his eyes again.

He swayed slightly and started to slide down the doorframe. Moving instinctively, Louisa had her shoulder under his arm in a moment, steadying him as he collapsed. He was much larger than she, and for a second she thought she would collapse with him.

She straightened and stared down, stunned, at where he sat propped against the doorframe. Hesitating only a moment, she leaned over him to smell his breath and detected a faint hint of alcohol. She brought a hand to his forehead and was alarmed to find he had a fever.

Another blast of the night air, uncharacteristically cold this early in September, had her shivering in earnest now. She would have to move the stranger inside and close the door. She didn't know what was wrong with him, but with his fever he couldn't afford to catch a chill. She wasn't strong enough, however, to carry him inside on her own.

Her decision made, she hurried upstairs and rapped on her brother's door. When he didn't answer, she entered the room and shook him awake.

"What's the matter?" he mumbled, his eyes still closed.

"I need your help. There's a man downstairs who is ill. He collapsed on our doorstep."

John jolted awake at the mention of the stranger. At eighteen, he was seven years younger than her, but since their father had died, he'd decided it was his duty to protect the family.

He dressed quickly and followed her downstairs to where the man sat, still propped up, in their doorway.

"Who is he?"

Louisa shook her head. "I don't know, but he's ill and

the cold can't be good for him. Help me bring him inside so I can close the door."

They managed to rouse the man enough to help him to his feet, supporting his weight between them. He was unsteady and their progress was slow, but at her insistence they managed to bring him to her room, still warm from her recently banked fire. He collapsed on her bed with a groan.

"I'll see to his comfort," she told John. "I saw a horse outside that must belong to our guest. The animal will need to be cared for."

John set his shoulders and she knew he was going to insist that she look after the horse. She cut him off before he could protest the impropriety of the situation.

"Do you actually believe this man is in any condition to do me harm?"

Her brother hesitated, but it was clear the stranger had lost consciousness. Grumbling something under his breath about bossy sisters, he turned and left to see to the horse.

Louisa occupied herself with rebuilding a fire in the small fireplace before turning to look at the man lying on her bed. Despite her assurances to her brother, she was nervous. She'd nursed their father during his long illness, but caring for this man was nowhere near the same.

She approached the bed and looked down at him, and her heart fluttered as she realized just how handsome he was. His hair was a dark brown, almost black, framing a face that had no doubt caused many other hearts to beat faster, as well. Despite his fever, he was very pale, his skin drawn taught over high cheekbones and a strong jaw that was already showing a hint of stubble.

She swallowed hard as her gaze traveled down the

length of him. He was asleep, but his presence filled the room. She shook her head to clear it and turned away, telling herself that caring for this man would be no different than caring for her father as she went to her washstand and poured water from the pitcher into the washbasin. Concentrating on the familiar task, she set the basin on her bedside table, dipped a washcloth into the water, and wrung it out. Her hands were not quite steady as she washed his face, hoping the cool water would bring him a measure of comfort. Her movements were brisk, but slowed when he moaned. His eyes opened and she froze as his black, inscrutable gaze caught and held hers.

She was spiraling downward, drowning in twin pools of darkness. The heat in the room seemed to increase as a flush spread through her body. The seconds ticked by, seeming to stretch into minutes.

Without another sound, the stranger's eyes closed again. She dragged in a shaky breath and shook off the paralysis that had stolen over her. She could not, however, shake off her sense of unease.

Her hands were still shaking when she dropped the damp cloth into the basin. Pushing aside her trepidation, she moved to the bottom of the bed to remove his boots. She hesitated only a moment before placing one hand on the heel of the black leather molded to his right leg and the other on his knee. A jolt of awareness surged through her at the contact and she jerked back. Her gaze flew to the stranger's face, and she breathed a sigh of relief when she saw he was still asleep. She would have died of mortification if he'd seen her foolish reaction to touching him.

She tugged off his boots before turning her attention to

removing his coat, but she knew her bravery did not extend that far. Her bedcovers were already turned down and it took only a couple of tugs to free them completely from under his legs. Concentrating on the blankets and not on his form, she covered him before exhaling the breath she'd been holding. Most of him was now hidden from sight, but she found it impossible to ignore the keen sense of awareness brought on by the knowledge that a very attractive man now slept in her bed.

Trying to ignore the less than chaste thoughts that rose, unbidden, to her mind, Louisa retrieved a blanket for herself from the trunk at the foot of her bed and settled into a chair to wait. When John returned from seeing to their unexpected guest's horse, he tried to insist on taking her place, but if the stranger's condition took a turn for the worse, John wouldn't know what to do. He helped her to remove the man's coat and loosen his cravat before returning to his own room, but only after extracting her promise to fetch him when the man woke.

It was a long night. The stranger's slumber was restless—interrupted, at first, by frequent bouts of thrashing and murmured words that were indecipherable. Eventually, he settled into a deep sleep and she was able to close her eyes and get some rest. She had just drifted off when a low moan woke her. She struggled up from her cramped position in the armchair by the bedside, and her blanket slid to the floor.

"Papa? Do you need anything?" she asked, disoriented after being pulled from the middle of a strange dream.

But the man lying in the bed, *her* bed, wasn't her father. She was confused for a moment and then the memories rushed back. After a year of failing health, her father had finally succumbed to death six months before. She leaned back in the chair and examined the stranger more closely in the faint morning light. She hadn't dreamt him after all.

The fire had long since gone out and she shivered in the cool morning air. She picked up the blanket from where it had fallen, wrapped it around her shoulders, and took the few steps to the bed. Leaning forward, she laid a hand on the man's forehead and breathed a sigh of relief when she found his temperature was normal.

She looked over at the window where the first rays of morning light were already creeping over the horizon and sighed softly. So much for a good night's rest, she thought as she began to work the kinks from her knotted muscles.

Nicholas Manning's head was killing him, but he was used to that. He raised a hand to rub at his temples, hoping to massage away the pain. Unable to stop himself, his thoughts went back to that time a few years ago, before his parents' deaths. They'd been content, their love still evident even after more than thirty years of marriage. But then his father started complaining of headaches and his health began to deteriorate rapidly. Nicholas had spent most of his time in London, away from Overlea Manor, but he'd witnessed his father's strange moods and increasing surliness on several occasions. Had witnessed how his father had pushed away all who'd loved him before the accident that had taken both of his parents' lives.

He remembered, too, how his older brother had developed the same mysterious ailment last year. An ailment that had led to his death.

His father had been sixty when he'd first started

complaining about headaches. His brother's attacks had started much earlier, at the age of thirty-two, and his illness had progressed more quickly. Nicholas was only twenty-eight, but he could no longer ignore the fact he was now showing signs of suffering from that same disease.

Pushing back his grim thoughts, he opened his eyes and squinted against the bright light streaming through the window. He began to sit up but froze when he took in the unfamiliar surroundings.

Vague images filtered back to him, most of them featuring a blond-haired, gray-eyed woman hovering over him. He frowned, trying to remember what had happened the night before, but his memory eluded him.

He surveyed the room around him. Where was he? Not in his London townhouse. He remembered receiving a letter from his grandmother the day before. While not unusual, his grandmother's letters were rare enough to make him wary since she never bothered him with good news.

He closed his eyes and concentrated on the memory. He'd arrived home yesterday afternoon, and a footman had presented him with the letter. He remembered wondering what bad news he was about to read as he proceeded to his study and threw the letter on the desk. He'd poured himself a brandy before picking up the letter again and breaking the seal.

And that was all. Try as he might, he couldn't remember what his grandmother had written. Nor could he remember anything after that. He must have read the letter. He always did. He'd learned long ago there was no point in putting off bad news.

He opened his eyes at the sound of the door opening to

find a woman standing there. Could this be the woman he remembered hovering over him last night? She was younger than he'd thought—not yet twenty if his guess was correct. Her long blond hair, tousled from sleep, trailed over her shoulders.

He frowned. Had he spent the night with her? He must have been truly out of his head, because he didn't usually dally with girls who were barely out of the schoolroom.

She was rubbing the sleep from her eyes when she entered. When her gaze met his, she froze. Her eyes were blue and wide with shock. Then, to his surprise, she opened her mouth and screamed.

Well, this was different. He'd made many women shriek in his day, but usually with pleasure.

CHAPTER TWO

Louisa had just finished setting the breakfast table when she heard the scream. So much for calmly explaining to her sister what had happened the previous night. Catherine was already awake and she must have gone to her room and discovered the man sleeping in Louisa's bed.

Her sister burst through the dining room door moments later.

"Louisa," Catherine said, her voice urgent as she came to an abrupt stop. "There's a man in your room. In your bed!"

Her sister's distress was genuine and Louisa tried to keep her voice soothing. "Sit down."

Catherine followed Louisa's orders and took a seat at the dining room table, her confusion clear. "You're not surprised." It seemed to take a few moments for that realization to sink in. "Why aren't you surprised?"

The door burst open again and they both turned to see their brother standing in the doorway. He was barefoot, wearing only trousers, a pistol clutched in his hand.

"What happened?" he asked, looking anxiously at the two of them. "Did he try to hurt you?"

Catherine's bewildered gaze went from John to Louisa, then back again. "Will someone tell me what is happening? Who is that man and why is he in Louisa's bed?"

"Calm down, both of you." Turning to her brother, Louisa pointed at his weapon. "Tell me you didn't go into my room with that thing."

"Excuse me," John said, his voice dripping with annoyance. "There's a strange man in the house, one you insisted on watching over all night without any help from me, so I loaded the pistol in case we should need it. Upon hearing one of my sisters scream, I don't know why I thought to investigate. When I found neither of you in the room, I came looking for you."

Louisa grimaced, imagining the scene.

"Well, you can put the firearm away now while I explain everything to Catherine. She was merely surprised."

With a parting glare at her, John left the room. Louisa turned to face her sister, who was staring at her, eyes wide with curiosity.

"Who is he?"

Louisa pulled out the chair across from her sister and sat.

"I don't know. He knocked at our door after everyone had gone to bed. He was ill and asked for our assistance."

"Why did you wake John and not me?"

"He'd collapsed, Catherine. I needed John's strength to help bring him to my room. And before you ask," she continued, seeing the question in her sister's eyes, "we brought him there because I'd only just put out the fire. It was late and my room was the only one that was still warm."

While her sister was mollified, Louisa could tell she was still annoyed at being left out of the night's excitement.

"How long is he going to be here?"

"As long as necessary."

"But how can we afford that? There's barely enough food for us and he doesn't look like the kind of person who eats little."

"We'll manage. We always have," Louisa said, standing. She started toward the kitchen to get their breakfast. "Besides, we may be able to get by with spooning some broth into him until he is better. He tossed and turned for most of the night and I have no idea when he'll wake."

"Oh, he's awake now."

Louisa spun around at the casual comment. "What?" she asked, trying to ignore the fluttering sensation in her stomach Catherine's news had elicited.

"He's awake," Catherine said. "What's for breakfast?"

Their mysterious guest was awake. She should go see him, find out who he was and how he was feeling. After Catherine and John's visits to her room this morning, he probably thought he'd wandered into a house filled with bedlamites.

She started for the door.

"Louisa?"

"What?"

A knowing smile touched Catherine's lips. "Never mind," she said, amusement evident in her tone. "You have more important things to look after than breakfast. Or should I say, more handsome things?"

Louisa left her sister without bothering to reply and

headed for her bedroom. At seventeen, Catherine was at the age where her thoughts often turned to her future husband. With the scarcity of eligible bachelors in the village and the knowledge they would never have a proper Season in London, she tended to latch onto every new face as a candidate for either her or her sister's affections.

When Louisa reached her room, she hesitated only briefly before pushing aside her nervousness and entering. She closed the door softly behind her and turned to face the man lying in her bed. Her breath froze. She was no longer certain he was as harmless as she'd have her brother believe. On the contrary, the man on her bed seemed too large for her small room and more than a little dangerous.

He was leaning casually against the headboard, his arms folded in front of a broad chest, his legs crossed at the ankles. He'd straightened his clothes, which molded lovingly to his body, but his cravat hung limply around his neck, revealing a tantalizing glimpse of skin at the base of his throat. His dark brown hair was tousled from his restless sleep, a lock falling across his brow. It was his eyes, though, that struck her most. Dark, unreadable and trained on her.

She tried to speak, to breach the heavy silence that hung between them, but she was captive to that gaze. Mercifully, he released her when he dragged his eyes down her figure. She became acutely conscious of her serviceable and long-out-of-fashion dress.

"How are you this morning?" she finally managed in a voice she hoped didn't reveal how much he'd disturbed her.

"I'm not sure. Why don't you tell me?"

"You don't appear to have suffered any ill effects."

His mouth quirked at that. "That good, were you?"

Louisa shook her head, confused by his obvious amusement.

"I had nothing to do with it."

Her words seemed to have a strange effect on him. His gaze traveled over her again, more thoroughly this time, and heat sprang to her cheeks. Then, to her surprise, he crooked a finger and whispered "come here" in a tone that sent a shiver down her spine.

"Excuse me?"

"Come here. I need you."

Worry overcame her unease. He seemed much better than he'd been last night, but he might have injuries that weren't obvious to the eye. She hadn't examined him that closely after her brother had removed his coat and left them alone. She rushed to his side and before she realized his intention, he grabbed her hand and tumbled her onto his lap. She froze, stunned, and their eyes locked.

"Why don't you refresh my memory about last night? I seem to be a little vague on the details."

As if in slow motion, his head tilted and descended toward her. Surprise kept her still when his mouth touched hers, his lips softly playing over her own. She opened her mouth to protest, but his tongue intruded and all reason fled.

She'd had a suitor before, when her father was still healthy, and they had shared a few kisses, but those kisses were nothing to this one. She should have been shocked at the intimacy of his tongue moving against hers, exploring her mouth. Instead, she found herself sinking against him and reveling in the feel of his strong arms around her. She moved her own tongue along his and his answering groan caused something new to stir within her.

His mouth left hers to travel across her cheek, then down the column of her throat, and waves of sensation roiled through her. The feel of his hand on her breast was a welcome relief, both soothing the aching need within her while stoking the flames higher. She clutched at his shoulders and shifted to give him better access. When his other hand traveled up the length of her leg and reached the bare skin above her stockings, however, she came crashing back to reality. What on earth was she doing? She pushed against his chest and scrambled off the bed when his grip loosened, ashamed of having forgotten herself so easily.

Cheeks flaming, struggling to right her breathing, she braved a glance at the man in her bed. His own breathing was as ragged as hers and he looked even more dangerous than when she'd entered the room.

"Surely you'll not deny me after last night?" His tone was short, his annoyance clear.

Confused, Louisa could only stare at him. Then understanding dawned.

"You don't remember what happened last night."

That was it, of course. His behavior now made sense. Not remembering what had happened, he'd jumped to the only logical conclusion as to why he'd be in a woman's bed. She, unfortunately, had no such excuse for her own behavior.

Very conscious of her shameful reaction to him, she rushed to explain.

"You came to our house late last night. You were ill, unable to stand, and had a fever. My brother and I thought it best to bring you here where you could rest. I was afraid

14

it might take you some time to recover, but I see now I needn't have worried."

She realized she was babbling and stopped talking. His gaze was intent upon her and she had to resist the urge to squirm.

"Yes, well," he said after several moments, "I'll thank you now and be on my way." He swung his legs over the side of the bed.

"No," Louisa said, rushing forward to lay a restraining hand on his shoulder. His gaze moved from her hand back to her face and one corner of his mouth quirked upward.

Reading his thoughts clearly, she dropped her hand and took a step back. She may have allowed him to kiss her once, but she'd been taken by surprise. There would be no repeat performance, a fact he'd do well to realize.

"You were very ill last night. You need to eat something to rebuild your strength. I'll bring you a tray."

He regarded her silently. She tried to imagine what he was thinking, but his expression was shuttered. She was about to leave to fetch his breakfast when he finally spoke.

"It appears I have misread the situation, and for that I apologize."

He stood and Louisa held her breath, watching for signs of weakness or fatigue. There were none.

"I suspect I was in no condition last night to formally introduce myself. The Marquess of Overlea, at your service," he said with a brief bow.

She could feel the color drain from her face. She stood very still, trying to calm her heart, which was now racing for a very different reason.

She didn't bother to return his courtesy when she replied. Instead, she straightened her spine and looked him squarely in the eye.

"I am Louisa Evans, my lord," she said, pleased that her voice was even. "I believe you have already met my brother, John, and my sister, Catherine."

He recognized her name and she could see it gave him pause. He recovered right away, but there was no doubt he knew what his family had done to hers.

"We haven't been formally introduced, but yes, I have had the pleasure."

She was amazed at how he could keep his manner so calm after being accosted first by a screaming woman, then by a madman with a pistol. Especially since he now knew the identity of the family who had taken him in. Yet there he stood, calmly facing her as though his family hadn't completely ruined hers.

"I heard about your father's death and I'd like to extend my condolences."

She could tell his words were sincere. His own parents had died two years before in a carriage accident and then he'd lost his only brother last year after a mysterious illness. Other than his grandmother, he was now alone. They shared a brief, unexpected moment of silent commiseration.

"I'll return in a few minutes," Louisa said before turning to leave.

"There's no need. I'll join you downstairs shortly."

She was about to protest, but when she looked back at him she could see from his expression that he would brook no argument.

She was gone. Nicholas sank onto the bed and cradled his head in his hands. Damn his headache. He'd almost disgraced himself in front of her, but had somehow managed not to sway on his feet.

She'd been right to insist he eat something before leaving. Each headache he endured took more out of him than the last. This one was the worst yet. He'd never lost consciousness before. He had a sudden image of his brother in agony, lying on his deathbed, but pushed it out of his mind. He was still alive and refused to give in to despair. He would enjoy what time remained, be it days, months, or years.

He turned his thoughts, instead, to Louisa Evans and experienced an uncharacteristic twinge of regret. It was bad enough he'd collapsed in her presence, an image he would not allow himself to contemplate, but remembering how he had taken her for a lightskirt was too much. Especially after what his uncle had already done to her family.

He would have to make it up to her. Thank her properly for taking care of him and for being so understanding about his error in judgment. Any other woman would have thrown him out on his ear. He couldn't imagine why she hadn't.

From his disjointed memories of the night, he knew she'd worn her fair hair loose about her shoulders. It was up now, but a few tendrils had escaped during their kiss. He remembered the uncertainty in her wide, gray eyes when she'd first entered the room. Those same eyes had darkened with desire when he'd kissed her. The memory of her response caused his body to tighten again.

She was obviously a passionate woman, but he could tell from their kiss that she was also an innocent one. He wouldn't take advantage of her. His family had already done hers enough harm.

He stood again, more slowly this time, and was relieved to find his moment of weakness had passed. With a bit of luck his strength would hold.

CHAPTER THREE

Louisa made it down the hallway, her legs threatening to give way with each step, before sagging against the wall for support.

Nicholas Manning, the new Marquess of Overlea, was in her house.

The Mannings were responsible for her family's diminished situation. She remembered it clearly, as though it had just happened. How Henry Manning, the marquess's uncle, had taken advantage of her father in a weak moment.

She'd been eight when her mother, who hadn't fully recovered after John's very difficult birth, died giving birth to Catherine one year later. Their father had shut himself in his bedroom for a whole week following the funeral while a neighbor stayed to look after them. At the end of that week, no longer able to bear the loss of her one remaining parent's company, Louisa had gone to him. Since he never opened his bedroom door when she knocked, she'd worked up the courage to walk in without knocking. She'd found him asleep in a chair, his beard overgrown, hair unkempt and an empty glass balanced precariously on one knee. She'd woken him, expecting her customary hug. Instead, he'd ordered her to leave the room. She'd left, shocked he had yelled at her. Her father never yelled. Worse, however, was the fact that he had raised his hand as though he'd been about to strike her.

She'd run to her room, thrown herself on her bed, and cried. Before long, her father came to her, gathered her into his arms, and promised to take care of them. That he'd never drink again.

He'd kept that promise until the night, years later, when Henry Manning had come across her father in the village. She remembered vividly the shame in her father's face when he'd later recounted what happened. They had started discussing her mother and Manning had taken him to the tavern and ordered a round of drinks. Not wishing to insult him, her father had decided there was no harm in having one drink. It had been almost ten years since Mama's death and he hadn't touched a drop in all that time. But one drink had turned to two, then three, and finally he'd lost count.

Louisa remembered how Henry Manning had brought him home, none the worse himself for having spent hours drinking with her father. She'd been angry at his smug demeanor that night. That anger had turned to despair the next day when he'd arrived to tell them they had one week to gather their belongings before he took possession of their home and their lands. He'd produced the promissory note her father signed the previous evening, and ashamed, her father had confessed what he'd done. He'd allowed Manning to talk him into joining a card game that was in full swing at an adjoining table. Losing steadily, he'd become more and more reckless with each drink until he'd lost everything. He'd behaved like an immature youth squandering his newly acquired inheritance.

They'd moved out of their manor house one week later, taking only what they could fit into the much smaller cottage Manning allowed them to have on the border of what had once been their estate.

"What's the matter?"

John's voice brought Louisa back to the present. She could see the concern on her brother's face and briefly considered not telling him what she'd learned. She quickly discarded the notion, though, knowing he'd find out soon enough.

"Our guest," she said, glancing quickly at her closed bedroom door. She lowered her voice so Overlea wouldn't overhear them. "I know who he is."

"And…?" John prompted when she paused.

There was nothing for it but to tell him straight out. "The new Marquess of Overlea."

John swore and started for her room. She threw herself into his path to stop him.

"What are you planning to do?"

"Throw the swine out on his ear, as he deserves."

"Lower you voice. He'll hear you."

"That was my intent," he said, his voice now louder.

Throwing her weight against him, she pushed her brother back into his room. Once there, she closed the door and leaned against it, barring his exit. She was surprised he'd allowed her to stop him, but her surprise turned to concern when he walked to his side table and picked up the loaded pistol that rested there.

"You are not throwing him out. He may be seriously injured from his fall."

"I don't care. I'm the head of the family now. Father never allowed a Manning in this house while he was alive, and nothing has changed now that he's gone." He took a step toward her. "Move away from the door, Louisa."

She was determined her brother would not have his way in this.

"I'm the eldest here," she said. "I've run this household for years now, and I'll continue to do so. I will not throw an injured man out on the road."

"Pity the Mannings have no such qualms."

"Overlea is no danger to us in his current condition. And in any case, he cannot be blamed for something his uncle did years ago, no more than you are to blame for Father's behavior the night he gambled away our home."

A flush of anger crept up his face, but she knew she'd made her point. As long as her brother never learned about what had transpired between her and the marquess in her bedroom, he wouldn't confront Overlea.

Breakfast was a tense affair. Louisa kept expecting her brother to say something harsh to the marquess and couldn't relax. He surprised her by holding his tongue, but what was more surprising was Catherine's silence. From the looks she cast in Overlea's direction, it was clear her sister was curious about their guest, but she seemed determined to remain faithful to their father's edict that all Mannings be treated as the enemy.

Louisa tried to fill the silence with small talk but gave up after a few attempts. The stilted conversation was almost worse than the silence. Overlea sat next to her and his presence made it difficult for her to concentrate on anything else. She caught herself watching his hands as he held his cutlery and her thoughts drifted back to how those same hands had felt on her breast and high on her thigh. Blushing, she forced her eyes away and tried to keep them on her still-full plate.

Overlea took their silence in stride, behaving as though nothing were out of the ordinary. When he'd first arrived downstairs she'd been acutely embarrassed by the fact that he'd soon learn how far they'd fallen. Even the poorest of genteel families had at least one servant, and she had no doubt this was the first time he'd ever stepped foot in a household that had none. She'd seen his surprise when he noticed the absence of servants, but he'd quickly masked it. If he had any disdain for the simple manner in which they lived, he didn't show it.

"Would you like some more, my lord?" she asked when she noticed his plate was empty.

She started to stand to tend to him, but Overlea's hand on her arm stopped her. He released her immediately, but she could still feel the imprint of his fingers. She didn't miss John's frown or Catherine's interested expression.

"I've already imposed on you too much."

Her thoughts flew back to the incident upstairs and she wondered if he was remembering it as well.

"Your horse," she said far too loudly.

He raised a brow at the abrupt change in subject and there was a heavy moment of silence before Overlea replied. "He should know his way home from here since it isn't too far. Of course, that would mean I'd have to impose further and ask if you know of another means of transportation."

"Oh, he's still here," Louisa said. "You needn't worry;

he's in the barn out back. John took care of him last night."

Overlea inclined his head and stood. "I'll go see to him now, then."

He took a step, stumbled, and reached for the back of the chair to steady himself. His eyes closed briefly and a grimace of pain flickered across his face. Louisa rushed to his side and braced her arm across his back. She returned the scowl John gave her with one of her own before turning her attention back to Overlea.

"Would you like me to help you upstairs?"

He stiffened and stepped away from her. "That's quite all right. It was just a brief twinge. You needn't concern yourself."

With that he turned and was gone.

Louisa turned immediately to John. "What is the matter with you?"

"You shouldn't be tending him. The new marquess has a reputation as a rake."

"How can you say that?" She was astounded by his stubbornness. "He is clearly still suffering from whatever illness caused him to collapse and you're concerned about his reputation?"

His hands were clenched into fists. "No, Louisa. My concern is for *your* reputation."

Louisa returned to her chair, looking away so her brother wouldn't see that his remark had struck home. He was right. Both Catherine's reputation and her own were at risk, but what other choice did they have? She couldn't send Overlea away, not until he was well enough to travel. After seeing him stumble, she didn't think that would be today.

Sighing, she reached across the table, took hold of John's hand, and squeezed it gently. "Your concerns are valid, I won't deny it, but we can't turn him out of the house when he is unwell. Surely you see that."

John pulled his hand from hers. "I'm not completely heartless, but I don't like having him here." He leaned forward, elbows on the table, shoulders slumped. "Papa would know what to do."

"Papa would agree with me," she said. She turned to include Catherine in their conversation. "I don't want either of you to worry. My reputation will survive as long as both of you are here."

She wouldn't think about the kiss she and Overlea had shared upstairs. It had been a mistake and would never happen again.

"I still don't like it," John mumbled.

Louisa let the comment go. "You two have things to do." She stood and began to clear the table. A quick glance at the clock told her it was already eight. "You'll be late for your lessons, John." They both knew how much Reverend Harnick disliked tardiness.

She watched as her brother finished the last of his eggs and, without another word, left. He was eighteen and should already have left for university. They couldn't afford it, but Reverend Harnick assured them John would be able to attend on a scholarship. After their father's death, however, John had been reluctant to leave Louisa and Catherine alone, and so, for now, he continued his studies under the reverend's tutelage.

"And you," she said, turning to Catherine, "there's mending to be done."

Catherine wrinkled her nose in distaste. "Someone will

miss the marquess while he is here."

She'd been so off-center since his arrival that it hadn't occurred to Louisa that Overlea's grandmother might be expecting him. Everyone in the area knew he'd been in London for the past few months. The fact he was here now could only mean he'd been on his way to his country seat, not far from their cottage. And even if his grandmother hadn't been expecting him, someone else would know about his movements and wonder where he was.

"Maybe we should send a note," Catherine continued.

"Yes, of course," Louisa said. "I'll speak to Lord Overlea about that. But for now, off with you."

Louisa sat heavily after her sister left the dining room. Why had she not thought about Overlea's grandmother? She would need to be told where he was. What was wrong with her?

But she knew exactly what was wrong with her. He was. Nicholas Manning, the new Marquess of Overlea, muddled her thinking. Confused her. That kiss upstairs was clear proof of that. She never should have allowed it, let alone permitted it to go as far as it had. She would have immediately put a stop to his liberties if it had been anyone else, but Overlea had a strange effect on her. One she did not like.

The soft chiming of the sitting room clock interrupted Louisa's concentration. She looked up from the sewing in her lap to see that it was already noon. Catherine had long since abandoned the mending to go work in the garden. It was her favorite place to be, and now that autumn was upon them and the gardening season was coming to an end, she spent most of her free time outside.

Louisa looked down at the morning dress she was working on, admiring the pale green muslin. Since her father's illness, she'd supported her family by taking in sewing. She didn't earn enough for extras, but at least the necessities were covered. She hadn't mentioned it to either of her siblings, but most of the sewing she took in was for the family who was responsible for their diminished situation. The dress to which she was currently adding the finishing trim was for Overlea's cousin, Mary Manning.

She couldn't be sure why the family allowed Louisa to make some of her dresses. They certainly had enough money to use only the finest modistes in London. While they did just that for the majority of Mary Manning's clothing, Overlea's aunt liked having Louisa make some of her daughter's day dresses. Louisa tried to convince herself that Elizabeth Manning did so to make amends in some small way for how her husband had ruined the Evans family and did her best to ignore the small voice that whispered the older woman had no such motives. That, instead, she enjoyed flaunting their position of superiority over Louisa's family. In the end, Elizabeth Manning's motivation didn't matter since Louisa relied heavily on the income her sewing brought in.

Unable to resist, she stood and held the dress against her. Closing her eyes, she twirled once, imagining what it would be like to own such a dress again instead of the dull, serviceable gowns she normally wore.

She opened her eyes and sighed deeply. She was being frivolous, hoping for things that could never be.

"That color suits you, Miss Evans."

Louisa spun around to find Overlea standing in the

sitting room doorway, one shoulder propped casually against the door frame. His glance swept over her and heat rose to her cheeks. She started to raise a hand to her hair, conscious of the tendrils that had escaped their pins, but stopped short.

"Thank you," she said.

To give herself time to regain her composure, she folded the dress with care and placed it on the settee next to the sewing basket before facing Overlea again.

He seemed to be studying her. "Is something the matter?" he asked when he finally spoke.

Other than the fact she had been caught preening like a silly school girl, Louisa thought, with a dress that was not and could never be hers, what could possibly be the matter?

"No, nothing, my lord. You need not concern yourself with me. But what about you? How are you feeling?"

At her words, his jaw tightened and a mask came down over his features. The warmth and concern she'd seen in his eyes only moments before was gone.

"I'm fine."

He entered the room and crossed to the window, his back to her.

She was not convinced he was telling her the truth. "Is there anything I can do for you?"

"Thank you, but no." He turned to face her, his hands clasped behind his back. "I have decided to return home. There are matters there that require my attention."

"When?"

"Now. After I take my leave of you."

She could only stare at him for several moments. The marquess had stumbled after breakfast, proving to everyone he was not completely recovered, and now he intended to ride home? Surely even he could see such an action would be foolhardy.

"Are you certain you are feeling up to it? Only this morning—"

"Yes," he said, an edge of impatience in his tone. "I am aware of what happened this morning. It was nothing."

"But—"

"Surely I do not have to explain myself to you?"

His words hit her like a slap, stopping her cold. The man who stood before her now was not the same person with whom she had shared breakfast that morning. He certainly wasn't the person who had understood the pain of having lost a father. The man she had found herself beginning to like. No, this man was a stranger.

She felt the loss of that man more deeply than she cared to admit. It was clear she'd been acting foolishly. He was, after all, a Manning. But despite his cool demeanor, she couldn't allow him to leave.

"No, of course not, my lord. You owe me no explanations. But perhaps you could wait until John returns. I expect him midafternoon. He can ride with you."

She didn't think it possible, but he seemed to stiffen even more.

"That will not be necessary," he said, his words clipped.

Louisa couldn't understand his anger, nor could she understand the cursed male pride that balked at showing any sign of weakness. Surely he realized she was just concerned for his safety. But if Overlea insisted he was well, she wouldn't be able to prevent him from leaving. Overlea Manor wasn't far by horseback and she could only hope his strength would hold until he reached it.

"I am in your debt, Miss Evans." He paused briefly. When he continued, his voice had lost its curt edge. "If there is ever anything I can do for you or your family, you need only ask."

Now it was her turn to stiffen. Distasteful as the thought was, they might one day have to rely on the charity of strangers. But she, too, had her pride, and she doubted they would ever be so desperate as to accept charity from the Mannings.

"Thank you," she said.

He looked at her for several seconds. His dark eyes seemed to see straight through her and she couldn't help but think that he knew what she was thinking. Finally, he looked away and reached into his coat pocket to produce a small gilt case from which he removed a calling card.

"Please accept this," he said, handing her the card. "I've written my direction in town on the back. I'm not sure how long I will remain in the country. If you change your mind—" She started to protest, but he spoke over her objection. "If you change your mind, please feel free to contact me."

She stared down at the card, a suspicion forming. "I will not accept payment for last night."

"No, of course not." He rushed to reassure her. "But you may very well have saved my life." His lips twisted slightly at that. "At the very least, your hospitality saved me from a cold, uncomfortable night on the side of the road. Hopefully you will never have need of my assistance, but I want you to know the offer stands."

She nodded. "Thank you," she said, taking the card and placing it on a side table.

There was a brief, awkward silence during which she

couldn't think of anything more to say. She had already expressed her concern for his safety and he had brushed it off. A strange expression crossed his face and for a moment she thought he was about to say something more.

He lightly took hold of her hand and bowed over it. The shock of his bare hand on hers sent a shiver of alarm down her spine. He looked deeply into her eyes and a fluttering sensation began in the pit of her stomach. Her breath caught and her thoughts went back to the kiss she'd been trying so hard to forget. When he released her hand, she let it fall to her side, ignoring the temptation to check if his touch had seared her skin.

"Good day, Miss Evans," he said softly.

Then he strode to the front door, opened it, and was gone. Louisa stared at the space where he'd been, trying to dispel the sense of loss that threatened to overwhelm her. She knew she was being silly. He hadn't even been here a full day. How could the house seem so empty now that he had gone?

She returned to the sitting room window and watched as he crossed the yard and strode, his back straight and his step unfaltering, to where he'd tethered his horse by a tree. She told herself she wanted to make sure he wouldn't stumble again, but she knew she was lying. It was probably for the best that Overlea was leaving. The marquess held an undeniable allure, a quality that no doubt drew many women to him. One to which it was clear she was not immune.

She watched him place a foot in the stirrup and swing onto the horse's back. She didn't realize she'd been holding her breath until she released it when he did not immediately fall off. Her gaze followed him until he was no longer in sight.

She shook her head then to clear her thoughts. She didn't have time for this. She had to finish Mary Manning's dress. She let the curtain fall back into place and was about to turn from the window when movement on the road caught her attention. Holding her breath, she waited, wondering if Overlea had realized he was not up to making this last leg of his journey alone and was returning.

She let out a long sigh, however, when she realized it was not the marquess returning, but his cousin, Edward Manning's, coach. Their landlord.

It was going to be a day for Mannings.

She went outside, preferring to meet him there. Unlike his cousin, Edward Manning was not ill and she had no intention of allowing him into her home. The coach came to a halt at the end of the lane, and she watched as the coachman descended and hurried to open the door. Edward Manning stepped down gingerly.

Having so recently been in Overlea's company, Louisa could not help but note the differences between the two men. From what she remembered, they were both of an age, but could not have been any more dissimilar than if there were no blood ties at all between them.

Overlea stood at least six feet tall with dark hair and eyes that were almost black. He was lean, yet surprisingly muscular, as she couldn't help but notice when she'd pressed herself against him that morning.

Edward Manning had a similar build to his cousin, but he was shorter and seemed softer. She knew Overlea's breadth of shoulders was natural, but suspected Edward Manning's was due to padding. His hair was a sandy brown and his eyes an icy blue that could cut right through a person. Unease settled in the pit of her stomach as those eyes now focused on her.

He came up the walkway, took hold of her hand, and bowed over it. "I trust you are well, Miss Evans," he said, squeezing her hand before releasing it. A shudder of distaste went through her. "I've been meaning to speak to you, but business kept me in London."

She could well imagine what that business was. No doubt he had been in town, throwing away the money he wrung from his tenants on any number of assorted vices.

"Thank you, I am well," she said, trying for that tone of civility she'd found increasingly difficult to maintain after her father had fallen ill and she'd taken over all dealings with Edward Manning. His interest in her had been evident from the start, and the last few months without his visits had been a relief. She couldn't imagine why he needed to speak to her now and hoped his visit wouldn't last long.

He licked his lips and glanced over her shoulder before returning his gaze to her. "Your brother, is he at home?"

She couldn't fathom why he would ask. He'd never dealt with John before now. "No, he is at his studies with Reverend Harnick."

"Good, good," he said. He cleared his throat before continuing and a slight smile played on his lips. "Your father has been gone for half a year, has he not? I imagine that means you are now out of deep mourning." He took a step closer to her. "I am sure you will appreciate that we have important matters to discuss. Perhaps we could step inside?"

His request was unexpected. Manning knew how things stood between their two families. He knew he wasn't welcome in their home and never would have suggested such a thing when her father was still alive.

"I am sure we don't have anything to discuss that would take that long," she said.

"Ah, but you are wrong about that, my dear. I am here to discuss your rent."

A chill swept through her. "Rent?" she repeated, hoping he was jesting. The look on his face said otherwise.

"Why yes. Surely you understand that I cannot allow you and your family to continue living here without paying rent?"

"But my father had an agreement with yours."

"Yes, but that agreement was between the two of them. Neither one is with us today. I have already been more than generous waiting this long before approaching you. Besides," he continued, his voice smooth but his eyes still cold, "I am sure your pride balks at the notion of such charity. This is the largest cottage on the estate and there are others who have shown interest in it. Surely you understand my position."

Though he tried to infuse his words with regret, Louisa could tell he felt none.

"How much?" she asked, forcing the words past the lump lodged in her throat.

He named a figure that had the lump moving down to settle firmly in her stomach. They would never be able to manage the added expense. As it was, she barely took in enough money from her sewing to feed them, which he no doubt knew.

"Mr. Manning," she began, trying to keep from revealing her rising sense of panic, "I am afraid that amount is beyond us at the moment."

He clucked his tongue at that.

"Such a pity," he said, shaking his head. "I have enjoyed having you and your family as neighbors."

He turned to leave.

Louisa blanched. Surely he didn't intend to cast them out?

"Wait," she said, her mind racing for a solution. He pivoted slowly, one eyebrow raised in question.

"Yes?"

"Perhaps we can come to another arrangement," she said, praying he would be reasonable. "One that would be mutually agreeable to both of us."

"Go on," he said, a smile beginning to form.

"I have some skill as a seamstress. Perhaps I could offer my services to your sister in lieu of any rent. She is paying me now, but she would no longer have to. And I would be happy to take on even more work."

Annoyance flickered across his face.

"Mary has more than enough dresses already," he said sharply. He seemed to catch himself then, for when he continued his voice had softened again. "No, I am afraid I can think of no solution." He looked pensive for a moment, then his eyes lit up. "Unless…"

"What is it?" she asked, eager to grasp at any way out of this situation.

A look of exaggerated concern crossed his face.

"It would be a shame for you to leave. I know you do not have other family to see you through this difficult time." The concern left his face to be replaced by a triumphant smile. "Where would you go?"

The beginnings of anger began to stir within her. The lying, deceitful wretch. He was enjoying her misery. He obviously had something in mind so she remained silent, knowing it would be unwise to anger him. She only hoped he would tire of his game soon and reveal his intentions.

She didn't have to wait long.

"Maybe there is something you can do for me." His gaze moved over her, lingering on her breasts. When he raised his eyes to hers again their piercing intensity caused her blood to freeze.

"I have always been very curious about you, Miss Evans. I have a feeling you are hiding more beneath that innocent exterior than you would have others believe."

She said nothing.

He took a step closer but she stood her ground. He would not see her cower.

"Surely we can find out," he said.

"I think not."

He stared at her intently for a moment before taking a step back.

"Of course not," he said. "Well, perhaps your sister will be of a different mind. She is no longer a child, after all. And I am sure she would be very eager to help keep her family from being tossed out of their home without a shilling to their name."

That will never happen, Louisa vowed silently. She would not allow him to approach Catherine with his lewd proposal.

She tried one last time to appeal to whatever scrap of decency he might possess, knowing all along it would be futile.

"Please," she said, trying to mask her desperation. "Hasn't your family taken enough from us? Can you not leave us in peace?"

His cool gaze flickered over her once more.

"I will be by on Friday. You will either have the rent then, or you will have to think of another way to pay me. Good day."

He strode toward his coach without a backward glance.

Sickened, she hurried into the house and closed the door behind her. Leaning against it for support, she closed her eyes and swallowed deeply, trying, without success, to achieve a measure of calm. She would never be able to solve this new dilemma if she panicked.

It was Monday. She still had four days to find a solution. But try as she might, she couldn't think of a way out of their predicament.

She needed to sit down. She took a few deep breaths to steady herself before moving into the sitting room. When she did, her gaze fell on the calling card lying on the side table.

CHAPTER FOUR

A flurry of activity broke out when Nicholas rode into the open courtyard of Overlea Manor. A groom rushed out to see to his horse, while the head gardener slipped away to let the staff know the marquess had returned. Within minutes every servant on the estate would know. He smiled wryly. His arrival had never commanded such attention before he'd inherited the title. When his father and brother were alive he'd been free to come and go as he pleased. He missed that freedom.

He dismounted and handed the reins to the groom, who bowed and led the animal away. He turned toward the manor house where the butler was waiting patiently by the open door.

Sommers bowed as Nicholas approached.

"Lady Overlea has been expecting you, my lord."

Nicholas knew that meant his grandmother wanted to see him as soon as possible. He had given up trying to remember what had been in her letter. He could remember breaking the letter's seal but had no memory of reading it.

The letter could only have been a summons or news that she was ill. Nothing else would have caused him to ride home to Kent on horseback while in the grip of one of his cursed headaches.

"Grandmother is well?"

"Yes, my lord, as always."

Of course. His grandmother had always been strong as an ox. She had outlived her husband, her two sons, and one of her grandsons. She would probably outlive him as well. That meant Grandmother had summoned him home, but why? She wouldn't have called him there on estate business. She left that side of things to him and he had never neglected his duties. She was up to something. Something he hadn't liked. He just wished he could remember what so he could meet her on even ground.

"Harrison arrived this morning," the butler continued. "He was surprised to find you had not yet arrived."

He grimaced inwardly. He couldn't remember the details surrounding his departure from town, but it sounded as though his valet's arrival had the entire household entertaining visions of yet another dead marquess. He only hoped they hadn't said anything to his grandmother that would cause her to worry. He glanced down at his badly rumpled and dusty clothes. He should go up and change first before seeing her, but at that moment all he wanted was to get this meeting over with as soon as possible.

"I knew Grandmother wouldn't be up when I arrived, so I decided to put up at an inn instead of coming here directly," he said by way of excuse. It wasn't a good one, but Sommers would never dare question him further. "I'll see her now."

"Very well, my lord," Sommers said with a slight bow. "She is in her sitting room."

Nicholas headed toward the staircase but stopped and turned back to the butler.

"One more thing, Sommers. Do you remember the Evans family? They had the estate bordering this one before my uncle acquired it."

"Certainly, my lord," Sommers said, hiding the disdain Nicholas knew he had for what his uncle had done. He'd learned most of the servants felt the same way after overhearing Sommers speaking of it once, years before, to the housekeeper.

"If a message should arrive from them, I would like to be notified immediately."

"Would that be this afternoon, my lord?"

"No," Nicholas said, frowning slightly. "I don't know when it will come, or even if it ever will."

"Yes, my lord."

With that, Nicholas turned back to the stairs and took them two at a time to the second floor and proceeded to the east wing where his grandmother had her rooms. He stood outside the door for several moments, attempting one final time to recall what she had written in her letter. He could almost see the words on the page, but the harder he concentrated, the more elusive the memory became.

Shaking off his frustration, Nicholas rapped twice on his grandmother's sitting room door. She answered immediately, bidding him to enter. He found her reclining on a chaise lounge, her eyes closed. Against the deep red of the chaise, her snowy white hair and pale complexion stood out in stark relief.

He could have kicked himself for not remembering his

grandmother had taken to resting in the afternoon. He should have waited to see her. Though she would never admit it, his parents' deaths, followed so closely by his brother's, had taken their toll on her.

She looked so small and frail and Nicholas felt a sudden rush of love for her. Aside from his cousins, with whom he had never been close, she was his only surviving relative.

She opened her eyes and looked at him.

"I see you received my letter," she said, drawing herself into a sitting position. She waved off the arm he held out to assist her. "I thought that would get your attention."

"Grandmother," he said, leaning down to kiss her cheek before taking a seat opposite her on a ridiculously ornate chair he wasn't sure would hold his weight. "I hope I didn't disturb your rest."

She frowned at him. "You aren't furious with me?" She peered at him closely. "What are you playing at?"

"Should I be angry with you?"

"Livid. Unless…" Her eyes lit up. "Unless you already have news for me?" She leaned forward and took hold of his hand. "Who is she?"

"Who is who?"

The dowager marchioness threw his hand back in exasperation.

"Don't toy with me, Nicholas. Who are you marrying?"

Surprise couldn't begin to describe his reaction to her question. He may have forgotten what she had written in her letter, but he wouldn't have forgotten a betrothal. His lapses in memory weren't that far along. Worried, he moved to sit next to her on the chaise. Grandmother was old, yes, but she'd never suffered from delusions before.

He knew some were prone to them as they aged, but somehow he'd never thought his strong-willed, mentally acute grandmother would be one of them.

"What makes you think I am getting married?" he asked, his tone gentle.

She stiffened. "Don't treat me like an old woman."

He smiled at that and she swatted his arm.

"I forbid you to say it." She frowned again. "Did you receive my letter?"

He wasn't sure how to hedge that one. He didn't want to lie to her, but he also didn't want her to worry. She didn't have to know yet that he'd started having headaches or that they were starting to affect his memory.

"Your letter?"

She sighed with resignation. "It must have missed you. But if you didn't come because of my letter, why are you here?"

"Maybe I just wanted to spend some time with my favorite grandmother."

"I am your only grandmother. And you are not going to want to have anything to do with me soon."

This was what he'd been waiting for. He stood and faced her, bracing himself for the worst.

"What have you done, Grandmother?"

"I have arranged for an announcement to appear in the papers tomorrow morning about the ball I'll be hosting here at the end of the month."

His confusion deepened. "Most people send out invitations to announce a ball."

She didn't react to the sarcasm in his tone. "I have sent out invitations, but I wanted everyone to hear our happy news before then."

Dread crept up his spine. "News?"

"Yes. News of your upcoming nuptials."

"My *what?*"

She really had gone mad. It was bound to happen at her age, but that it should occur in so public a manner was beyond embarrassing.

"Please, Grandmother, say you didn't."

The dowager marchioness held firm. "I did."

His mind began to race. He paced to the door, hands combing through his hair. He darted a glance at the clock on the mantel. It was almost one o'clock.

"If I leave now I might be able to reach London before they go to press." Presuming, of course, he didn't suffer a relapse. His headache was only marginally better, but he did feel steadier on his feet. He had no idea how a newspaper was run, but he had to try to stop that announcement from appearing.

"You'll stay right here," his grandmother said, her tone firm.

Nicholas spun to face her.

"I may be old, Nicholas, but I haven't lost my senses. Tomorrow's item is not precisely an announcement. I merely arranged to have it known that you plan to announce your betrothal at this ball. It will appear as a bit of gossip."

That admission went a long way toward relieving some of his concern.

"Surely you don't expect me to manufacture a bride-to-be before then," he said, exasperated by her meddling. She'd been trying to get him to marry since his brother's death, but this was going too far.

"I know the Earl of Raymond would consent to a

match between you and his eldest daughter. And Lady Strathmore has been hinting broadly that her daughter would favor a match with you. My preference would be for you to wed your cousin Mary, as your brother had planned to do, to mend the rift between the two families. I cannot force you to do that, however."

"How kind of you," Nicholas said, unable to keep his annoyance from his voice.

His grandmother continued as though he hadn't spoken.

"I am sure speculation will be rife. I suggest you finalize who your betrothed will be soon."

Nicholas could only stare at her, incredulous. The memory of what had been in that damnable letter had come crashing back to him as she spoke. How could he have forgotten the announcement of an upcoming marriage? His marriage. Of course, Grandmother had led him to believe she would soon be making a formal announcement. She had also neglected to mention she'd already set her plan into motion.

"I will not be forced into marrying someone I cannot tolerate, and I most definitely will not be marrying my cousin. James was the martyr in this family, not I."

He ignored the stab of guilt that went through him when he saw the sorrow that crossed her face at the mention of his older brother. It had only been a year since his death.

"I hate to mention this, but you must be aware that I have not led a monkish life and am not unused to having gossip connected to my name. Surely you know someone's speculation that I intend to marry would hardly be enough to force my hand."

His grandmother sighed deeply. "Nicholas," she said, her tone now a placating one, "please understand. I have always wished for you to find someone special. Someone you could love as your grandfather and I loved each other and as your parents loved. I do not want to do this."

"Then why do it?"

"You are twenty-eight years old. It is time for you to be settled and beget an heir."

Twenty-eight was hardly an advanced age, but he knew his grandmother was thinking of his father and brother's unexpected deaths.

"We already have an heir if something should happen to me."

The dowager marchioness grimaced.

"Edward is my grandson and I love him, but your cousin would never be a good marquess."

"We agree there, but I will not allow you to force me into this." He turned and strode toward the door. "I will be returning to London tomorrow."

He was about to leave when his grandmother's words stopped him.

"I have told you my plans in advance this time, Nicholas. If you do not comply now, there will be no warning next time. The first you hear of it will be a formal announcement that will include the bride's name."

"I see," he said stiffly, turning to face her. "I suppose I should be grateful you've allowed me some choice in the matter."

"Nicholas…"

He didn't stay to hear more. He opened the door and walked out, closing it soundly behind him. A swift, burning anger had replaced the concern he'd felt for his grandmother upon entering her sitting room. He couldn't believe she actually sought to blackmail him into marrying.

He wanted nothing more than to head for the stables and ride off some of his anger. He needed to clear his head and think of a way to dissuade his grandmother from her current course of action. Instead, he turned and headed for the library. It would serve no purpose to ignore the fact that his damned head still ached. He'd managed the ride home from the Evans cottage because he'd ridden with care, but he was in no frame of mind at the moment for such caution.

He collapsed into the armchair before the fireplace. It wasn't yet cool enough to light a fire during the day, so he stared, instead, into the empty hearth. His lips twisted with wry amusement as he remarked how the lack of warmth from the fireplace seemed an apt metaphor for his own life. He couldn't remember the last time he'd been genuinely alive. Oh, he'd made a fine show of it while in town, but his frivolity had only been on the surface. With all the death that had surrounded his family, his newfound, never-expected responsibilities, and now the threat of a similar death hanging over his own head, he was as cold and lifeless inside as the dark ashes in the hearth before him.

He'd recently decided he could never risk marrying. It was clear some illness was striking down the men in his family and he didn't want to pass that illness down to his own children. He wondered if his grandmother suspected he had come to such a decision. He'd never discussed marriage with her before today, but she was astute enough to guess at his thoughts on the subject. He wondered if she would release him from her schemes to marry him off if he told her he was beginning to show signs of the same illness that had already killed his father and brother.

He couldn't risk having children. There had been women, yes, but he'd always taken care so as not to sire any bastards. He was grateful now for that caution.

His grandmother was right about Edward, though. He couldn't inherit. He was selfish and irresponsible, traits he had no doubt inherited from his father, but they had flourished under his aunt's cosseting. And he had only grown worse with each passing year.

No, he had to take steps to keep his cousin from becoming the next Marquess of Overlea, and he had to act before his own illness left him incapacitated. His pride balked at what he knew had to be done, but he could no longer afford to put it off.

His thoughts turned to the beautiful Louisa Evans and the kiss they had shared that morning, and for one insane moment he wondered if he should consider proposing to her. But then he remembered how stiff she had become when she thought he was offering her charity. If she was determined to refuse any assistance or thanks from him for her care of him the night before, she would certainly never accept a proposal of marriage.

Besides, he knew he was being ridiculous. One shared kiss did not mean they were compatible. Granted, it had been a very nice kiss, full of passion and the promise of delights to come.

He shook his head to clear his thoughts. Given what he would need to do to procure an heir, it was probably better to marry someone to whom he was not quite so attracted. He wondered whether either of the ladies his grandmother had mentioned would agree to the kind of arrangement he had in mind.

Louisa had nowhere else to turn. She'd tried unsuccessfully to find more sewing to take in or to think of some other way to pay Edward Manning the rent he demanded. His suggested alternative was too repulsive to contemplate, let alone accept, and she wouldn't allow him to approach Catherine with his vile proposition.

In a moment of frustration she'd almost told her brother about their landlord's visit. The temptation to have someone with whom she could share this burden was great. She knew, though, that John wouldn't have been able to help, and he was brash enough to do something foolish like challenge Edward to a duel for the proposition he'd made. She couldn't allow that to happen.

She brought the horse she'd borrowed from a neighbor to a stop at the end of the drive and looked across the manicured gardens that spread out before Overlea Manor. Their former home, while respectable in size, was not nearly as grand as the house before her now—three stories in height, two wings sweeping out at the sides, and an impressive portico that rose up to the roofline, all in a rich honey-colored stone. She could only stare at it in wonder, the knowledge that she was completely out of her depth solidifying.

Asking for Overlea's assistance had been the only path open to her. She'd managed to maintain her equanimity during the ride, but now that she was here, her heartbeat quickened. She took a deep breath in a vain attempt to quell her nerves before starting down the drive to the front of the house. When she dismounted, a groom was already headed toward her. She smiled as she handed him the reins.

Back straight, feigning a confidence she was far from feeling, she turned and proceeded up the short stairway to the main entrance. She paused at the top, smoothing a hand over the dark blue skirt of her riding habit. The style was more than a few years out of date now, but there was no point in having a habit in the current style when they didn't even own a horse.

She took another deep breath before lifting the heavy brass knocker and letting it fall. The door was opened immediately by a footman. He looked at her and then glanced beyond. She could see him stiffen when he realized she was unattended. She could only imagine what he must be thinking.

"I am here to see Lord Overlea."

The footman did not bother to hide his disapproval. "The marquess is not in."

He was actually going to close the door on her. Out of sheer desperation, Louisa stepped into the doorway. He would have to physically remove her if he wanted her gone.

"Could you please tell him that Louisa Evans is here to see him?"

She was surprised when his demeanor changed almost instantly. He opened the door wider and stepped back to allow her to enter, all solicitousness now.

"Of course, Miss Evans."

He led her to the drawing room and retreated, closing the door behind him.

Louisa drew in a shaky breath. She'd crossed the first barrier, gaining entrance, but her nerves were still unsettled. The toughest part lay ahead. Asking Overlea for assistance she wasn't certain he would provide. Edward Manning was, after all, his cousin, and given the marquess's reputation he might see nothing wrong with the arrangement Edward had proposed. It was, after all, very common for men of their stature to have mistresses.

She wondered if Overlea had a mistress and found the idea bothered her more than she cared to admit.

Her thoughts were so full of her upcoming meeting with Overlea that she barely took in her elegant surroundings. She perched on the edge of a cream-colored settee and it took all her focus to keep from fidgeting. As the minutes passed, she found herself growing more anxious. She had been waiting a full quarter of an hour before it occurred to her that Overlea might refuse to see her.

She waited another quarter hour before deciding to seek out the footman. She had just reached the drawing room door when it swung open. Startled, she took a step back.

She'd thought the Marquess of Overlea a handsome man before, but the last time she'd seen him, his clothes had been rumpled from a night of tossing and turning and dark stubble had covered his jaw. He had seemed approachable then. Now, clean-shaven and impeccably dressed, he took her breath away. He wore a coat of deep green that stretched across shoulders that seemed broader now, a waistcoat in a lighter shade of that same color, and fawn buckskins that molded to his muscled thighs and disappeared into boots she suspected were the same ones she remembered removing from him. She was acutely conscious, as she had not been before, of the difference in their stations.

That Overlea was surprised to see her was evident, especially as she was alone. He couldn't know, then, that her reputation was already on the verge of being ruined. That she could very well find herself with no alternative than to accept Edward's proposition if he refused to help her.

"Miss Evans," he said, inclining his head.

She acknowledged his greeting but found herself unable to speak for a moment.

"Please," he said, indicating the settee she had abandoned, "make yourself comfortable."

She sat and watched as he settled himself into a chair opposite her.

"I would ring for tea, but I sense this is not a social call."

"No," she said, before lapsing into silence again. Now that she was here she didn't know how to begin. How could she tell him what his cousin had proposed?

"You appear well today, my lord," she said in an attempt to stall the inevitable uncomfortable conversation. "I assume that your illness has passed?"

"Yes," he said.

His posture was stiff and it was clear he didn't wish to discuss it. She had no alternative but to get straight to the reason for her visit.

"I know you weren't expecting to see me so soon."

"I hadn't expected to see you at all." He shifted forward in his chair, a slight frown pulling at the corners of his mouth, and continued. "You will excuse me for being direct, but what could possibly have happened in the past two days to bring you here? You left me with the impression that you didn't wish to have further contact

51

with me or my family."

She resisted the urge to squirm under his intent gaze.

"It must be quite serious for you to come here unescorted. I thought I would be dealing with your brother, if anyone."

"My brother and sister cannot know I came to see you."

His eyebrows rose at that. His gaze never left her as he leaned back in his chair.

"I've had a visit from your cousin."

"Mary?" he asked, his confusion evident.

She shook her head.

"No, your cousin, Edward Manning."

His frowned. "Why would that bring you here? Are you not his tenant?"

"Not precisely." She hesitated a moment before continuing. "How much do you know about what happened between my father and your uncle?"

"A fair bit," Overlea replied, his features shuttered.

She was grateful to be spared having to relay the details of what had transpired all those years ago.

"After... well, after what happened, we moved from our old house to where we now live. I suppose after everything he'd taken from us your uncle decided to show us some mercy." She failed to hide the note of bitterness in her voice. "The cottage is one of the larger ones on the estate. I remember my father being worried about the rent now that he didn't have the income from the estate, but your uncle allowed us to live there without having to pay it."

"And now?"

From his almost unnatural stillness, it was clear he

suspected what she was about to say.

"Your cousin has informed me that we are to start paying rent immediately."

"And you cannot afford it."

"No," she said, her voice barely above a whisper.

It was several moments before Overlea replied. "Why are you here, Miss Evans? I know you're not here for charity. Would you like me to speak to Edward? Convince him to give you more time? Or perhaps to continue to allow you to remain in your home under the same conditions as when you father was alive? If that's the case, I'm afraid I'll have to disappoint you. I don't have that much influence over my cousin's actions."

She would have to tell him everything. The subject was already an uncomfortable one, but the kiss she and Overlea had shared on that morning after he woke in her room made it even more so. Keeping silent, however, might have grave consequences. Especially for Catherine.

"There is something else," she said, her embarrassment acute. Unable to broach the subject just yet, she stood and walked over to the window. She gazed out at the perfectly manicured grounds for a full minute before taking a deep breath and turning to face him again. Overlea stood, but he didn't say anything, giving her the time she needed. She was grateful for that. "Your cousin did offer me an alternative to paying rent. One that would involve using a currency of a different, much more unpalatable sort."

It took him only a moment to catch her meaning. He scowled and swore softly, but she continued before he could say anything. "John and Catherine know nothing about this, and they must never hear of it. John is hotheaded enough to do something foolish. And

Catherine—" Her voice hitched. "He offered to approach her directly and make her the same offer if I refuse."

"Surely she would never agree to such a thing. Not if you speak to her first and give her your support."

"Mama died in childbed during Catherine's birth. A part of her believes she is responsible for the series of events that led us to where we are today. That Papa never would have fallen into your uncle's trap if she'd never been born and Mama hadn't died. Papa never would have turned to drinking, never would have gambled away the estate and our home. Of course," she added, rushing to reassure him lest he think she shared that belief, "Catherine is not to blame for our father's actions, but she might accept your cousin's offer as a way of atoning for all that has happened."

His dark eyes settled on her for what seemed an eternity. She squirmed, uncomfortable being the sole subject of that inscrutable gaze. Finally, he spoke.

"I believe I can help you."

Intense relief washed over her and she had to close her eyes for an instant. She started to thank him, but his words stopped her.

"You may want to hear my conditions first."

An icy finger of dread snaked up her spine. Had she made a mistake in coming here? Was it possible he was as despicable as his cousin?

"Perhaps you should be seated for this."

She stiffened. "That is quite all right. I am comfortable here."

She threw a hasty glance at the door, wondering at her chances for escape, but realized she was being foolish. This man had spent a considerable amount of time under her roof and he'd had several opportunities to make unwanted advances. Other than the one kiss they had shared when he'd woken and mistaken their relationship, an action for which he had later apologized, he had been circumspect in his attentions.

Nevertheless, she shivered when he approached her. His movements were smooth, almost predatory. There was no hint of the caution with which he had moved on that other occasion.

He stopped a few feet from her. She couldn't make out what thoughts lurked behind his dark, intent gaze, but she sensed he was coming to a decision. She didn't have to wait long for him to reach it.

"You require my assistance and I am inclined to offer it to you, but I have something to ask of you first. Without your agreement, I fear I will be unable to help you."

Louisa couldn't believe what she was hearing. He was about to make her the same offer Edward had made. She was disappointed. For some reason she'd expected better of him.

He was silent for a moment, as if he were choosing his words carefully. When he finally spoke, they were the last she expected to hear.

"I need a wife."

CHAPTER FIVE

He'd shocked her. He didn't need to see the color drain from her face to know that a proposal of marriage was the last thing Louisa Evans expected, or wanted, from him.

Damn his cousin Edward for being an unscrupulous bastard, and damn him for using Miss Evans's distressed circumstances to his own advantage. He knew that in her eyes he was little better than his cousin. Once she became aware of the full terms of their marriage that opinion would solidify, but for now it would be best to keep those terms to himself. He just needed her to accept his proposal. He would deal with the matter of his heirs later.

"You require my protection and I require a marchioness. It is the perfect solution."

She looked at him as though he had grown two heads. It wasn't an expression he was accustomed to seeing. Even though he was aware of the justified animosity her family had always held toward his, he felt the sting to his male pride. Any other woman would have leapt at his offer of marriage, and not just for his title. While he was now pursued relentlessly since becoming the Marquess of Overlea, he had never wanted for female companionship.

He could have chosen from among any number of women, but for some reason Louisa Evans was the one he wanted. It wasn't just that she was attractive, though she was that, with her slim figure, her long, pale blond hair, now worn up, her wide gray eyes and that full mouth. A mouth meant for kissing, as he had discovered.

He was attracted to her, more than he should be for the type of union he had in mind. However, that attraction wasn't the reason he wanted her for his wife. In fact, he was sure it would prove to be a major inconvenience. No, he had proposed to her because Louisa Evans was an intelligent and practical woman. She was a breath of fresh air after all the simpering, marriage-minded females of London. Most important, however, was the fact that she was also a desperate woman. One whom he was certain would ultimately agree to his terms.

She remained silent and he watched the play of emotions that crossed her face. The shock had faded quickly enough, only to be replaced by confusion and uncertainty. Then she turned away from him again, her back ramrod straight.

He waited patiently. He knew what her answer would be. She had no other choice.

Finally she turned, chin held high. Nicholas felt relief, and to be honest, a sense of admiration. There would be no histrionics here, no pleading. She would deal with him plainly.

"Why me?"

"Why not you?"

His equanimity gave her pause. "We both know you are

the catch of the Season. Any number of women would agree to be your wife, most of them, no doubt, better suited to the duties such a position entails than I. So," she continued after a brief pause, "I ask you again. Why me?"

"I can think of no one better suited to be my marchioness," he said, glad he could be honest with her on that score.

Her eyes narrowed as she stared at him intently. "You're not telling me something."

A quick stab of guilt pricked him, but he quickly suppressed it. He had no choice. Both their hands had already been dealt.

"Becoming my marchioness is the only way I can guarantee you are safe from my cousin's whims."

He could see her weighing his words and pressed his advantage.

"Of course," he continued, "I realize your responsibilities to your family and I am willing to provide for them. They will live here, with us. Catherine will have a Season in London and John…?"

"John would like to attend Oxford."

Nicholas smiled. "Then he shall."

He could see the indecision vanish from her eyes.

"Very well, I accept your proposal."

She was trying so hard to be brave, but Nicholas could tell she was feeling overwhelmed. Life had dealt her more than her share of hardship. He was willing to relieve her of at least a few of those burdens. She wouldn't thank him once she knew all of it, but for now he could help her.

The strength of his desire to take care of her caught him off guard.

"Congratulate yourself," he said, striving for levity.

"You are about to become the Marchioness of Overlea. Women everywhere will hate you on sight."

The ghost of a smile touched her lips before she sobered.

"Your aunt will not be pleased when she hears of this."

He frowned. "Why would she care?"

"Was there not an understanding that your brother was to wed Mary? The betrothal was never formalized and I'd assumed…"

He couldn't hide his stab of annoyance at her words, and her voice trailed off when she saw it. First Grandmother had suggested he marry his cousin, and now Louisa Evans, a stranger to the complicated intricacies of the Manning family dynamics, was intimating as much. It made him wonder how many others also assumed he would be marrying his cousin.

"I am not my brother."

"But surely the reasons such a union was proposed in the first place still exist."

"My brother was willing to sacrifice himself to make peace within our family, but as you know, I was not raised the heir. I am not nearly so noble."

She tilted her head and gazed at him, an odd expression on her face.

"I am not so sure about that."

Her comment pleased him more than it should have. It was too bad he didn't deserve it.

"I believe we will get on very well together," he said. "There are a few matters I need to attend to before we can discuss the details of our arrangement. Can I call on you tomorrow afternoon?"

She inclined her head. Turning, she made her way

toward the room's exit.

"Believe it or not," he said, his voice causing her steps to falter, "I had not thought of asking you until I saw you here."

She didn't turn to face him.

"If it weren't for your cousin I wouldn't need to be here. And I would not have accepted."

Then she was gone.

As Louisa finished setting the table for dinner she couldn't keep her gaze from moving to the chair closest to the door, where Overlea had sat on the morning he'd had breakfast with them. She found it impossible to believe that had only been two days ago. So much had changed in such a short time.

She still found it almost impossible to believe that Overlea had proposed to her and that she had actually accepted. Of course, given the alternative presented by Edward Manning, marriage to the marquess was the better option. The only option. And marrying Overlea would secure Catherine and John's futures. John would not need to wait to see if he could secure a scholarship to attend Oxford. And with Overlea's backing, she was certain Catherine would be considered quite a catch. She would be able to choose a husband from any number of candidates.

She was not unaware of the irony of their situation. One Manning had stripped away almost everything from their family, leaving them only their dignity. Then that man's son had threatened to take even that from them. It seemed strangely fitting, then, that another Manning would return everything they had lost.

Somehow she would have to convince John of that.

She wasn't looking forward to telling him her news. She knew Catherine would go along with her decision once she'd gotten over her initial surprise. Her sister had no memory of what their life had been before, so the loss of everything they'd once had was not so devastating to her. John, though only a year older, seemed to remember all too clearly.

Louisa looked about the small dining room with its simple furnishings. Soon they would leave here, the cottage to which they'd been exiled all those years ago that was now their home. Tomorrow, when Overlea arrived to discuss the details of their arrangement, she'd learn just how long it would be before their circumstances changed yet again. This time, however, it would be for the better. She had to hold onto that belief.

She pushed back the suspicion that Overlea was hiding something from her. For her own peace of mind it was better not to waste time worrying about what it might possibly be before she had to.

Giving herself a mental shake, she brought herself back to the task at hand. Catherine would be downstairs soon and John home from his lessons. She had just enough time to clean up before dinner. She was starting up the stairs to do so when John burst through the front door.

"Louisa," he called, halting her progress. "I need to speak to you and Catherine."

"Can this wait until dinner?"

The expression on his face gave her pause. He looked both guilty and determined, and it made her uneasy.

"We need to talk," he said. His gaze went to the top of the stairs. "Good, Catherine is here. We can settle this at once."

Unease swept through her. Somehow her brother must have found out about her visit to Overlea Manor. Either that or he'd learned of Edward's proposition. Neither alternative boded well.

"Let me explain—" she started, but John cut her off.

"You won't dissuade me this time, Louisa. My mind is made up and I have already spoken to Reverend Harnick."

She looked at Catherine who was now standing, silent, beside her, but it was clear she, too, had no idea what their brother wanted to discuss.

"I told Reverend Harnick that I will not be applying for a scholarship to Oxford, but hope, instead, to find some way of supporting us. He knows of some families that he believes would be willing to hire me to tutor their children in Latin and Greek."

It she still had doubts about her decision to accept Overlea's proposal, they were gone in that moment. She'd hoped to put off telling her siblings about that decision until she'd spoken to Overlea again and they had settled the details, but time was no longer a luxury.

"That won't be necessary."

"Yes, it is," John cut in. "I'm the man of this family now and it's time I started acting like it."

"Listen to me, John—"

"I'm done listening. I should have done this a long time ago, but I let you convince me that Father would be upset if I gave up my studies." He paced to the door and back, his young body filled with a vibrant energy. He swept a hand through his blond hair. "You were probably right about that. But you have sacrificed for too long, Louisa. It is now my turn to take care of the family."

Louisa placed a hand on her brother's arm.

"I don't mind," she said. "You cannot give up your studies. I know how much going to Oxford means to you."

"I think everyone here knows that will never happen. How could I leave you two here, alone, without any income? What kind of man would that make me?"

The bleakness in his eyes further strengthened her resolve.

"John is right," Catherine said. "We can't allow you to continue taking sole responsibility of caring for the family. Surely I can find a position as a lady's companion or a governess."

"No." The vehemence in her tone surprised her siblings. "I am to be married and my future husband has assured me your futures are secure."

Her words dropped into the room with deafening finality. It was Catherine who found her voice first.

"Who?"

"The Marquess of Overlea."

If she weren't so worried about her brother's reaction, the expression on his face would have been comical. She knew, however, that this was no laughing matter.

"What are you saying? How could this have happened?"

Louisa knew that, above all else, John must never learn of Edward Manning's proposition, nor of her visit to Overlea that afternoon. Her siblings would never believe that her upcoming nuptials were the result of a love match, and she had no doubt John would not accept the marriage if he thought she was sacrificing herself for them. She would have to give them enough of the truth to satisfy their disbelief.

"Overlea has decided he is of an age when he must marry and secure the future of his title. He has proposed and I have accepted."

Her brother swore and she flinched at his vehemence.

"The decision has been made," she continued. "He will be here tomorrow to discuss the details."

John's scowl deepened. "I do not consent."

"I don't require your approval. I am old enough to marry where I will."

"You would give yourself to a Manning?" His disgust was palpable. "They stole everything from our family. They are the reason we've had to live hand to mouth for years."

Louisa shook her head.

"The marquess is not to blame, nor was his father or brother. It was his uncle who cheated Papa."

John shook his head, his anger only increasing the more she tried to make him see reason.

"It matters not. He is a Manning and they are all alike."

"Lord Overlea is *saving* us, John. After our marriage we will never again want for anything."

"I have already made plans to take care of us. It is my responsibility, not yours."

Louisa wanted to scream with frustration, knowing her brother would never see reason on this subject. Catherine had remained silent during their exchange, but it wasn't hard to read her thoughts from the expression on her face. Guilt and hope. Clearly, she could see the advantages of her sister marrying the Marquess of Overlea would be plentiful. Ignoring her brother for the moment, she grasped Catherine's hands.

"It will be fine. I want to do this. We have yet to settle

the details, but the marquess has promised that you are to have a Season. Just imagine! You will put everyone to shame. You will have the choice of any man you desire."

"What about you, Louisa? You, too, could have your choice of any man."

Louisa shook her head.

"I am five and twenty, far too old for a Season. And we all know that without a dowry and someone's patronage I would never secure a match."

Catherine was about to protest, but Louisa forestalled her.

"Overlea is not unattractive," she said, trying to ignore the heat she could feel creeping into her face. "I do not think marriage to him would be a great hardship."

John bristled at her words, but she ignored him. She had meant her assurances to put her brother and sister at ease, but as she said them she realized it was the truth. She remembered, again, the kiss she and the Overlea had shared and her flush deepened. And aside from the fact that he was a very attractive man, he had shown her and her family great kindness.

She had approached him for help and his response had far exceeded her expectations. Rather than merely ensuring her family would continue to have a roof over their heads, he had decided to provide her with the means to secure all their futures. It was true that her relationship with Overlea would be a practical one, but most marriages began in such a manner.

Their upcoming marriage would also give her what she had most wanted—a family of her own. She had long ago given up hoping that should would one day marry and have children, but now that dream was within her grasp.

She believed she and Overlea would get on well, despite the niggling doubt that he had not been completely honest with her. Whatever he was hiding, she would deal with it later. For now, she had to provide for John and Catherine.

She turned back to her brother.

"The marquess can guarantee your entrance into any school you desire. I've already spoken to him and he will see to it that you are able to attend Oxford."

John said nothing, but his arms were crossed and his expression mutinous. Louisa didn't miss, however, the brief flicker of longing that had crossed his face at her words. Oh yes, she was definitely doing the right thing.

She turned back to her sister. "I have already set the table and dinner should be ready. Could you see to it while I speak to John alone for a moment?"

Catherine cast a doubtful glance in John's direction, but she shrugged and headed into the kitchen with a soft "good luck" meant only for Louisa's ears. When she was gone, Louisa led John to the sitting room and closed the door.

"You have already put off your education because of Papa's passing, and as you pointed out, you don't want to leave us to fend for ourselves. Now there is nothing to keep you from continuing your education."

"The price is too high," he said.

"I am old enough to know what I'm doing and you know I have always been a good judge of character. If I had any reservations at all I would never have accepted Overlea's proposal."

"You cannot be serious. You barely know the man."

She tried a different approach. "Have you not thought about Catherine?"

"What does she have to do with this?"

"You know the guilt she carries. She has always blamed herself for Mama's death."

"Catherine is a child. Father is the one to blame for his actions. He didn't have to drink himself into the ground and gamble away the house and estate."

"How long do you think it will be before she throws herself at some man who she believes will save us? She is seventeen and I've seen the way some of the men in the village look at her."

The color drained from her brother's face and he clenched his fists.

"I will kill anyone who attempts to take advantage of her."

"The best course of action—nay, the only course of action—is the one I have chosen. Once we have Overlea's protection, Catherine's guilt will ease."

"And what of you? How are your actions any different from what you fear she might do?"

She couldn't believe how stubborn her brother was being.

"Overlea isn't taking advantage of me. I am no fool, John. He needs a wife and an heir and for whatever reason he has settled on me. Ours will be a respectable union and no different from the marriage arrangements that are often made between families."

"I still don't approve," John said.

Louisa sighed. It was clear her brother was determined not to be swayed.

"Everything will work out. Overlea will be paying us a call tomorrow to discuss the details of the marriage contract. You can act as chaperone when he does and see for yourself that his intentions are honorable."

Louisa said a silent prayer that her brother wouldn't pick up on her suspicion that Overlea was keeping something important from them.

CHAPTER SIX

The morning seemed to drag on forever. At breakfast Louisa found it almost impossible to eat, but somehow managed to choke down a few bites of toast while Catherine prattled on about nothing in particular and her brother sat glowering at her from across the table. She was relieved when he left for his studies, but he promised to be home that afternoon for Overlea's visit. She knew John was hoping Overlea would change his mind, but she was confident he wouldn't. Overlea would be there.

Catherine wasn't surprised to hear that she wouldn't be present during the discussion of the marriage contract, and Louisa was relieved when she announced she was leaving to visit one of their neighbors. It had strained her almost to the breaking point to listen to her sister's normal chatter about plants and about her plans for the garden next spring. Although she'd tried to behave as usual, she was sure Catherine could tell that her mind was on Overlea's upcoming visit.

It was after one in the afternoon when she heard male

voices outdoors. She groaned when she recognized they belonged to her brother and the marquess. She dropped the mending she'd allowed to pile up back into its basket and rose with haste, hoping to intercept their conversation before John said something to offend the marquess.

The front door opened and she was relieved to see Overlea follow her brother into the house. It was clear John wasn't happy he was there, but at least he hadn't tried to turn him away. Her gaze locked with Overlea's and for a moment she almost forgot to breathe. The knowledge that this man was actually going to be her husband struck her with renewed force.

"My Lord," she said, dropping her gaze and dipping into a brief curtsey.

He raised an eyebrow in silent comment at the change in her demeanor before inclining his head in acknowledgement. She hadn't seen his companion until he turned to the man beside him.

"This is my solicitor, Mr. Stephens. I thought it best to include him in our discussion since he will be drawing up the marriage settlement."

"We won't be signing anything until we have someone else look it over," John said. He didn't come out and say that he believed Overlea was trying to take advantage of Louisa, but the implication was there.

"John—" she started.

"That is quite all right," Overlea said. "I would expect nothing less. One must be thorough when it comes to such things."

"Especially when one is dealing with a Manning," John said.

Louisa glared at her brother, embarrassed by his

rudeness, but the marquess didn't acknowledge the insult.

She greeted Mr. Stephens before turning back to Overlea. "I'm afraid we have no study. Would you care to wait in the sitting room while I speak to my brother for a moment?"

She thought she detected a hint of amusement in Overlea's eyes, but it was gone so quickly she was left wondering if she had imagined it. She watched the two men go into the sitting room before turning to walk down the hallway. She didn't have to tell her brother to follow.

She tried to keep her annoyance from her voice when she faced him. "I know this is difficult for you, but you must promise to stop being rude to Overlea. He has shown us nothing but kindness."

Her brother's expression, already mutinous, became darker.

"Make no mistake, John, I *will* marry him. All our futures depend on Overlea's generosity. You would do well to think about that the next time you try to antagonize him."

John remained silent and all she could do as they joined the two men in the sitting room was hope that he would refrain from making any further negative comments.

Overlea was deep in conversation with his solicitor, but they broke off and stood when she and her brother entered the room. She didn't miss the assessing gaze Overlea swept over her drab brown outfit and she found herself wishing she'd given in to her impulse to wear the dress Overlea had caught her admiring the last time he was there. She hadn't yet delivered it to Miss Manning and the temptation had been great to don it for today's meeting, especially since he had remarked on how the color suited her.

She hesitated for a moment, flustered when she saw that Overlea's solicitor had chosen to sit in the room's one armchair while Overlea sat on one end of the settee. She recovered quickly and, hoping he hadn't noticed, took a seat on the other end. She watched him from lowered lashes as he resumed his seat.

Despite the fact that there was a respectable space between them, she was very aware of how near he sat. She imagined she could almost feel the heat radiating from his body. She hoped he couldn't tell she was a nervous wreck. By contrast, he seemed to be taking their situation completely in stride. If he had any doubt about the wisdom of marrying a stranger or if he was at all affected by her presence, it didn't show. If they were going to deal with each other in marriage, she would have to get over her nervousness around him. After all, it wasn't as though theirs was a love match. She had no doubt that Overlea expected her to deal with him in a straightforward manner.

While his solicitor drew papers out of his case and sorted through them, she took advantage of the delay to examine him again. She didn't see any sign of the weakness he had exhibited when he'd shown up on her doorstep and she wondered again what could have caused his illness. Her gaze traveled back to his face, where she saw that he was taking in her perusal, one brow raised. She looked away again, cursing her fair skin as heat swept over her cheeks.

She fixed her gaze on Mr. Stephens, who handed her a small sheaf of papers. The meeting didn't take as long as she would have expected. Overlea must have met with his solicitor right after he'd spoken to her, because the details she had discussed with him—a Season for Catherine and provisions for John's education—were already included. He had also settled upon Catherine a very generous dowry, one that would ensure she made an excellent match.

"It is too much," she said, meeting the marquess's gaze for the first time since the meeting had started.

He shrugged. "It is to be expected for a member of my family, and once we are married your sister will become my family. I will not shirk my responsibility to her."

Logically, she knew he was correct, but she was beginning to feel as though she were taking advantage of him. True, she was promising to try to provide him with the one thing he wanted most, an heir, but that was something he could have had from any number of women. Women who would actually bring assets of their own to the marriage.

"When is the happy event to take place?" John asked.

He'd been so quiet that she'd almost forgotten his presence. He was leaning against a wall, but every line of his body was tense, as though he were ready to strike out at any moment.

She looked at Overlea, unaware of the protocol for marriage after the death of one's parent. "Father died six months ago. Should we wait until a year has passed?"

He shook his head. "Six months is enough if we keep the ceremony private."

Louisa had thought she'd have more time to adjust to the idea of her upcoming marriage, hoping that in that time she'd get to know her future husband better. It was a vast understatement to say he unsettled her and left her feeling unbalanced.

She realized she was biting her lower lip when she

noticed Overlea's gaze had settled on her mouth. She stopped, worried that he disapproved of the nervous gesture. His eyes met hers and she blushed when she saw the heat reflected in their depths. This time it was he who looked away first.

"I imagine a wedding will take some time to arrange," she said, trying to order her scattered thoughts.

"Grandmother is planning a ball for the end of the month. She was hoping to announce our engagement at that time."

Panic rushed through her at the thought, for she wasn't sure she was ready for the whole world to learn about their engagement so soon. There was also the fact that she had nothing to wear to such an event.

"So soon?"

"The invitations have already gone out." There was a flicker of something in his eyes as he spoke, but she couldn't define it. "There is no point in waiting. I thought we could have a small ceremony that morning. Just family, of course. And instead of presenting you as my betrothed during Grandmother's ball, you will be presented as my wife."

"What?"

Louisa and her brother spoke at once. Her voice held a hint of panic, while her brother's was low with anger. John shifted away from the wall and glared at Overlea.

"It is out of the question. If you marry so soon we all know what people will say, especially if it becomes known you recently spent the night here."

Louisa hadn't even considered that aspect of the situation, but her brother had raised a good point.

Overlea's expression was almost one of boredom. "I do

not conduct my affairs based on the fear of what others might say."

"That is an interesting choice of words." Her brother spat out the words.

Louisa's thoughts went to the kiss she and Overlea had shared on the morning of his stay. She wondered if he was thinking about the same thing, but didn't have the courage to look at him.

Overlea stood, his movements slow, and approached John. She feared her brother had gone too far.

"You do your sister a disservice if you believe her actions that night were anything other than circumspect."

His statement startled her. Was that why John was so angry? Did he believe she and Overlea had already behaved inappropriately? While the kiss they had shared was outside the bounds of propriety, it surprised her that her brother believed much more than that may have transpired.

"I know your reputation," John said.

"But it would appear you do not know your sister."

John was about to reply, but Louisa could no longer sit there and listen to them argue. "That is enough, John."

Overlea took a step back when she stood and went to her brother.

"Three weeks, Louisa. You know what people will say."

"What do *you* think happened that night?"

"I try not to think about it."

She was hurt that he thought so little of her but tried not to show it.

"People will talk no matter how long our betrothal. After a while, the rumors will cease and people will find something else to gossip about."

"I don't like this. Why the hurry?"

She gave Overlea a pleading look then, which he deciphered correctly. He went back to the settee and turned to speak to his solicitor. Louisa faced her brother again and when she spoke her voice was low.

"Edward Manning has informed me that he is thinking of renting this cottage to someone else. If he does, where would we go? We would be the subject of gossip then as well. Worse, we would be an object of everyone's pity. I know you would hate that."

His eyes widened briefly with surprise before narrowing again. His hands clenched at his side. "You were planning to keep that piece of information from me."

It was clear he didn't appreciate the fact that she'd thought only to shield him from worry about their future.

"It no longer matters," she said.

John looked away from her then and was silent for what seemed an eternity before finally replying.

"I have to get out of here. I can't stand to hear you talk about selling yourself to a Manning."

Louisa didn't try to stop him. She could only hope he would soon adjust to the path their lives must now take. She wouldn't allow herself to think about what could happen if he didn't.

When she turned back to face her guests, Mr. Stephens was already gathering up the paperwork. Overlea approached her.

"I believe we have covered everything that needs to be included in the marriage settlement. Mr. Stephens will draw up the agreement as soon as possible and have a copy delivered to you. You will, of course, have someone review the contract for you to make sure everything is in order."

Louisa nodded. "Reverend Harnick is John and Catherine's guardian. At five and twenty I don't require one, but I'm sure he will know of a solicitor who can act on my behalf."

"Good," he said. "Perhaps it will ease your brother's mind somewhat."

She had to concede he was right. Everything was happening too quickly. She felt as though her life were spinning out of control. The appearance of a mysterious stranger in need of help, followed closely by Edward Manning's indecent proposal that had forced her to turn to Overlea for help. And now it would appear they were to be married, and much sooner than she had expected.

Overwhelmed, she sank onto the settee. Overlea took it upon himself to see his attorney out before returning to speak to her in private. He lowered himself next to her.

"Will you be all right, Miss Evans?"

She gave a small laugh, one that she feared would soon turn to hysteria if she didn't get her emotions under control.

"It is all happening too fast. I fear I am out of my depth."

He smiled at that and reached to take hold of her hands.

"You will do well," he said, squeezing them gently. "You are a practical and resourceful woman. I wouldn't have proposed if I didn't believe you would make a fine marchioness."

Louisa frowned at his unromantic words. Practical and resourceful. Well, she supposed it could have been much worse. She stared down where his thumbs were drawing little circles on the backs of her hands. The sensations caused by that small movement made her intensely aware of the fact she was alone in the house with him. Suddenly all she could think about was how those same hands had cupped her breasts and started to caress her inner thighs. Her breath hitched at the unexpected longing that swept through her.

"I don't know what I'm supposed to do now," she said, tugging gently at their joined hands until he released them.

"I have some unfinished business in London I must attend to. I expect to return within two weeks."

"How on earth am I to prepare for a wedding?"

"Do not concern yourself. Grandmother is already planning the ball and after leaving here I am going to speak with Reverend Harnick." He paused briefly before continuing. "Your brother is correct. Tongues will wag, but I think we will be able to weather the storm together."

She stifled a gasp as a thought occurred to her.

"What is the matter?"

"I will need a dress... oh, and Catherine and John also need new clothing. I will have to buy material—"

"Miss Evans... Louisa."

She stopped and stared at him. He was leaning toward her, his gaze holding hers captive. His use of her given name added an intimacy to their conversation that hadn't been there before.

"I will speak to Grandmother tonight. I will be leaving first thing in the morning, so I am afraid I won't be able to introduce you to her myself, but I am sure she will send word about when you may call on her." A corner of his mouth quirked up. "She had given up hope of my ever marrying and is looking forward to meeting you. She will help you to make all the arrangements. Grandmother could move mountains through sheer will alone."

There was a rueful twist to his lips when he uttered that last statement and it left Louisa thinking that he had often been on the opposite side of that will.

"Was your grandmother terribly shocked at your news?"

"She was surprised when I mentioned your name, yes."

"Does she disapprove? It's no secret that I will bring nothing to the marriage. I am certain she wishes you to make a more advantageous match."

"She has made no secret of the fact that she wants me to marry, but she knows it would be better for all parties involved if I chose my own bride. Would you not agree?"

He looked at her directly as he spoke, and she acknowledged the truth of his words. She couldn't imagine trying to force this man into marrying against his will. In fact, she thought it would probably be impossible to force him to do anything he didn't want to do.

There was one more worry she had to discuss with Overlea before he left.

"Your cousin will be expecting a reply soon to his… proposition." The word left a bitter taste in her mouth. "We may find ourselves cast out before you return, or worse. He may approach Catherine directly."

Overlea's jaw tightened. "I will deal with my cousin. He won't come near you or your family."

"Thank you, my lord," she said, her relief vast.

Sensing that their meeting was at an end, she stood and walked with Overlea to the front door. She turned to face him and found she was at a loss for words. The next time she saw him they would be within days of marrying. She imagined Overlea was thinking the same thing.

Her gaze met his and she felt herself being pulled toward him.

"Miss Evans?"

"Yes, my lord?"

"Perhaps we should do away with the formalities. My name is Nicholas."

She balked at the intimacy. "Perhaps... I can call you Overlea."

He shook his head. "I wasn't raised to be the next marquess. Overlea was my father and then my brother, not me. I would prefer it if I weren't reminded of them every time you said my name."

Couched in those terms, his request did not seem unusual.

"Very well, my lord... Nicholas."

He smiled, a wicked, coaxing smile that served as testament to his reputation as a rogue.

"That wasn't so bad now, was it, Louisa?"

Standing this close to him, drawn in by his knowing gaze and wicked smile, she was in danger of losing her detachment. Theirs was not a love match, yet at this moment that fact didn't matter to her. His head lowered and for a moment she thought he was going to kiss her again. His mouth hovered over hers and she closed her eyes, waiting. Abruptly, he took a step back and disappointment swept through her. She took a deep, shaky breath and tried to ignore her jangled nerves. When she looked up at him his mask of cool detachment was firmly in place again.

"I will see you in two weeks," he said.

She watched as he left. This time there was no fear for

his safety. Whatever weakness had overcome him that other night, it was clearly gone now.

Nicholas cursed at himself as he rode away from the home of his future wife. Good lord, he had almost kissed her. Again. And afterward he had fled from her presence like an untested, infatuated youth. The very last thing he could afford to do, however, was to become romantically involved with Louisa Evans. The future of the marquisate depended on it.

He didn't know what had come over him. He had meant only to bridge some of the cool formality that was between them. After all, it wouldn't do for her to call him "my lord" at their wedding. He'd looked into those gray eyes of hers, however, and forgotten his intentions. Perhaps he was losing his mind.

He tried to shake off his unsettled feelings surrounding Louisa Evans and concentrate on the meeting ahead. It was time to deal with Edward, and he found he was looking forward to the encounter.

As he rode to his cousin's manor house, he tried to remember when he had last visited. It had been several years since his uncle had been alive, his death predating that of Nicholas's parents. Although his father and uncle were twins, they had never been close. His uncle had spent his whole life knowing his brother would become the Marquess of Overlea because he'd been born ten minutes earlier. Instead of the closeness that twins often shared, there had been nothing but acrimony between them. Being a second son himself, Nicholas knew all too well how everyone favored the eldest. He had been happy not to have his every move monitored and had never coveted the extra responsibilities that came with the position. His uncle, however, had felt differently and his lifelong bitterness had been passed down to Edward.

His brother, James, had agreed to marry their cousin Mary in an effort to mend the rift by uniting the two branches of the family. When he died, Nicholas had become the new Marquess of Overlea. He had avoided the subject of marriage at all costs, but since his brother's betrothal had never been formalized he suspected his aunt and cousins were under the impression he would step in and wed his cousin. There was sure to be a scene when they learned he was to marry another. Normally he avoided that side of the family and all their drama, but today he was looking forward very much to informing Edward of his upcoming marriage.

When he arrived, the butler led him into the drawing room where Nicholas expected his aunt and cousins would keep him waiting. He was surprised, therefore, when his aunt appeared within minutes.

"Nicholas!" she exclaimed. "We did not expect to see you here today."

He returned a short bow, more than a little surprised at her effusive welcome.

Edward had inherited his coloring from his mother. Elizabeth Manning had the same ice-blue eyes and light brown hair, but hers was threaded through now with liberal streaks of gray. He could almost see the wheels turning behind those eyes as she weighed the various possibilities for his visit. She would have to wait, however. He wanted to see the look on Edward's face when he made his announcement.

"Are my cousins at home?" he asked. "There is some

news I wish to share with them."

He was amused at the gleam that entered his aunt's eyes. Clearly she had settled on the belief that he planned to offer for Mary.

"Of course," she said, her smile bright.

He waited while she rang for tea and requested that his cousins join them. Her manner was overly friendly, something that had always irked him even as a child when he realized how quickly that façade could—and did—change.

His cousins didn't make him wait long. Edward greeted him with a curt "Overlea," the name sounding almost like a curse. Mary was right behind him. She met his eyes only briefly before curtseying and joining her mother on the settee.

Nicholas marveled at how anyone could imagine he would want to wed Mary. She was pretty, yes, having inherited her father's dark hair and her mother's pale blue eyes. She'd also inherited the best features from both her parents, but it was her personality that made him cringe. Or rather, her lack of one.

"I have some happy news that I wanted to share with you."

Edward appeared bored. Mary sat unmoving, her eyes cast down. His aunt, however, didn't bother to hide her anticipation.

"I am to be married," he said. "I believe you all know my intended."

"Oh, Nicholas—" his aunt started.

"Her name is Louisa Evans."

There was a moment of stunned silence. His eyes were on Edward when he'd shared his news and he saw the way his cousin's jaw clenched. He found it interesting that Mary's stiff posture relaxed almost immediately. It appeared she, too, did not wish a union between them. His aunt went through the motions of wishing them well, but she couldn't hide her anger. She made her excuses and escorted a silent Mary from the room.

Nicholas paid little attention to them. His eyes were fixed firmly on Edward, who wisely chose to remain silent. Nicholas could tell he was wondering if Louisa had told him about his proposition.

"I believe you know my betrothed," he said.

"Of course I know her," Edward replied, not bothering to mask his annoyance. "She's lived in the area since she was born, and she does some sewing for my sister."

"True. And there is the fact that this used to be her family's home."

Edward sneered. "It was a fair card game. If her father couldn't afford to lose, he never should have played. They're fortunate Father allowed them to live in their cottage rent free. He didn't have to be so generous."

Nicholas raised a brow. "You can stop pretending. I know he did that only at my father's insistence."

Edward shrugged but said nothing.

"And what are your intentions toward the Evans family."

Edward hesitated only a moment before replying. "Father made a promise, and I upheld it."

"And now that Joseph Evans is gone?"

Nicholas could see the hint of apprehension that crossed his cousin's face though Edward did his best to hide it. "There was no understanding that the rest of the family could stay there forever without paying rent. I very generously waited until their period of mourning was over, but things change."

Nicholas took a step toward his cousin, allowing the tight rein he'd been holding over his temper to slip. The corners of his mouth turned up in a grim smile at the flash of fear in Edward's eyes.

"I know about your proposal to my bride-to-be."

He wasn't surprised when Edward tried to lie. "I don't know what you mean. What did she tell you?"

Nicholas took another step forward and was satisfied when his cousin took a corresponding one back.

"I will be marrying Louisa Evans very soon. She is under *my* protection now. You are not to approach her or any member of her family ever again. Do I make myself clear?"

Edward sputtered briefly before allowing his own anger to show.

"You do not control me. You may hold the title, but you do not have the right to tell me what I can and cannot do. If the delightful Miss Evans or her sister decides—"

Pure, unadulterated rage pumped through Nicholas's veins. His hands shot out and he grasped his cousin by the throat. He lowered his head so his face was only inches away from his cousin's.

"Make no mistake," he said, his voice low with menace, "if you ever so much as look at Louisa or her sister again, it will be the last thing you do."

He flung Edward away from him in disgust and watched as the man grasped at his throat, coughing.

"You will regret threatening me," Edward said between fits of wheezing.

Nicholas spared the man only a brief, contemptuous

glance before striding from the room and away from the house, his fists still clenched in impotent fury. He longed to smash them into Edward's smug, superior face. To pummel the man to within an inch of his life. The only thing that had stopped him was the knowledge that doing so would disappoint his grandmother. If Edward dared to look at Louisa again, though, even that wouldn't stop him.

CHAPTER SEVEN

It had been two days since Louisa had gone to Overlea Manor to ask for the marquess's help. The very last thing she'd expected to come from that meeting was a proposal of marriage. She'd been desperate but had somehow managed to control her nerves. Now, however, the task proved nearly impossible. Catherine, on the other hand, was brimming with anticipation.

She aimed a shaky smile at her sister before stepping down from the carriage Nicholas's grandmother had sent to collect them. The butler ushered her inside right away, bidding her to wait in the drawing room while he notified the dowager marchioness of her arrival.

They had to wait some minutes before Nicholas's grandmother swept into the room. She was shorter than Louisa and her slim figure and snow-white hair should have given her an air of frailty. Instead, however, the older woman possessed an unmistakable air of authority that made Louisa feel completely out of her depth.

She and Catherine stood to greet her.

"I apologize for keeping you waiting," Lady Overlea said after she had rung for tea. "I was in the conservatory tending to the roses and Sommers did not know where to find me."

Catherine's interest was immediately piqued, and she was almost glowing with excitement when she spoke. "I love to garden as well. I have read about conservatories, but have never actually seen one."

"We must not impose," Louisa said, afraid Nicholas's grandmother would be annoyed at Catherine's exuberance.

"It is no imposition," the older woman said. "I am quite proud of the Overlea conservatory and would like nothing more than to give you a tour. Unfortunately, we will not have time today. Perhaps on your next visit."

"I will look forward to it," Catherine said. "I saw some of your gardens on the way in and would like to have a closer look. I can see that you have some plants I have never seen before."

"You have discovered my secret love," Lady Overlea said, her smile warm and open. "I think you will enjoy exploring the plants in the conservatory. Many have come from much warmer climates and must be brought indoors before the winter."

Catherine's own smile widened and Louisa began to relax. She froze, however, when Lady Overlea turned her attention back to her. The weight of the older woman's perusal was almost a palpable thing.

"I was so very sorry to hear about your father's death, Miss Evans."

A lump rose in her throat at the other woman's words, especially since it was obvious she meant them.

"Thank you, my lady," she said. "And since we are

soon to be family, you must call me Louisa and my sister Catherine."

Nicholas's grandmother waited several moments before asking, "How did my grandson come to propose marriage to you? I was not aware that he had even met you." A frown creased her brow.

Louisa's mind went blank and she strove to collect her scattered thoughts. It hadn't occurred to her that Nicholas wouldn't have told his grandmother how they'd met. He must have been trying to spare her from worrying about his health. She would have to come as near to the truth as possible without revealing the details of her other grandson's proposition.

"In truth, we have known each other only a short while. He rode by our house earlier this week while returning from London and stopped by our cottage. He expressed his condolences on our father's death." She ignored the curious look Catherine aimed at her and continued. "I was surprised, myself, when he proposed marriage to me two days ago."

Lady Overlea nodded as though the explanation made perfect sense and smiled, amusement lighting her features. "That would be like Nicholas, unable to pass by a beautiful young woman without stopping to talk to her."

Louisa blushed at the compliment.

The dowager marchioness's mood changed, becoming somber. "I have a confession to make. I am afraid I didn't leave my grandson with much choice. It was time for him to marry and I forced the issue."

Her revelation surprised Louisa. She couldn't imagine Nicholas being forced to do anything against his will.

"I will be blunt with you. My grandson probably didn't

tell you, but the Overlea line is in danger. If Nicholas does not produce an heir the title will go to his cousin. Do not mistake me, I love all my grandchildren, but the notion of Edward as the next Marquess of Overlea..." She closed her eyes briefly. "Well, let us just say that it is important Nicholas produce a son to secure the inheritance."

Louisa could almost feel the weight of that responsibility being transferred squarely onto her shoulders.

"I cannot guarantee the marquess a son, but I will do my duty," she said, unable to hold back her blush.

Lady Overlea reached over and patted Louisa on the arm. "That is all we can ask. Now," she said, rising to her feet. "We have a wedding to plan and a wardrobe to secure. I have already sent word to London and the modiste will be here tomorrow. Please come with me. We have not a moment to spare."

Nicholas's first action on reaching his London townhouse was to send word to Richard Harding, the Earl of Kerrick, that he was in town again. When he arrived later that afternoon, Nicholas led the way to his study.

"It's a little early for drinking, is it not?" Kerrick asked when Nicholas walked over to the sideboard and poured two brandies.

"It was an interesting visit," Nicholas said as he handed his friend one of the drinks.

"It was certainly a short one, even for you. I hope you straightened out all that nonsense about getting married. What did your grandmother have to say for herself?"

Nicholas waited until Kerrick had raised the glass to his lips before replying.

"Congratulate me," Nicholas said. "I am to be wed."

He smiled when his friend choked on the drink. Lord knew there was little enough to find amusing about the whole situation.

"Damn," Kerrick said when he'd regained his composure. "That wasn't funny."

"I wasn't making a jest."

Kerrick stared at him in horror. "Bloody hell."

"Yes, well, hopefully it won't be quite that bad."

Kerrick shook his head in amazement. "I can't believe the old lady outmaneuvered you. Your aunt must be over the moon."

Nicholas scowled. "I am not marrying my cousin."

"Good," Kerrick said. "I have to say I was never crazy about that side of your family. Edward is a vile creature, and Mary is much too meek and nondescript for you."

Nicholas could not agree more wholeheartedly.

"To say they were displeased when I told them would be a vast understatement." A small smile of satisfaction touched his lips as he remembered the scene.

Kerrick laughed. "Leave it to you to turn the announcement into a production."

"Yes, it was very amusing."

He didn't bother to tell his friend about Edward's proposition to Louisa. That matter was dealt with and his cousin would be a fool not to heed his warning in future.

"So tell me, who is the fortunate woman? One of the many who have been dangling after you since your brother passed away?"

"No," Nicholas said. "It is a neighbor in Kent."

"Really?" Kerrick's brows rose as he speculated on the importance of that revelation. "Have you been keeping secrets from me?"

"I wish it were something that interesting," Nicholas replied. "You won't know the family."

He downed the remainder of his brandy. He'd had some time now to consider this discussion with Kerrick, but had been unable to think of a way to ease into it.

His friend picked up on his change in mood immediately.

"Why are you here, Nicholas? It doesn't bode well for your upcoming marriage if you feel the need to escape her presence right after your betrothal."

Kerrick was aiming for levity, but Nicholas was in no mood for jests.

"I have returned to town for a special license. The ceremony will take place at the end of the month."

Kerrick whistled. "Is she with child?"

Nicholas winced at those words. "No, thank God."

He paced to his desk, then turned to lean against it.

"You may want to sit down."

Kerrick raised a brow but did just that.

"I need a favor."

"You have it," Kerrick replied without reservation.

"You haven't heard what I am asking of you."

"It matters not. Whatever you need—short of murder, and even then it would depend on who you wanted me to kill—you have it."

Nicholas smiled. He knew he could depend on Kerrick to do just about anything he asked, but what he was asking of him now… Nicholas knew that in the end he would agree, but he also knew Kerrick would try to talk him out of his plans.

"I had an episode on the way home," he said.

"How bad?"

"Bad. I passed out. When I awoke, I couldn't remember where I was or why I was on my way to see Grandmother."

Kerrick remained silent for a moment, taking in the importance of this piece of news. Nicholas was glad he didn't offer trite words of sympathy. With this latest episode he could no longer deny that he had inherited the condition that had led to the deaths of both his father and his brother.

"Were you on the road at the time?"

Nicholas nodded. "Fortunately, I saw a cottage as my light-headedness worsened and was able to seek shelter before losing consciousness."

"You might have lain on the road for hours."

"Yes, that would have been most inconvenient. And you'll appreciate the poetry of the situation. I ended up on the doorstep of the woman I'm about to marry."

"I'm having a very difficult time picturing you falling prostrate at the feet of a woman, then turning around and asking her to marry you." Kerrick shook his head at the image. His demeanor became somber, though, as he continued. "I know you don't want me to speak of it, but surely you can find someone who can help you with this illness."

Nicholas shook his head. This was a subject he hated to think about.

"Both my father and my brother consulted all the leading physicians and no one knows what this illness is. Apparently they've never seen anything like it. The only thing they do know, and even that was a guess after my brother fell ill, is that the condition is inherited."

"What do you need me to do?" Kerrick asked after a moment of silence.

"Before I continue, I need you to promise you'll hear me out."

"You're beginning to make me nervous. Just tell me what you need."

Nicholas nodded and pushed away from the desk. He walked around it, pulled out his chair, and sank into it heavily. "Overlea needs an heir."

"I presume that is why you are marrying."

"In part. My recent bout of illness, however, did make me realize one thing. I cannot risk having a child of my own."

Kerrick was clearly confused by his words.

"If you are not intending to father children, why are you marrying? You already have an heir."

"No," he said, his tone emphatic. "Edward cannot inherit."

Kerrick leaned forward. "You're not making sense. I can see why you don't want Manning to become the next marquess, but the only way to avoid that is to have a male child of your own."

Nicholas shook his head.

"Not quite. It is my wife who will produce the heir. Everyone need only assume that the child is mine."

Kerrick sat back, stunned. "You would do that?"

"I have no other choice."

"Yes, Nicholas, you do. You are speaking nonsense. You actually want your wife to pass off someone else's child as your own? When it is not even certain that you would pass on your illness to your children?"

Nicholas laughed, the sound bitter. "That is not a

chance I am willing to take. And the father wouldn't be just anyone. It would be someone of my choosing. Someone with impeccable bloodlines himself."

Nicholas knew the moment Kerrick understood what he was saying. His expression changed from confusion to incredulity, then anger. He stood abruptly, moved to the desk and leaned over it, his face mere inches from Nicholas's own.

"You are insane. Does your wife-to-be know you plan to whore her out to some other man? To me?"

The words were calculated to make him cringe and they hit their mark. He'd been careful not to think about what Louisa Evans's reaction would be. Unlike Kerrick, however, she would have no choice in the matter after she signed the marriage contract and promised to provide him with an heir.

"Have a care what you say."

"The hell I will," Kerrick said, pushing himself away from the desk.

Nicholas had been expecting the disbelief. He'd even known Kerrick would be angry. What he hadn't expected was the flash of disgust he'd seen on his friend's face. He said nothing as Kerrick paced across the room. For a moment Nicholas thought he was going to storm out the door, but instead he turned abruptly and stalked back to the desk.

"I won't do it," he said, his mouth a grim line.

Nicholas had expected his refusal, but he was certain he could make Kerrick see reason.

"Then I will find someone else."

Kerrick's jaw tightened. "Who?"

Nicholas shrugged, pretending a casual indifference he

was far from feeling.

"I am sure there are any number of men who would gladly do the deed. I would have preferred it to be someone I knew could be counted on to keep his mouth shut, but…" He shrugged again as he allowed his voice to trail off.

"Don't do this, Nicholas. Think of the scandal if word were to get out"

"It matters not. You know there will be rumors anyway after Louisa and I marry so quickly, but her position as marchioness will serve as a nice buffer against those rumors." He braced his arms on the desk and leaned forward. "My heir will survive those rumors. He would hardly be the first by-blow to assume a title. Overlea, however, would not survive Edward as the marquess. He would drive the estate into the ground. And you've heard the rumors that are swirling around town about him. From what I've recently learned, I daresay most of them are true."

Kerrick sank into his chair again and buried his head in his hands. It was almost a full minute before he looked up.

"Have you so little regard for this woman you are to marry? From what you've told me, she may have saved your life. You probably wouldn't have survived a night out on the road, not in the condition you were in."

"She won't be happy. In fact, I expect her to be furious, but she is a practical woman. She will do what needs to be done. And when I die she will give thanks every day that she will never have to watch her own child and grandchildren succumb to the same illness. Grandmother has already lost a son and a grandson to that illness. Soon, she'll have lost two of her four grandchildren. Louisa

Evans will not have to suffer that same fate. Better she should think me a bastard now than suffer what my grandmother has."

Kerrick had stilled during his speech. Without conscious thought, Nicholas had risen at some point. He had never before spoken so passionately about what was to come. He had always avoided the subject of his eventual death.

He turned and stalked to the window, trying to get his emotions back under control.

Neither spoke for what seemed a very long time, the two men locked in a silent battle of wills, neither willing to admit they might be in the wrong. In the end, Kerrick approached Nicholas and laid a hand on his shoulder.

"I can make no promises," he said, "but I will return with you to Kent."

Nicholas closed his eyes in relief. Everything was going to work out as he'd hoped.

CHAPTER EIGHT

The morning of the wedding dawned and Louisa was surprised at the calmness that had settled over her. She'd been overwhelmed at first by all the wedding details, but just as he'd promised, Nicholas's grandmother had taken care of everything.

Lady Overlea had already arranged to have most of the Evans family's personal belongings moved to Overlea Manor. John had been sullen and silent during the last weeks but he hadn't protested, and for that Louisa was grateful. That night her brother and sister would be sleeping in their new rooms at Overlea manor. She knew Catherine, at least, was very excited by the prospect.

She, on the other hand, would be spending the night here with her new husband. Before leaving, Nicholas had informed his grandmother that he wanted privacy after tonight's ball, and since some of the guests would be spending the night at the manor house before departing on the morrow, it was decided they would get that privacy only by retiring to the Evans cottage. A group of servants were there now, preparing the house for her honeymoon night with her new husband.

She shied away from thoughts of the upcoming wedding night. She had expected to see Overlea at some point during the last week, but he'd sent word that he was delayed in town. A part of her had half expected to learn he'd changed his mind and that there would be no wedding. She'd been relieved, therefore, when he'd sent her a second note apologizing for his delay but promising to arrive last night.

She stood now in front of her mirror as the housemaid Lady Overlea had sent over flitted about her, adjusting the folds of her wedding gown and adding a pearl necklace and ear bobs. Louisa could only stare in wonder at her reflection, barely able to recognize the elegant woman in the mirror. Since the wedding was to be a small family affair, they'd chosen a simple white dress. Louisa had worried that with her fair skin and hair she'd look pale and colorless, but the silk fabric had a subtle rose undertone that brought out a hint of color in her cheeks and complemented her gray eyes. A few tendrils of her normally straight hair had been cut and now curled becomingly around her face, and flowers she didn't recognized had been woven into her hair. Louisa knew Lady Overlea and Catherine had enjoyed picking them out from the flowers that grew in the conservatory at Overlea Manor.

An abbreviated knock at the door was her only warning before Catherine burst into the room with an excited flourish. Louisa could only stare in wonder as her sister twirled in front of her, showing off her pale rose gown and the elaborate upsweep of her hair. She dismissed the maid and greeted her sister with a hug.

Catherine drew back with a laugh and looked her over.

"You are beautiful, Louisa," she said with a sigh.

Louisa smiled. She hadn't had had any doubts, but seeing Catherine so happy and excited about the future reaffirmed that she was doing the right thing. She wouldn't be able to feign the excitement her sister was feeling, but at least she'd banished her nerves. If only she'd been able to speak to Nicholas one more time before the wedding. It seemed like such a long time since she had last seen him.

"I spoke to John," Catherine said, "and I warned him not to scowl today."

"I'm sure that once everyone learns Overlea has married someone he barely knows and who is so far beneath him, tongues will start wagging in earnest. What is a frown or two from a disapproving relative after that?"

Louisa aimed for levity, but in truth she tried not to think about the ball that would be held later that night. Lady Overlea had explained that everyone thought Nicholas was going to be announcing his betrothal tonight. The news that he had already married would come as a surprise.

"Yes, well, I told John that I would never speak to him again if he ruined your wedding."

Her sister's vehemence surprised her.

"Don't worry," Catherine said. "I probably wouldn't last more than a couple of days without speaking to him. I don't want him to know that, though."

Louisa couldn't help but laugh. At some point in the last three weeks her sister had taken on the role of champion of her upcoming wedding. She knew Catherine was looking forward to her upcoming Season next spring and hoping to have a similar wedding in the not-too-distant future.

"I am trying not to think about John," Louisa admitted. "He's been so quiet these past few weeks and rarely speaks to me anymore."

"He loves you, but he thinks he has failed us. Just when he had determined he would sacrifice his education for the well-being of the family, you snatched that away from him with your own sacrifice. His pride is a little put out."

Louisa could only stare at her sister in amazement. "When did you grow up and become so wise?"

Catherine smiled fondly at her. "I have had a very good teacher."

Louisa dabbed at the tears that sprang to her eyes at her sister's words, which caused Catherine to frown at her.

"There's to be no crying," she said, waving a finger in front of Louisa in mock admonition. "Today is a day for happiness only."

Louisa took a deep breath and gave her sister a weak smile. "I will do my best."

Another knock sounded at the door and her heartbeat sped up. It was foolish, but she wondered if Overlea had come to see her. She was disappointed when the maid entered and announced that the carriage was ready to take them to the chapel.

"Is my brother ready?" she asked.

"He has already left and asked me to let you know he would meet you there."

Louisa nodded and turned back to Catherine. "Are you ready?"

Her sister's haste in leading the way was answer enough.

The drive to the chapel was blessedly quiet. Normally Catherine liked to fill any silence with chatter, but she must have sensed Louisa's need for quiet. As the carriage came to a stop, however, Catherine reached across the seat and squeezed her hand. "Everything will be fine."

Louisa smiled, relieved that for once she could sit back and allow someone to give her comfort. It was clear she no longer had to worry about her sister.

A footman opened the carriage door and held out a hand to help first Catherine, then Louisa, down. It was a perfect fall day. The air was crisp but not too cold. The leaves were beginning to change color and she couldn't help but note that she, too, was changing. Her old life was dropping away, soon to be replaced by a new one. She only hoped she would not have to go through a barren, metaphorical winter before that happened.

She looked up at the chapel. It was a small country church, a fact for which she was grateful. Given his position in society, the Marquess of Overlea could have insisted they have their wedding in a London cathedral in front of heaven only knew how many guests.

"Aside from your brother, everyone is inside, my lady," the footman said.

Louisa spotted John then. He'd been waiting at the side of the chapel and was coming around to meet her. This was the first time she had ever seen him dressed in formal attire, and it made him appear older than his eighteen years. He stopped when he was a few feet away.

"If you are determined to do this, I would like to give you away."

Profound relief swept through her and she closed the distance between them to embrace him. A sense of peace settled within her. Everything was going to be fine now.

The small group followed the footman into the chapel. Louisa and John waited in the vestibule while Catherine was shown to her place. John's expression was intent as he searched her features, and she knew that her brother was looking for any sign of doubt. She smiled at him and took his arm.

The music started and together they stepped into the main area of the chapel and started down the aisle. Overlea was true to his word and the wedding was a small one. As expected, only her family and his grandmother were present. She didn't recognize the man standing by his side, but she spared him only a quick glance before her attention became riveted on her future husband. His dark gaze locked with hers and she could see the approval in his eyes.

She must have made a little sound because her brother swung his head to look at her, his brows raised in question. Knowing he would like nothing more than to spirit her away from the chapel, she shook her head in a small, abbreviated movement and turned her attention back to the man waiting for her at the end of the aisle. She wasn't certain, but she thought she detected a hint of relief in his expression. It seemed she wasn't the only one who'd thought the other might have changed their mind about the marriage.

The walk down the aisle was a short one and before she knew it, her brother had placed her hand in Overlea's. In a low voice John warned him to take care of her before he retreated to his seat. Nicholas squeezed her hand to reassure her and she couldn't stop the smile that sprang to her lips.

She tried to keep her attention on the reverend, but Overlea drew her eyes and attention like a magnet. Despite the preparations of the last few weeks, she still found it difficult to believe she was actually standing here, about to marry him. He was more handsome than any man had a right to be and could have any woman he wanted. With his black hair and dark eyes, he also exuded an intriguing hint of danger. There was a provocative edge to the man that was almost impossible to resist.

Before she knew it, they were married.

Overlea bent to kiss her. It wasn't a long kiss, merely the light brushing of his lips against hers, but it served as notice that her future and that of her siblings were now in his keeping. In a daze, she remained silent while Overlea placed her hand on his arm and led the way out of the chapel. The small group of witnesses gathered outside where Lady Overlea swept her into a surprisingly firm hug and welcomed her into the family. Overlea spared a moment to introduce her to his good friend, the Earl of Kerrick, before leading her to their waiting carriage. She couldn't help but wonder at his haste.

He handed her in before following and taking the seat opposite her. In the small space, she was very aware of how he seemed to fill the entire carriage. Of his scent and the way his long legs seemed to take up all the available space. She leaned back in her seat, closed her eyes and concentrated on her breathing in an attempt to hold back the nerves that were threatening to surface now that they were alone. It was difficult to take a deep breath because of the tightness of her stays, but the undergarment did wonders to accentuate her bosom.

She opened her eyes again when the carriage began to

move. Nicholas was staring out the carriage window, but upon sensing her gaze he turned his complete attention on her.

"How does it feel to be the new Marchioness of Overlea?"

She frowned. "I didn't marry you for your title."

"True," he said, his voice devoid of emotion, "but I am sure it will be of great consolation to you."

Something was different about him, but she couldn't say what.

"I wasn't sure you would return," she said after a short pause.

"I had little choice in the matter."

"You are the Marquess of Overlea. You could have done whatever you wished."

His lips twisted ruefully at her words. "There are some things that are beyond even my reach."

"Such as?"

She was curious about what had caused his strange mood. He was silent for a long time and she didn't think he was going to reply, so was surprised when he finally said, "My illness."

Was he going to tell her what had happened to him that night? And his phrasing made it sound as though it was not something that was in the past.

"Are you feeling unwell, my lord?"

"Nicholas, remember?"

She licked her lips. "Of course. But you haven't answered my question."

He shrugged. She hoped he was about to confide in her, but the carriage began to slow then.

"We're almost there." There was a subtle shift in his

demeanor and she knew they wouldn't be returning to the subject of his health. "Has my grandmother told you what to expect today?"

She nodded. Since there would be a ball later that evening, they were doing away with the traditional wedding breakfast. Instead, she would go to her new bedroom, where the same maid who had helped her to dress earlier would be waiting to assist her in changing out of her wedding dress. Later that evening, after the guests arrived for the ball, she and her new husband would enter together and she would be formally introduced as the new Marchioness of Overlea. Invitations had gone out to those families who lived within a few hours' drive of Overlea Manor, which included those who had town homes in London. It seemed that upon hearing the rumor Overlea would be announcing his betrothal at this ball, a number of families had returned to town just so they could attend the event.

"This will be your first ball?"

She nodded, trying not to think about all the eyes that would soon be on her. When she failed, she covered her face with her hands. "Everyone will be whispering about me."

She heard him move, and he was beside her when he pulled her hands away and tilted her face up to his.

"They can think what they like, but no one will dare insult you and risk displeasing Grandmother and me."

She sighed. "After tonight everyone will know that ours is not a love match. I suppose it doesn't matter. Such arrangements are made all the time."

He tilted his head and looked at her, a slight frown marring his brow. "That was important to you? Marrying for love? I thought you were more practical than to wish for such nonsense."

She blushed under his intense scrutiny. "Most women hope for as much. They may not say so, but the desire is there nonetheless."

His voice lowered as he asked his next question. "Do you regret agreeing to marry me?"

He seemed to genuinely want to know. She thought back to the last three weeks. To the doubts she'd had and the internal struggle that would follow where she told herself she was being practical and doing the right thing for her family. She remembered her unease as the days passed and Nicholas hadn't returned from London. Her worry about whether he'd changed his mind, and her intense relief when she'd received his letter telling her that he would be returning the day before the wedding. At the time she'd told herself she was only worried because of the uncertainty surrounding what would happen to her family if he called off the wedding, but then she thought about the jolt of awareness she'd experienced when she saw him again today, waiting for her at the end of the aisle. And there was also the undeniable attraction between them now.

"No, I have no regrets."

He seemed relieved at her assertion. Her breath caught and held when he lowered his head.

"I'm glad," he said before his lips met hers.

It was the merest brush of his lips against hers, no different than the kiss they had shared at the end of the wedding ceremony, yet a jolt of awareness coursed through her body at the contact. He pulled back to stare down at her and the very air seemed to thicken around them.

The carriage came to a halt, interrupting the moment of intimacy, and Nicholas looked away.

They remained silent as a footman handed her out of the carriage and Nicholas escorted her up the short flight of stairs to Overlea Manor. She hesitated when Sommers opened the door and she saw that the staff was waiting, lined in two long rows along the hallway. She had already met many of them over the past weeks, but couldn't help feeling self-conscious when she was formally introduced as Lady Overlea. She'd spent the last three weeks surrounded by preparations for today's wedding and the ball that was to follow tonight. During that time she'd tried not to think about her future role as the Marchioness of Overlea, but she could no longer ignore how much her life would change. The reality was overwhelming.

She managed a few words to the staff, although she couldn't say afterward what they were, before Nicholas dismissed them. She expected him to have her new lady's maid accompany her to her rooms and was surprised when he escorted her himself. It occurred to her, then, that he might intend to consummate their marriage right away, and the thought caused her to stumble on the stairs. He reached out to steady her, his warm hand on the small of her back, and a shiver of awareness went through her. If Nicholas noticed he didn't say anything, but he did remove his hand when they reached the landing.

She already knew the way to her rooms, which adjoined Nicholas's, and preceded him down the corridors. With every step she was conscious of his very masculine presence at her side. The silence that stretched between them threatened to suffocate her and it only grew more oppressive with each step. Desperate for something to break through that stillness, her thoughts settled on the one unhappy face she couldn't help but notice after their arrival at the manor.

"Your valet doesn't like me," she said.

Nicholas stopped and she turned to look at him. He was frowning, but his face cleared before he spoke. "Harrison is like that with everyone."

He started to walk again and she had to hurry to catch up.

"Why did you hire him, then? Surely you'd prefer someone who wasn't so…" She searched for the right word to describe him and finally settled on "sour."

Nicholas shrugged. "I didn't hire him. He was my father's valet, and James used him as well when he inherited. I didn't have the heart to let him go when I became marquess. He was loyal to them and I have doubts he'd be able to find another situation. Just ignore him, his negativity isn't personal."

Louisa wasn't so sure about that, but she tried to shrug off her unease. They'd finally reached her bedroom and there was another moment of awkward silence when Nicholas turned to look at her.

He spoke first. "I'll take my leave of you now. I'm sure Grandmother has seen to it that your rooms will be satisfactory."

She looked up at him. "You're not coming in?"

His expression was shuttered and she couldn't tell what he was thinking. It left her feeling at a distinct disadvantage.

He raised a hand, brushing the back of his fingers against her cheek. "You look tired."

She swallowed hard before replying. "I slept very little last night."

He dropped his hand and took a step back, and she felt the absence of his touch acutely.

"You should rest, then, before tonight's celebration."

She could only nod in reply before slipping into her room.

Nicholas made his way to the study and sank heavily into the oak chair behind his desk. He leaned back and stared up at the ceiling, seeing again the way Louisa had looked at him in the carriage. For a moment he'd allowed himself to believe she was with him because she wanted to be there and not because her family needed his protection. She'd been surprised just now when she realized he wasn't going to join her in her bedroom, but not nearly as surprised as he'd been by the strength of his desire to make love to her. It was true that there were ways to avoid pregnancy, but he could not risk fathering a child and passing on his illness.

No, it would be better for everyone involved if he stayed away from his wife. Theirs could never be a real marriage.

He'd been attracted to Louisa from the start, but today, watching her walk down the aisle, no longer enshrouded in drab colors, he'd been struck anew by her beauty. He didn't regret choosing her for his marchioness, but he now realized how dangerous she would be to his peace of mind. He needed Kerrick to agree to his plan, and with any luck she would conceive a son with her first pregnancy.

He hated the thought of his wife and his good friend together. They had only been introduced briefly after the wedding ceremony and already he wanted nothing more than to send Kerrick away. He'd never given any thought to marrying, but he'd always assumed that one day he would wed. He never would have imagined, though, that he would then have to stand back and hand his wife over to another man.

He stood and walked over to the small cupboard where he knew his brother had kept a bottle of brandy and poured a small amount into a glass. It was still early, but he needed the extra strength to get through the hours until the evening's celebrations.

He turned when the door opened. His grandmother eyed his glass with obvious disapproval. He placed the drink on the desk before turning back to her.

"You chose well," she said. "It was almost worth the tongue-lashing I received from my daughter-in-law."

Nicholas's mouth twisted in distaste. "I cannot believe everyone thought I would wed Mary. I've never developed a taste for self-sacrifice."

A strange expression crossed his grandmother's face. For one panic-stricken moment he thought she suspected what he planned to do, but he quickly dismissed the thought. Grandmother would never approve and she would waste no time in telling him so.

"She is going to be a fine wife and marchioness," she said. "And perhaps, in some small way, this makes up for what Henry did to that family."

He hoped his grandmother never learned about Edward's most recent proposition to Louisa. His fists clenched just thinking about it, but he forced himself to relax. A change in subject was definitely in order.

"The Evans cottage will be ready for tonight?"

"Of course. I can't imagine why you would want to

spend the night there. Your rooms here would be infinitely more comfortable."

Yes, but along with that comfort came a staff that would notice the marquess and his new marchioness hadn't spent their wedding night together. He also knew that he wouldn't be in any mood to continue the pretense of newly wedded bliss with the few guests who would be spending the night and departing for home sometime tomorrow.

He shrugged, hoping the movement appeared casual. "I thought a little privacy would be nice. I am sure you understand."

His grandmother smiled and he experienced a twinge of guilt at deceiving her.

Nicholas waited for her at the base of the stairs, but this time Louisa was prepared for the strength of her reaction to him. He was dressed in black, the somber color stark against his white shirt and cravat. His dark brown hair, worn a little long, seemed to blend into the black of his topcoat. She hadn't noticed the slight bronze tone to his skin before, but against his snow-white cravat it was proof that he enjoyed the outdoors. She already knew he liked to ride. He was truly one of the most handsome men she had ever met.

When she reached the bottom of the staircase, he held out his arm and she took it. She knew to expect the frisson of awareness that went through her.

He smiled down at her, but she noticed that his smile didn't reach his eyes. "I will be the envy of every man here."

She knew her dress complemented her fair coloring.

The light blue silk gown, with its low bodice and skirt that flowed over her slim form, shimmered with every step she took. She had never seen fabric quite like it, and it was by far the most beautiful dress she had ever owned.

"And I, no doubt, will be the object of much resentment from the single women present who had hoped to attract your attention."

Nicholas laughed at her words, and she was happy to see that a little bit of warmth had crept back into his face.

"I will only become more nervous the longer we delay," she continued.

"You'll do well. You can take comfort in the fact that Grandmother has given you her seal of approval."

"She has been most kind to me," she said, though the truth was "kind" was a vast understatement. The Dowager Marchioness of Overlea had welcomed her with open arms into the family. Had it not been for her aid and tutelage over the last three weeks, Louisa feared she would be hiding in her rooms right now.

Nicholas led the way to the ballroom. When they entered, a hush fell over the room and all eyes turned to them. Speculation hung dense in the air as everyone tried to get a good look at her. After what seemed an eternity, Sommers announced them. The words "The Marquess and Marchioness of Overlea" dropped into the room with the force of a cannon blast. There was a moment of suspended silence, then there was a cacophony of whispers, gasps, and people pushing forward, hoping for an introduction. It was too much, but Nicholas had only to raise a hand and silence fell once again.

He drew her closer to him. "We are so glad you could all come to celebrate what is the happiest day of our lives.

You will all have the opportunity to meet my lovely bride, but first I must beg your indulgence as I promised her a dance before you all steal her away from me."

Together, they made their way to the center of the room and Nicholas turned to face her. With butterflies rioting inside her, she stepped into his arms and tried to push back the knowledge that every person in the room was looking at her. It was her first time waltzing in public since learning the dance from the dance master Lady Overlea had hired and she sent up a silent prayer that she wouldn't trip. It was soon clear to her, however, that Nicholas was not a novice to the dance. He was careful to maintain a suitable distance between them as he glided with her across the ballroom floor, but Louisa could not help but be aware of how close their bodies were. She remembered, again, that first kiss she had shared with him, when he had pulled her into bed with him, and how she had pulled away just when the kiss threatened to become so much more. Tonight, however, she would not stop him.

Curious if he was thinking about the same thing, she looked up into his eyes and was disappointed to see that the warmth had disappeared again. He had asked her earlier if she regretted agreeing to marry him, but now she couldn't help but wonder if he was the one having second thoughts.

The music came to an end and Nicholas bowed over her hand, brushing a soft kiss on its back. Aware that everyone was watching them, she smiled and tried to convince herself as well as their audience that nothing was amiss.

The Earl of Kerrick stood off to the side, making small

talk with some of his and Nicholas's mutual friends. They had all been shocked to learn of Nicholas's hasty marriage and more than a few had tried to prize the details of their courtship from him. They all assumed the bride-to-be had been compromised and that Overlea had no choice but to marry her. Kerrick knew better, but he would never reveal the real reason behind the marriage.

It had been almost three weeks since Nicholas had laid his shocking proposal before him, yet he still couldn't believe that his friend was serious. Under normal circumstances, Nicholas was not the type of man to stand by and allow another man to bed his wife.

He was only half-listening to the conversation around him as he watched the newly wedded couple dance. A few others joined them in waltzing, but the majority were occupied with their speculations. He glanced toward a group of older women, some of whom had hoped to ensnare Nicholas as a prize for their own daughters. Their disdain for the new marchioness was plain to see. When Nicholas's grandmother joined them, however, their expressions changed. They might disapprove of Nicholas's wife, but they would never display that disapproval to the marquess or his family.

The last notes of the song played and most of the men in his small group broke off to claim their partners for the next dance, a quadrille. Kerrick choose to keep his attention on the newly married couple. He knew no one would question his interest. As the groom's closest friend, they would assume he was horrified at the idea of his friend having been ensnared and forced to wed.

Kerrick was circling the dance floor, trying to see where the guests of honor had gone, when the next dance began.

As he passed the refreshment table, however, his attention was captured by a woman who appeared to be arguing with a young man. Their voices were low and they were partially hidden behind a column, so their argument had not been noticed by those around him. Kerrick was appalled at how cavalierly the man was treating the woman.

He abandoned his quest to find Nicholas and rounded the column. The pair stopped arguing and turned to look at him. The woman bore a marked resemblance to the bride. He'd only met them briefly earlier today, but the arguing couple appeared to be the bride's siblings.

The woman, Catherine Evans if he remembered correctly, was clearly embarrassed at having been caught engaging in such unseemly behavior, but her brother showed no sign of remorse.

Kerrick turned to the girl, who was just as beautiful as her older sister. Pale blond hair curled becomingly around her face, her skin creamy as silk, and her eyes… good heavens, he had never before seen eyes that were such a vibrant shade of blue. How had he failed to notice that this morning?

"Can I be of assistance?" he asked.

The young man answered for her.

"Thank you for your concern, but my sister and I were merely having a minor disagreement."

Kerrick had two sisters of his own and he still remembered how some of their arguments had reached almost epic proportions.

"If I noticed your argument, others might as well. You should probably go somewhere more private if you plan to continue."

He bowed briefly before retreating. He couldn't help but think it was a pity Miss Evans was so young. Not yet fully out, if he wasn't mistaken.

CHAPTER NINE

The rest of the evening flew by in a blur for Louisa. Aside from family members, she hadn't known any of the guests, most of whom were members of the ton who had traveled to Overlea Manor for what they'd thought was a ball to announce Nicholas's betrothal. Lady Overlea had taken Louisa under her wing and introduced her to everyone. As the hours wore on, her head began to ache from the effort of trying to remember the names of all the people she had met.

Louisa had caught only glimpses of her husband after their dance. She'd danced with many of the men at the ball, but Nicholas hadn't danced with any of the women. She wasn't the only one who noted that fact.

She couldn't help but be aware of the glares some of the women cast in her direction. The worst were those who didn't bother trying to be discreet in examining her midsection. She knew there was speculation about the reason behind the haste of their marriage, but no one said anything directly to her. She would have to pretend not to notice. When no baby appeared before the ninth month of their marriage, anyone who thought she was already with child would know they were wrong.

By the time the late-night supper was to be served, Louisa's energy was starting to flag. She hadn't been able to sleep the night before and the nap she had taken that afternoon hadn't been a long one. She was exhausted and Nicholas noticed. After the supper, when everyone else returned to the ballroom, he drew her aside.

"You're tired," he said.

"I'm afraid I am not used to keeping such later hours, and the nap I took earlier was not a very long one."

As if to give proof to her words, she yawned. The corner of his mouth lifted as she colored with embarrassment.

"Would you like to cause a few more tongues to start wagging?"

She wasn't certain if she should be courting more gossip, but the glint of mischievousness in his eyes had her curious.

"What are you thinking?"

"I think we should slip out the servants' entrance and make our way to your cottage."

Louisa's stomach turned over at the suggestion and a new set of nerves assailed her, but there was no point in putting off their wedding night. She nodded her assent.

He beamed at her and Louisa could see a hint of what he must have been like as a child. She wondered if their son would have that same gleam in his eye when he was up to mischief.

He grasped her hand in his much larger one and led the way out of the ballroom and down to the kitchen. They passed a few servants on the way, but he raised a finger to his lips to silence their questions. Louisa did not miss the amused glances the servants aimed at them as she and Nicholas escaped out the kitchen door.

Caught up in the moment, she laughed as they made their way to the stables. Nicholas had thought ahead and a curricle had already been prepared for their departure. It did not take long for the horses to be brought out from their stalls and harnessed. His eyes were still sparkling when he helped her into the conveyance and climbed in after her.

There was a blanket on the seat between them, which he unfolded and tucked in around her. The intimacy of the act put all her senses on high alert. He must have felt it, too, for his hands stilled and his eyes locked with hers for an unbearably long moment before he looked away and took up the reins.

She'd never ridden at night before. The evening was cold, but clear, the sky filled with a thousand stars. She was filled with exhilaration as they drove away from the Overlea Manor like two thieves.

She must have dozed during the half hour trip for the next thing she knew the curricle was slowing to a stop outside the cottage and she found herself pressed against Nicholas's side. She straightened with a jolt, embarrassment flooding through her.

Nicholas sprang down from the curricle and reached up to help her down. His hands at her waist were warm and they remained there for several moments after her feet were on the ground. Their gazes locked. Gone was his playful mood. He looked down at her in silence, his expression serious. She found herself hoping he was going to kiss her. Instead, he dropped his hands after several seconds and took a step back. She felt the loss of his touch keenly.

"The grooms will be busy at Overlea Manor, so I'll see to the horses," he said.

Louisa could only nod before entering the cottage. She shouldn't have been surprised that the door was opened by a footman. She'd thought they would be alone, but the hushed voices coming from the kitchen told her that at least a few servants had been dispatched to see to their comfort.

Other than that, everything was still as they had left it that morning. She made a mental note to speak to Reverend Harnick about donating the cottage's furniture to other families in need.

She made her way above stairs and headed to her parents' bedroom, which she knew had been prepared for the wedding night. When she entered the room she was amazed at the transformation. The coverlet was a rich blue, threaded through with gold. It was turned down and she could see that the formerly threadbare sheets had also been replaced with sheets made from a fine, satiny material of pure white. She ran her hands over the cool fabric, then over the new plump pillows, and sighed. She had never imagined sleeping on such material before, but of course, sleeping was not all she would be doing on it.

She turned to take in the rest of the room. The furniture was the same, but all the fabrics and accessories had been changed. The windows were covered with drapes in a blue brocade that matched the coverlet. There was even a new carpet on the floor. She took a peek inside the wardrobe, which now housed an impressive collection of clothing for both Nicholas and herself. She found it difficult to believe that so much work had been done for one night's stay and wondered if Nicholas planned to stay longer.

She closed the wardrobe firmly. She knew she was expected to call for her maid, who she imagined was waiting somewhere downstairs to help her out of her gown and into her nightclothes, but she didn't have quite that much bravado. Feeling more than a little self-conscious, knowing she was doing this all wrong, she went back downstairs to the sitting room to wait for Nicholas.

When he entered a short time later, he was surprised to see her.

"You were tired. I thought you would be in bed already."

Louisa couldn't quite meet his eyes. "My short nap on the drive seems to have renewed my energy."

And it was true. She was not feeling at all tired at the moment, though she suspected it would catch up with her soon.

"Perhaps you would like something to drink before retiring?"

She hadn't noticed the sideboard was now stocked with bottles of sherry, brandy, and she didn't know what else. They hadn't been able to afford the luxury of having spirits in the house themselves.

"Sherry, please," she said. Perhaps it would help to ease her nerves, which were now in full revolt.

Nicholas moved to the sideboard and poured a glass of sherry for her and brandy for himself. He handed her the glass and raised his own in a salute.

"To the marquisate," he said before bringing the glass

to his lips.

She thought it an odd toast, but raised her glass as well, sipping at a more leisurely rate. She watched in silence as he put down his glass and walked over to the window. He seemed somehow to be more on edge than she. How was that possible? Nicholas had a reputation for having been with many women. Why would he be nervous with her?

When she finished her drink, he walked over to her and took the glass from her hand. She wasn't sure what to expect next, but it certainly was not what followed.

"You should retire," he said softly.

She marshaled her courage before asking, "Will you be joining me?"

He shook his head. "We need to talk tomorrow about my expectations for this marriage."

She didn't like the sound of that. She wanted to press the issue now, but she could see that he wasn't in the frame of mind for such a discussion. Besides, fatigue, aided by the sherry she'd drunk, was beginning to creep over her again.

Confused, more than a little worried about the next day's conversation, she bid her new husband an awkward goodnight and went up to her room. She rang for the maid to help her undress and went to bed alone.

The sheets were a little cold at first, but overwhelmed by the events of the day, bone-tired from her lack of sleep the night before, she fell asleep right away. She wasn't sure how long she slept before she was jerked awake. The darkness and the feel of the cool bed sheets against her skin disconcerted her and it took her a moment to remember where she was. She heard another noise, a scraping sound, and then the bedroom door slammed open. Louisa covered her mouth to stifle the scream that had almost escaped. In the dark she could just make out a shadow.

"Nicholas?"

There was a murmur of assent and Louisa sat up in bed.

"Help me," he said.

Her eyes had grown accustomed to the darkness and she could see he was gripping the door handle to keep himself upright. She jumped out of bed and hurried to his side.

"Are you having another episode?"

As soon as the question was out of her mouth she realized how foolish it sounded. It was obvious he was suffering, again, from whatever ailment had assailed him that other time. She leaned into him and draped his free arm around her shoulder.

"You can let go of the door," she said.

He did so and Louisa struggled to remain upright under his weight. The position was awkward but she managed to lead him the few steps to the bed. When they finally reached it, he released her and stumbled onto it.

Louisa placed a hand on his forehead and was shocked to find him running a fever. How was it possible that he was so ill when he had been fine only a few hours before? She turned, but he stopped her with a hand on her arm.

"Don't leave," he managed, his voice barely above a whisper.

"I'll be right back," she said.

She rushed to the washstand and poured some water into the bowl. Dipping a washcloth into the cool liquid, she wrung out the excess water and returned to place it on

Nicholas's forehead. He moaned at the contact. She stood there, uncertain what to do. His eyes snapped open and ensnared her in their depths.

"Don't leave… please," he said before closing his eyes again.

Louisa looked at the chaise, thinking she could sleep there, but then swiftly discarded the notion. She and Nicholas were now husband and wife. There would be nothing wrong with sharing the same bed. She would be able to get some much needed rest and if he should need her she would be right there.

Before she could change her mind, she drew the covers over Nicholas and went around to the other side of the bed. She slipped between the sheets. This time she lay awake for a long time, listening to her husband's steady breathing, before finally falling asleep again.

Nicholas became aware of the warm body beside him. Louisa. Unlike other women who saturated themselves with heavy perfumes, her scent was clean. She was nestled against him, her back to his chest and her bottom snug against his manhood. His hand snaked around her abdomen, pulling her more closely against him. Her backside wiggled against him and he groaned.

He placed his mouth on her shoulder and kissed his way to her neck. She made a small sound of encouragement and he trailed his hand up her torso, finally cupping her breast through the fabric of her nightgown. He continued to kiss her throat as he enjoyed the way the weight of her breast filled his hand. His fingers toyed with her nipple, drawing it into a tight bud.

"Nicholas," she breathed softly.

His name on her lips inflamed him. He rolled her onto her back and stared down at her. Her pale hair spread across the pillow, framing a face that was flushed from sleep. Her gray eyes had darkened with passion. He traced the line of her full lower lip with his thumb.

He was supposed to remember something about Louisa, but it lurked just out of reach. She brought her hands to his shoulders and arched against him, and he found he didn't care about whatever it was he was supposed to remember.

He kissed her then. He knew it was her first time with a man and that he had to go slowly, but he found the effort more than he could manage. Her mouth opened under his and he took the opportunity to plunder its depths. Her response was tentative at first, but it wasn't long before she was meeting his kisses with her own impassioned response—long, drugging kisses that only stoked the fire of his desire higher.

He rolled onto his back and draped her over him, taking advantage of the position to untie the ribbon at her neckline so he could push down her nightgown. When her breasts spilled free, he groaned and shifted her so he could take one rosy tip in his mouth. Louisa inhaled loudly in surprise, but her hands came to his head and she held him there, arching further into his mouth. He moved from one breast to the other, pushing her nightgown down further as he suckled. When it was past her hips, he rolled her onto her back again and dragged the garment from her body.

His mouth left her breast and quested lower. She gasped when he stroked one hand up the inside of her thigh and stroked her between her legs. God, she was already wet. Nicholas fought against the urge to take her right then.

When he moved lower, Louisa stiffened with surprise. One glance was enough to tell him that he had shocked her. Deciding she obviously wasn't ready for what he had in mind, he kissed his way back up her body, stopping long enough to pay homage to her breasts again. They were not overly large, but neither were they small. The sounds she made as he drew on them drove him to the edge of sanity. He brought himself up over her completely and kissed her again, his passion a living thing. She instinctively opened her legs wider as he reached down to unbutton his breeches. They were married now and he didn't have to worry about bearing a child out of wedlock. He had been with many other women in the past, but at that moment he could not remember any of their faces. There was only Louisa. He could sate himself within her fully and didn't need to worry about pulling out. She had, after all, promised to give him an heir.

He froze as his hand reached the last button. An heir. Good God, what was he doing? He couldn't make love to Louisa and risk conceiving a child who would eventually develop the same illness that seemed to plague his family.

Slowly, every fiber of his being protesting, he rolled away onto his back beside her and threw an arm over his eyes. He struggled to right his breathing.

She made a sound of protest that echoed his own deep disappointment. Staying away from Louisa was going to kill him.

She shifted position. Although he didn't remove his arm, he knew she was looking at him.

"Nicholas? Are you still not feeling well?"

He laughed bitterly at the question. That was the understatement of the century. He tried to remember what had happened last night, but the details were vague. After sharing a drink with Louisa and sending her off to bed alone he wasn't sure. A horrifying thought occurred to him. Was it too late? Had they already made love?

He removed his arm and looked at his wife, who held the bedclothes clutched to her chest. Her forehead was creased with worry.

"What happened?" he asked. Louisa blushed and he rushed to elaborate. "What happened last night? Did you and I…"

She shook her head, her embarrassment clear.

"You sent me up to bed."

He took a steadying breath before continuing.

"Did I join you afterward? I had meant to allow you to rest."

Louisa studied him for a moment before replying. "You fell ill again. You managed to make your way to the room and wake me up."

So that explained why he was there.

"And you decided to join me?"

"You asked me not to leave," she said, her voice soft. "And the bed looked far more comfortable than the chaise."

He couldn't fault her for thinking it would be fine with him if they shared a bed. They were married, after all, and he had never even hinted to her that he didn't want that kind of relationship with her.

A corner of his mouth lifted in wry amusement. Who was he fooling? It was becoming clear to him that he very much wanted a physical relationship with his wife. He was still hard and knew he had to get away from her before the intimacy of the situation provoked him into continuing where they had left off.

It was only then that he realized he was still dressed. If he had been thinking clearly earlier, he would have realized that nothing of consequence could have happened between them last night.

Nothing of consequence. Except that she had watched over him twice now while he was ill. The episodes had never come this close together before.

"Stay in bed," Louisa said. "I will get dressed in my old room." She frowned before continuing. "Would you like me to have a tray brought up for you?"

It rankled that she was treating him like an invalid. Given the alarming frequency with which he collapsed in her presence he could scarcely blame her, but it rankled nonetheless.

"I'll join you downstairs shortly," he said before covering his eyes with his arm again.

He heard a rustle of movement before she slid out of bed and went to the wardrobe. He shifted his arm slightly and was disappointed that she'd donned her nightgown again before leaving the bed. Sunlight streamed through the window and she was standing within its circle of light, unaware that the outline of her body was visible through the thin, gauzy material.

Groaning softly, he covered his eyes again and listened for her departure. He wasn't sure he was strong enough to stay away from his wife.

She couldn't get used to having servants in the cottage. Only her new lady's maid and Nicholas's valet had spent the night, but one of the kitchen staff from Overlea Manor had arrived early that morning to cook breakfast and a footman was stationed by the dining room door. After preparing her plate from a sideboard that had never seen so much food, Louisa dismissed the footman and sat at the table. It had only been a day, but with all the changes in the cottage it no longer seemed like home.

She gave herself a mental shake at her sentimentality. The changes were probably a good thing. She needed to accept that Overlea Manor was now her home.

She had just poured her tea when Nicholas entered. He murmured a greeting and went to the sideboard to prepare his own plate. He wouldn't appreciate her hovering over him, but she couldn't keep her eyes from following his movements in case he should need her assistance.

Her attempts to make conversation during breakfast were met with monosyllabic responses. She wondered if she'd done something wrong but quickly discarded the thought. She hadn't known him long, but she already knew Nicholas wasn't the kind of man to display any signs of weakness. The fact that she had now seen him fall ill twice would bother him more than a little.

She gave up on engaging him in conversation, so was surprised when he turned to her after clearing his plate.

"The guests who spent the night should be departing after breakfast. Given how late some will sleep, I think we can avoid most of them if we depart midafternoon."

Louisa murmured her agreement and watched as he pushed away from the table and strode from the room. The feeling she'd had that her husband was hiding something from her, something other than his illness, had returned in full force. If she didn't know better, she'd think

Nicholas was uncomfortable around her.

CHAPTER TEN

Nicholas was grateful for two things. First, that the drive back to Overlea Manor was a short one, and second, that he'd chosen to drive his curricle last night. The latter meant he could concentrate on the task of handling the horses instead of finding himself in the far more intimate setting of the Overlea carriage with his wife. He was still almost painfully aware of her, especially after what had nearly happened that morning, but he wasn't in a position to do anything foolish.

He realized now that he had been an idiot to ask Louisa to be his wife. Perhaps he should have proposed to Mary after all. But no, he discarded that thought almost as soon as it occurred to him. Mary might be meek, but she never would have agreed to the arrangement he had in mind and would have wasted no time telling her mother and brother about it.

He tried to imagine other alternatives, but in the end he knew Louisa had been his only choice. Her lack of parents, the fact that she had two younger siblings to care for, her desperate situation—all combined to present him with the one woman he knew would agree to the proposition he was about to put to her.

He glanced at her, but her face was turned away. His mind shied away from any thought that he was treating her as shabbily as his cousin. However, remembering the hurt confusion he had seen on her face when he'd rebuffed her attempts at conversation over breakfast made him feel like a bastard who'd kicked a wounded puppy.

He went over their upcoming conversation in his mind. The conversation he'd had with Kerrick was nothing compared to the one he was going to have with his wife later that day. He knew that soon enough she would hate him, and he would be unable to blame her.

He breathed a sigh of relief when the curricle finally approached the manor house. He'd sent his valet and her maid back to Overlea Manor that morning with a message about when they'd be returning, but it was still a surprise when his grandmother met them in the front hall.

"I'm glad the two of you are back so soon. We need to speak with you," she said before turning and entering the drawing room.

He met Louisa's bewildered gaze.

"Do you know what this is about?" she asked.

For a moment he suspected his grandmother had somehow learned about his plan for an heir. The only other person who knew, however, was Kerrick, and his friend wouldn't have told her.

He shook his head. "No."

Looking a little nervous, she went into the drawing room and Nicholas followed. Catherine was already there, sitting on the settee, and she looked miserable. Lady

Overlea sat in a chair, opposite her, but she remained silent.

"Catherine?" Louisa went to her sister and lowered herself onto the settee next to her. "What happened? Why are you so upset?"

Nicholas remained standing by the door, hesitant to intrude.

Catherine raised her head. The deep breath she took before replying was shaky. "I'm so sorry, Louisa. I tried to stop him, but he wouldn't listen to me. We argued about it. Your friend," she said, turning to look at Nicholas, "he saw us, but he didn't know why we were arguing."

"Are you talking about John?" Louisa asked.

Catherine nodded and held out a small, folded piece of paper he hadn't noticed she'd been holding in her lap. Louisa took it, bewildered. She unfolded it, her hands trembling, and began to read. Nicholas moved behind the settee and read the note over her shoulder.

Louisa,

Now that you have married Overlea, it wouldn't be appropriate for me seek employment as a tutor. Fortunately, I remembered about Father's old friend, Captain Farrows. I believe he is in London now, or he was when he sent his condolences a few months ago after hearing about Father's death. I know we'd decided not to take him up on his offer of charity, but now that you and Catherine are taken care of, I need to make my own way in the world. I plan to approach him about sponsoring me in purchasing a commission in the military.

My mind will not be changed. You have chosen your own path. Please allow me to do the same.

John

"No," Louisa said, shaking her head as she stared down at the paper and reread it. "He can't do this. He's supposed to go to Oxford." She turned to Catherine. "When did he leave? We might be able to stop him."

Catherine shook her head. "He left last night, shortly after we noticed you and Overlea were missing. He asked one of the guests who didn't stay over if he could join them when they returned to London."

Louisa stood and moved around the settee to where he was standing.

"You can stop this," she said to him. "You must stop this. You can send someone to follow him. He'll be with Captain Farrows. I can give you his direction—"

Nicholas reached for her hands, which were clutching the note, and stilled their trembling. He took the note and handed it back to Catherine before turning back to Louisa.

He said the words he knew she wouldn't want to hear. "He is old enough to make this decision. We can't force him to do what he doesn't want to do."

She made a strangled sound and Nicholas had to resist the urge to pull her into his arms.

"No," she said, shaking her head. "He wanted to go to Oxford. To enter the clergy."

"That may have been true at one point, but no longer."

"His mind was made up," Catherine said. "I threatened to tell you, but it was no good. He said there was nothing you could say or do that would make him change his mind, and I didn't want to ruin your wedding night."

"You did the right thing," Lady Overlea said, speaking for the first time since they'd entered the room. "Nothing would have been gained, and John would still have left, only he would have done so on bad terms with you and Louisa."

"This wasn't supposed to happen," Louisa said. "We had it all planned out."

"Things don't always go according to plan," Nicholas said, speaking from his own cynical knowledge of just how off course one's life could go.

Needing to offer her comfort, he raised her hands to his lips and brushed soft kisses on their backs. His eyes locked with hers and the power of her mournful gaze went right through him. Shaken, he dropped her hands as though he'd been burned.

"My head tells me you're right, but my heart…" She shook her head, unable to continue for several moments. "I need to be alone right now."

Nicholas watched her leave, yearning to go after her but knowing he couldn't do so.

"You did the right thing," he said, turning to Catherine.

The corners of her mouth lifted a fraction in response, but the weak smile didn't meet her eyes.

He left the room then, knowing that Grandmother would do what she could to comfort Catherine, and made his way to the study. Going over the account books for the estate was the very last thing he wanted to do at that moment, but the job had to be done. The tedium of the task would also help to take his mind off his wife and the mess that was his life for the afternoon.

Nicholas sat down at his desk and opened the estate

ledgers. It would take him the rest of the day to wade through the accounts, a task he always hated. He ignored the headache that was starting to pound at his temples, knowing it to be an aftereffect of the episode he had suffered the previous night.

It was an hour later when a knock sounded at the door. Without waiting for his reply, Kerrick entered. Normally Nicholas wouldn't have minded the interruption, but the cursed throbbing in his head always made him irritable, to say nothing of the reminder about why Kerrick hadn't returned to London with the rest of the guests.

"How long are you planning to hide in here?" Kerrick asked.

"You have an estate. You know they don't look after themselves."

Kerrick either couldn't tell he was annoyed or he didn't care. He closed the door behind him and took a seat across the desk.

Nicholas made a show of closing the ledger and giving his friend his attention. "Is there something I can do for you?"

"You wife is a beautiful woman," Kerrick said.

A jolt of annoyance shot through him, but he strove to ignore it. This was what he'd hoped for, after all. His longtime friend was more likely to agree to his proposal if he found the woman in question attractive.

"Have you seen her today?"

"No. I thought it best to speak to you first. Have you told her what you have planned for us?"

Nicholas shook his head. "I'm planning to tell her tonight." He hesitated only a moment before asking, "Are you agreeing to help me?"

Kerrick shook his head. "I haven't made up my mind. Besides, the point might be moot if she decides to leave you after you tell her."

Nicholas knew Louisa wouldn't leave. She had nowhere else to go. She could, though, outright refuse him.

Kerrick made a great show of examining his nails before continuing. "It seems to me that you're putting off telling your very lovely wife that you wish her to bed your best friend."

Nicholas found it difficult not to flinch at the words. His idea for conceiving an heir hadn't seemed quite so objectionable when he'd originally thought of it. The more time that passed, however, and the more he was around Louisa, the more distasteful the whole thing was to him.

"You wouldn't happen to have any idea how best to introduce the subject, would you?"

"Me?" Kerrick said with a bark of laughter. "This is your insane idea, one I have not yet agreed to help you with. You're going to have to figure this one out on your own."

"Did you come here just to harass me, then?"

"Actually," Kerrick said, leaning forward in his seat, his expression serious now, "I came here to see if you had come to your senses."

"It was while I was lucid that I realized this was the only way I could fulfill my duty and provide an acceptable heir to the title."

Kerrick waited a moment before saying, "I saw the two of you together last night."

Nicholas raised a brow. "I believe everyone saw us together last night. That was rather the point of the whole thing."

"You know what I mean."

"No, I don't. Why don't you enlighten me?"

Kerrick leaned back in his chair. "I believe your new wife has developed a *tendre* for you. And if I am not mistaken, I think you are not unaffected by her."

"I will be the first to admit that Louisa is a very beautiful woman. She barely knows me, however, and certainly not enough to have developed any romantic feelings for me. I have taken care not to encourage her in that direction."

He had to tamp down on the guilt that speared through him when he remembered how hurt she'd been when he'd rebuffed her attempts to engage him in conversation. It was better for everyone involved if his wife learned that the last thing he wanted or needed was for them to become close. It was difficult enough staying away from her now.

Nicholas met his friend's curious gaze, careful to keep his own neutral. Kerrick exhaled loudly and stood.

"Will you be at dinner? Since I know you won't be otherwise engaged with your new wife, I thought you'd want to spend some time making sure your best friend doesn't expire from boredom."

Nicholas frowned when his thoughts went immediately to what Kerrick might soon be doing to relieve his ennui. He struggled to keep his voice casual when he replied.

"I'll see you at dinner. It will be a good opportunity for you and Louisa to get to know each other before I speak to her tonight."

Kerrick merely nodded before leaving.

Nicholas sat staring at the door through which his friend had departed for some time before turning his attention back to the ledgers. He didn't want to think about the conversation he would soon be having with his wife.

John's leaving had shaken Louisa to her core. Things weren't going at all as she'd hoped. The very last thing she'd wanted was for John to sacrifice his future. She still couldn't quite believe he'd tossed aside the opportunity to attend Oxford, which had been guaranteed by her marriage to Nicholas. The irony was not lost on her that she'd tried to keep the knowledge of Edward Manning's proposition from her brother, knowing he would confront Manning if he learned of it, because she'd wanted to keep him safe. And now he had run off to enlist in the military.

She was also having a hard time anticipating husband's moods. She never knew from one moment to the next if he would be the open, friendly man who she had glimpsed from time to time, or the man who seemed to barely tolerate her presence.

She hesitated outside the dining room door, smoothing a hand over her dress reflexively. The pale yellow color complemented her coloring and she found herself hoping Nicholas would find it becoming. She wondered what mood he would be in tonight.

She relaxed slightly when she entered the room and saw her husband hadn't arrived yet. Catherine and Lady Overlea were already seated and were chatting about some of the plants in the conservatory. It comforted her to know that her sister, at least, was finding herself at home in Overlea Manor.

She'd just taken her seat when Nicholas and Lord Kerrick arrived. She'd been told her husband's friend would be staying for a visit but hadn't seen him yet since returning. Perversely, she wondered briefly if he, too, were avoiding her.

Nicholas greeted her with a smile, but she noticed it didn't reach his eyes, which appeared to be shadowed with strain. She wanted to ask him how he was feeling but knew he wouldn't welcome her concern.

In her position seated across from Nicholas, she had an excellent vantage point from which to observe him, although she tried not to be obvious about it. He was avoiding her again, engaging everyone in conversation but her. He spoke to her only briefly and only when necessary. His friend, however, who was seated next to her, seemed to go out of his way to make up for her husband's lack of attention.

Lord Kerrick was very amusing and it didn't take him long to tease her out of her somber mood, even causing her to laugh out loud. Her husband's eyes swung in her direction at that, but he turned away again quickly, a slight frown on his face. She sighed, all too aware of the impassable gulf that seemed to be growing between her and Nicholas. After that, Lord Kerrick failed to tease even a smile from her.

Preoccupied with her own thoughts, Louisa nonetheless noticed that her sister seemed to be taken with Lord Kerrick. Catherine and he exchanged pleasantries, but it was obvious to her that she was intrigued by the man.

Dinner seemed an interminable affair and she was glad when it was finally over. Nicholas and Lord Kerrick retired the library afterward while the ladies went to the drawing room where Nicholas's grandmother was content to listen to Catherine play the piano. Louisa pled a headache and escaped to her room.

She was about to ring for her maid when a soft knock at the door startled her. Expecting that the maid had learned she'd already retired for the night, she bid her to enter and was surprised when the door opened to reveal her husband instead. He closed the door softly behind him.

"Nicholas," she said, her pulse starting to race, "I didn't expect you tonight."

"I needed to speak to you in private."

Something in his tone alarmed her. She had thought, no she had hoped, he was there to finally consummate their marriage. It would appear she was wrong and she chided herself for being a fool.

They stood there for several long, awkward moments. Louisa remained silent, waiting for him to broach whatever subject had brought him there. Finally, when she could no longer bear the silence, she asked the question that had been uppermost on her mind all day.

"You asked me a question yesterday. Now I would ask the same of you."

He raised a brow.

"Do you regret marrying me? If you do, I am sure a man in your position would have no problem in arranging to have the marriage annulled. You could go on with your life as though I had never existed."

He didn't answer right away and her spirits sank.

"I do have regrets," he said after a moment, his voice low.

She wanted to die of mortification. "I see," she somehow managed to say.

She started to turn away, but he crossed the distance between them and took hold of her hands in his.

"I regret that I cannot be the kind of husband you deserve."

He dropped her hands and indicated she should sit. She was grateful, for she wasn't sure how much longer she'd be able to remain standing. Lowering herself onto the bench at the foot of the bed, she wished now that she hadn't asked the question.

Taking a seat on the bed, he turned toward her. Their eyes met and she could see the bleakness there.

"I need an heir and you have agreed to provide me with one."

She was confused. That wasn't what she'd expected to hear.

She nodded, unsure where this conversation was headed. A moment before she had expected him to tell her that he wanted to end their marriage, and now he was talking about having children.

"Would you rather have a different woman as their mother?"

He shook his head. "No, you will be the mother to my heirs."

Louisa licked her lips, waiting for further explanation. His eyes followed the movement, but he didn't continue.

"Have you come here, then, to…" Her hand swept over the bed and her cheeks began to heat.

"No," he said softly.

Was that regret she saw in his eyes?

"I don't understand. How am I to provide you with an heir if you will not lie with me?"

He squared his shoulders and continued. "Louisa, you

know I suffer from an illness."

Concern warred with her confusion. "Should I call someone?"

She stood to ring for a servant, but he stopped her.

"No, I am feeling well at the moment."

She sat again on the bench and took a deep breath to calm her nerves. "Pray, continue."

"You have seen me fall ill twice now," he said, his words slow and measured. She nodded and he continued. "My father and my brother suffered from similar episodes. The doctors do not know what caused them, but it is likely my illness will kill me, just as it did the previous two marquesses."

From the stark expression in Nicholas's eyes, she could see he believed what he said. She couldn't understand how he could calmly accept such a fate.

"Surely there must be someone who can help you."

He shook his head. "My father and my brother consulted all the best doctors. It is a mysterious ailment, one for which there appears to be no cure."

To say she was shocked would be a vast understatement. She struggled to gain control of her turbulent emotions before speaking again, knowing that Nicholas did not want sympathy from her.

"I don't know what to say." She reached out to place a hand over his.

He looked down at their hands and one corner of his mouth quirked upward sardonically. Self-conscious, she removed her hand and placed it in her lap.

"I appreciate your concern, but think of what I have told you. My father and my brother both suffered from this illness, and now I do as well. That means it is very likely any children I father will also suffer from it."

A pang went through her at the thought of having a child who might die from Nicholas's mysterious illness. She took a deep breath and tried to consider the full implications of what he was saying. Was this why he'd stopped this morning while they were making love? He was afraid that their children would develop the same illness?

"It is not a certainty, Nicholas," she said. "We can none of us predict the future."

She watched as he shook his head, unmoved by her words.

"My mother died in childbirth," she said, continuing when he didn't reply. "She died while giving birth to Catherine. Does that mean that I should not try to have my own children? That I should refuse you my bed out of fear of something that may never happen?"

"It is not the same thing."

Louisa stood and moved closer to him. Taking a deep breath, intensely aware of her husband on a physical level despite the bleak topic of their conversation, she sat next to him on the bed and reached for his hand again. At first she thought he was going to pull away, but in the end he allowed her the comfort she was so eager to impart.

"It is the same thing. We cannot allow fear of the future to stop us from living in the present."

He looked away from her before she could define the emotion she'd seen in his eyes. Anger? Frustration?

"You do not display any signs of weakness, Louisa. You are a healthy young woman in the prime of her life. Death in childbed is a possibility for everyone, but it is not a certainty. I, however, am exhibiting the same symptoms of an illness that has already killed two of my closest family members. Unlike you, I am not healthy, and I will not risk passing this illness to my children."

Louisa wanted to comfort, but didn't know how. He'd pulled away from her and was now clenching his hands into fists on his thighs. She wondered if time would dissuade him from his conviction or further entrench it in his mind. Likely the latter, especially if he continued to suffer attacks.

"What are we to do then?" she asked. "As you have stated, you are in need of an heir. Unless…" Her breath caught as she considered one possibility. When she continued her voice was cautious. "Edward is next in line, is he not?"

He turned to stare at her in disbelief. A lock of his black hair had fallen onto his forehead. Louisa's fingers itched to smooth it back, but instead she kept her hands folded in her lap.

"Do you honestly believe I would allow my cousin to become the next Marquess of Overlea? After what I know of him? After what he tried to do to you and Catherine? That would put you back under his power when I die."

"I realize that," she said, her voice trembling at the thought of once again having to rely on Edward Manning's notion of generosity for her survival. "But you have already said that you will not father any children."

A hint of wariness crept onto his face at her words.

"What is it?" she asked.

"I cannot risk passing my illness on to my children, that is true, and on that matter I remain firm."

There was something he wasn't telling her. "But?"

"But there is nothing stopping you from having

children."

He stared at her intently as he spoke, watching for her reaction. At first there was none. His words made no sense. Then, when understanding of what he was proposing dawned, anger began to course through her.

She did not bother to hide it from him. She stood and turned to face him, hoping fervently that she was mistaken. That somehow she had misinterpreted his words.

"You are not suggesting what I think you are," she said, the words tight and clipped.

He was unmoved by her anger. "It is the only way. I must have an heir. And remember, you agreed to give me one. You signed a marriage contract to that effect."

He was out of his mind. How could he sit there and calmly suggest that she… She couldn't even finish that thought.

"No."

"I intend to hold you to your agreement," he said.

"I agreed to give you an heir, not some man I don't know."

"You would be giving me an heir. I will recognize the child as my own."

Panic began to set in. "Don't make me do this, Nicholas."

His voice softened slightly.

"I would never force you to sleep with someone else." His face was a mask of non-emotion as he spoke. "You barely know me, yet you agreed to become my wife. I know you find me desirable. Surely it is not outside the realm of possibility that you would find another man attractive in the same way."

Louisa turned away from him. He actually expected her to do this. To sleep with another man and to pass off the child of that union as theirs. Yes, what he'd said was true, she was willing to make love with Nicholas. Wanted it more than she was willing to admit at that moment. What he didn't know, what she wouldn't tell him, given the cavalier manner in which he was discussing the possibility of her lying with someone else, was that her feelings for him went beyond merely finding him attractive or desirable. She was surprised, considering how little time she had known him, but she was drawn to Nicholas Manning in a way she had never been drawn to another man. She very much doubted that it would happen again.

A horrible thought occurred to her and she turned to face him again.

"Who?"

She didn't need to elaborate. He knew exactly what she was asking.

"Kerrick."

It was as though he had slapped her. Somehow she kept her voice even. "Please leave."

Nicholas stood and raised his hands in supplication.

"Louisa—"

"Get out. Now." She couldn't bear to hear any more about this.

She watched as his hands dropped to his sides and he moved to the door. He paused with a hand on the doorknob and for a moment she thought he wouldn't leave. The foolish romantic in her hoped he would take it all back. Say that he didn't expect or want her to do such a thing. That he wanted her only for himself.

In the end, after only a moment of hesitation, he

opened the door and left. Louisa held herself together just long enough to cross the room and turn the lock. The tears came then. Not caring that she was still fully dressed, she crawled into bed and pulled the covers over her.

CHAPTER ELEVEN

The next morning, Louisa considered asking for a tray to be bought up to her but decided against it. She couldn't hide from her husband forever. Steeling herself to face him, she dismissed her maid after dressing and made her way to the breakfast room. She was more than a little relieved to learn he had already eaten and gone out for an early morning ride, and she wondered if he were normally an early riser. She realized yet again just how little she knew about Nicholas. Given that he clearly didn't wish to have a conventional marriage, it was likely they would always remain strangers.

As the new Marchioness of Overlea, the duties of overseeing the household now fell on her. However, since Lady Overlea hadn't expected her back from her honeymoon so soon, the menus were already set for the week and there wasn't much to be done. The dowager promised to go over Louisa's new duties with her soon, but she had already promised Catherine, who was having the time of her life learning about the exotic plants housed in the conservatory, that she would spend the morning with her.

With nothing better to do, Louisa decided to explore the house on her own. It was late morning and she was in the gallery examining the long line of Manning ancestors when Sommers found her and informed her that she had guests. He presented the calling card to her and she groaned inwardly when she saw it belonged to Elizabeth Manning, Edward Manning's mother.

Dreading the encounter, she made her way to the drawing room and found Nicholas's aunt and his cousin Mary seated on the settee. They were deep in conversation, but their voices were too low for her to overhear what they were saying. She watched them from the hallway, undetected, for a few moments. From the impatient expression on the older woman's face, she knew this was not going to be a friendly call. Both these women had expected Nicholas to offer for his cousin. Still, she was now part of the Manning family and would no doubt see them often. This first meeting would be an awkward one. Neither had attended the Overlea ball and the last time she'd seen them was to take measurements for the morning dress she'd been commissioned to make for Mary. Still, she hoped that once they got past this first meeting everything would be fine.

She took a deep breath and entered the room.

"My lady," she said, dropping a brief curtsey before turning to the younger woman. "Miss Manning. What a pleasant surprise."

Elizabeth Manning pinned her with a gaze that was far from cordial. Mary's expression, however, was impossible to read. Elizabeth stood as Louisa moved into the room.

"My daughter and I are here to wish you well on your new marriage. Had we known the ball my mother-in-law recently hosted was in honor of my dear nephew's marriage, we would have declined the invitation that took us away from home."

Louisa could tell the woman's words were insincere but thanked her nonetheless.

"We do have a request to make of you," Elizabeth continued. "In the past, Lady Overlea has allowed us to take cuttings from some of her plants. Since you are now in charge of the household, I thought I should apply to you first before taking any more samples. I fear some of the more exotic plants just don't do very well without the extra sun you get here in your conservatory, but Mary does love the plants so we keep trying."

"Oh, of course," Louisa said, rushing to reassure her. "But there is no need to be so formal. We are, after all, now family."

"I am glad you think so," Elizabeth Manning replied with a smile that was not at all genuine. She turned to her daughter. "Please be a dear, Mary, and get the plants. If you see your grandmother, perhaps you could coax her to join us for a visit."

"Yes, Mama," Mary said, her eyes lowered as she hurried from the room.

Elizabeth waited for her daughter to leave before dropping her mask of civility. Louisa searched for something to say to relieve the tense atmosphere. "The weather has been surprisingly warm for this time of year. I wonder if we will have a late winter."

The expression on Elizabeth's face was one of contempt. "I should congratulate you on managing to ensnare my nephew."

Louisa was shocked at the other woman's open hostility. She'd known that Nicholas's aunt would resent the fact that he had chosen to marry her, but she hadn't expected to be insulted so openly.

"I did not ensnare Nicholas," she said, doing her best to keep her tone even. "In fact, no one was more surprised than I when he asked me to marry him."

"I find that difficult to believe." When Louisa didn't reply, she continued. "When is the baby due?"

The audacity of the question stunned her. Abandoning her attempt to pacify the older woman, she straightened and replied with more force than she'd thought herself capable of.

"That is none of your concern."

A gleam entered Elizabeth's eye. "I see I am correct."

Her gaze traveled to Louisa's stomach, but the loose style of her dress would easily hide an early pregnancy. Louisa chafed under the other woman's scrutiny, resenting the implication she was a conniving woman who had trapped Nicholas into marrying her.

"If you must know, I am not with child."

The very last thing Louisa wanted to think about was the question of the future heir to the marquisate. If Nicholas persisted in his desire not to have a true marriage, it was inevitable that she would never have a child. That thought brought with it a pang of grief.

Louisa hadn't heard Nicholas's grandmother enter the drawing room until Elizabeth's gaze strayed to the doorway.

"It is good to see you again, Elizabeth," Lady Overlea said as she crossed the room to greet her daughter-in-law.

She turned to Louisa then. "Are you still feeling unwell, my dear? I hope that headache isn't still plaguing you."

It took her a moment to realize Lady Overlea was speaking to her. She must have overheard part of her conversation with Elizabeth and was giving her an excuse to leave. She could have hugged her. Instead, she raised a hand to her temple.

"I'm afraid so," she said.

"Well, I'm sure Elizabeth will understand if you go and rest. We'll entertain each other in your absence."

Louisa pressed a kiss to Lady Overlea's cheek and said her goodbyes to Nicholas's aunt before leaving the drawing room. Before seeking refuge in her bedroom, she headed for the library. A good book was just the distraction she needed at the moment.

She stopped abruptly on the threshold when she found Lord Kerrick in the room. He was seated in an armchair, reading. Apparently he'd had the same idea. He glanced up at her arrival and smiled.

"Lady Overlea," he said, closing the book and placing it on the table beside him. "I was hoping for an opportunity to speak with you."

She was tempted to use her excuse of a headache and leave, but there was something in his expression that made her stay.

He rose but didn't approach her. She left the door open before moving farther into the room.

"Nicholas spoke to you?"

It would appear there was nowhere she could go to hide from this painful subject.

"Last night," she said.

He sighed. "From your expression I take it the

154

discussion didn't go well."

Louisa found it impossible to gauge the intent behind Lord Kerrick's words. "How would you have expected such a conversation to go?"

"Well, I imagine you'd have thrown something at him. Or perhaps kicked him."

Louisa couldn't help but smile at his words.

"I'm afraid not."

"Are you considering his suggestion?"

Her stomach dropped at the question. "I'm sorry to disappoint you. The only man with whom I will…" Her voice faltered as heat flooded her cheeks. "I intend to remain faithful to my wedding vows."

Was that relief on Lord Kerrick's face?

"Good for you!"

She was well and truly confused. "I thought you wanted to…" She floundered for words.

A look of horror crossed his face. "Good God, no. Despite what Nicholas told you, and despite what he may want to believe, I think he would kill me if we followed through with this scheme of his. And, I must add, I am relieved he has chosen so well for his wife."

Much as she wanted to, she wasn't sure she could believe him. "You are wrong. My husband seems very eager for me to conceive a child with someone else. With you."

She couldn't believe she was standing there, discussing such an intimate thing with a stranger. The entire situation in which she found herself was ridiculous. Rushed into a marriage with someone she barely knew, someone she very much wanted to get to know better, but who apparently didn't want her. She'd been surprised by the intensity of the emotions that overwhelmed her when Nicholas kissed her. It had come as a blow to her to realize he didn't feel even a little of what she did. If he did, he wouldn't have been able to suggest she become intimate with someone else.

"I can't believe we are having this conversation," she said, covering her hot cheeks with her hands.

The smile on Lord Kerrick's face was a kind one. "I felt the same way when he first told me. And now that I've met you..." He shook his head. "Nicholas is a bigger fool than I'd thought possible."

Louisa turned away from him before continuing.

"It is obvious he feels nothing for me."

Lord Kerrick came up behind her, placed his hands on her shoulders, and turned her gently to face him. When he spoke, his voice was soft but firm.

"I don't think that's true."

"It must be. He must have chosen me to be his wife because he knew he would have no difficultly allowing me to do this thing."

She hated that she was discussing this with Lord Kerrick. Given the difficult position Nicholas had put them both in, however, she had no choice.

"I've seen the way your husband looks at you. I believe he may care for you more than he'd like to admit."

"No," she said, shaking her head.

"Yes," he said, more firmly. "There is a way to find out for sure."

Louisa wasn't sure she liked the gleam in his eyes, but the promise in his words was too much for her to resist.

"How?" she asked, unable to keep the hint of hope, however foolish, from her voice.

She watched as Lord Kerrick walked to the doorway. He glanced quickly into the hall before closing the door firmly and turning to answer her question.

"We give him what he thinks he wants."

She didn't know what she'd expected, but it hadn't been those words. She shook her head. "No. Absolutely not."

"Of course not," he said with an exaggerated shudder. "I have grown rather fond of my hide. And even if Nicholas allowed me to keep it afterward, I am certain I would no longer be welcome here."

"Then what exactly do you propose?"

"It's quite simple. We will both act the part he wants us to play." When he saw her negative reaction to that suggestion, he hastened to add, "Not to the end he has chosen. No, I won't do that to him. Only enough to make him think we are going along with his plan. If he asks me again for my decision, I will tell them that I am willing to proceed if you also agree to it. Since we both know that will never happen, it wouldn't be a lie."

"And I?"

"You can tell him what you choose. Either that you cannot decide until you get to know me better, or you can choose not to discuss the subject at all."

She was still unsure. "What would such a pretense gain us?"

"When your stubborn husband sees us growing closer, when he believes you and I will fall in line with his plans, I think his true feelings for you will come out. Nicholas may be playing it cool at the moment, but he won't be able to keep his jealousy at bay. I have no doubt that his true feelings will come to the surface. I just hope he doesn't come to hate me too much when they do."

For the first time since Nicholas had rebuffed her on their wedding night, Louisa felt a real spark of hope. Was Lord Kerrick correct? He did know her husband better than she. Was it possible that he was not as indifferent to her as he would have her believe? She remembered again the kisses they'd shared. How close they'd come to consummating their marriage the morning after their wedding night. If there was even the slightest chance Lord Kerrick's plan would lead to her husband realizing he wanted what she did, a real marriage, she knew she had to go along with it.

She was about to tell him as much when she heard a noise at the library door. She started to turn to see who was about to enter when Lord Kerrick took a step closer to her and grasped her hands in his.

When the door opened, he dropped her hand and took a step back. Worried one of the servants had seen Lord Kerrick holding her hands, Louisa turned to the door and was horrified to see her husband standing there.

His face was an emotionless mask. He bowed briefly, apologized for interrupting, and left, closing the door behind him.

She spun back to face Lord Kerrick. "You did that intentionally."

"I did," he said. "If we are to force Nicholas to reveal his true feelings, we're going to have to waken his jealousy."

She considered her husband's lack of reaction and the hope she'd experienced just moments before dimmed. "He didn't appear to mind."

"Oh, he was definitely surprised and not at all happy to

see us together. I caught a flicker of it before he hid it."

"He was surprised because I told him I wouldn't even consider this. And now he has seen the two of us together."

"Have faith. Nicholas is stubborn. He is hiding his feelings even from himself. I fear this may take a little time."

Louisa straightened her shoulders and nodded, resolved to follow Lord Kerrick's plan.

"Can I ask you for your permission to call you by your Christian name?"

She was surprised by the request.

"We don't know each other that well—"

"Yes, but I think it will annoy your husband."

She considered for a moment. "Are you sure?"

"You have a choice, Lady Overlea. Sleep with me now and have done with it, send me away, or draw out the pretense. If you choose the first, I think we will both cement ourselves in your husband's disfavor forever. With the second, Nicholas will continue to avoid you and you'll never have a real marriage. Choose the third, however, and you may uncover the depth of his feelings for you. And with some luck, Nicholas will still be on speaking terms with me after it is done."

He was right. Of the three options open to her, there was only really one choice she could make. "When do we start?"

"We already have. You should go now. Given your reaction when he approached you yesterday, Nicholas will expect you to feel guilty after being caught alone with me. It wouldn't feel right if you remained here with me."

"I hope we are doing the right thing," she said before

turning to leave.

"As do I," Lord Kerrick replied.

Louisa was careful to keep her distance from Lord Kerrick for the rest of the day. In turn, Nicholas continued to avoid her. Of course, he'd been avoiding her for some time, so she had no way of knowing if his current behavior was due to the scene he'd witnessed in the library.

Dinner was an awkward affair. Louisa hadn't wanted to worry her sister with the truth about her and Nicholas's relationship, but it was clear she sensed something was wrong. Catherine had always been intuitive, picking up on the mood of others very easily. She chattered on in a cheerful manner, though, no doubt in an attempt to raise the spirits of everyone else.

Louisa said very little. Her gaze drifted to her husband, where he sat silently at the head of the table, for what felt like the hundredth time. She tried to guess his mood, but it was impossible. Contrary to what Lord Kerrick had suggested, he didn't show any signs of being jealous. He appeared calm and collected.

Lord Kerrick bantered back and forth with Catherine. Louisa could see the infatuation in her sister's expression when she looked at him. Kerrick seemed to be enjoying himself, but he could very well be putting on a show for her husband. She glanced at Nicholas again and caught him looking at his friend, a frown on his face. His gaze turned to meet hers then and his expression returned to its impassive mask. The telltale sign of emotion had been so brief she wondered if she'd imagined it.

After dinner she joined Catherine and the dowager marchioness in the drawing room. Nicholas and Lord

Kerrick remained behind, and Louisa couldn't help but wonder if they were discussing her.

As she had the previous evening, Catherine went immediately to the piano and began to play. They'd had a pianoforte in the cottage until last year, when they'd had to sell it after their father fell ill. At the time Catherine had said she didn't mind, but seeing the joy on her face as she sat on the piano bench told Louisa that she had missed it very much.

Louisa sat on a settee and took out a new handkerchief she planned to embroider. It had been years since she'd done any kind of needlework other than mending, and she was looking forward to the decorative work as a welcome change of pace. Nicholas's grandmother sat next to her. They'd been listening in silence to Catherine's playing for about a minute when Lady Overlea turned to her.

"Is something amiss between you and my grandson?" Her voice was pitched low so Catherine wouldn't overhear.

Louisa's hands stilled on the embroidery, and it was several moments before she could meet the older woman's gaze.

"It is not something I can discuss with you," she said when she finally replied.

Lady Overlea's lips tightened into a thin line.

"I will speak to my grandson and settle the matter."

"Oh, no, please do not trouble yourself," she said, anxious to reassure the older woman. "It is merely a misunderstanding."

She didn't think Nicholas would take well to his grandmother interfering in his romantic life.

Lady Overlea looked at her. It was clear she was

measuring her words when she spoke again. "You know of his illness?"

She was about to admit she'd witnessed two episodes, but something stopped her. Nicholas's grandmother wouldn't have asked her question if he'd told her about those episodes, and Louisa guessed he was trying to shield her from any additional worry.

"Yes," she said.

Lady Overlea merely nodded in reply. For a moment Louisa was afraid she was going to be subjected to yet another lecture about the pressing need for an heir, but Lord Kerrick entered the room at that moment. Her gaze moved past him when her husband's tall form moved into the doorway behind him. She was struck anew by just how handsome he was. With his dark hair and dark eyes, he had the appearance of a dark angel. Her dark angel. Only he was doing everything in his power to push her toward another man.

A horrible realization came over her as she met Nicholas's gaze. She wasn't sure how or why, since she barely knew him, but she was certain of one thing. She cared for him very much. Perhaps even loved him. At that moment she knew she would do whatever was needed to discover whether Nicholas Manning had even a small amount of affection for her.

Looking from her husband to Lord Kerrick, she couldn't tell what had passed between them during the few minute they'd spent together before joining them in the drawing room. Neither showed any sign of having had a disagreement. Lord Kerrick met her gaze and gave her a reassuring smile before turning his attention to Catherine, joining her at the piano. Louisa caught her sister's telltale blush under his attention.

Louisa took up her embroidery as they listened to her sister play, but she was very conscious of her husband. He stood by the fireplace, holding himself aloof from the others in the room. At times she could almost feel his eyes on her, but when she glanced up from her work he was always looking elsewhere. She ached to reach out to him, but knew such an overture wouldn't be welcome.

Catherine finished her piece to enthusiastic applause from Lord Kerrick. She blushed again and stood.

"It would be wonderful if we could play whist," Catherine said. "We haven't played in so long. Not since Papa fell ill and we no longer had four players."

A smile touched Louisa lips as she remembered their frequent games.

"What a splendid idea," Lord Kerrick said. He turned to Louisa and continued, "As the only guest present, I am going to impose on your hospitality, Nicholas, and claim the lovely new marchioness as my partner."

A twinkle of merriment danced in his eyes. Louisa glanced at her husband and was heartened to see a brief flicker of annoyance cross his face.

Nicholas turned to Lady Overlea. "Would you like to make up the foursome, Grandmother? I know how much you enjoy a good rubber of whist."

Lady Overlea shook her head and stood, her movements slow. "I exerted myself today and think I should retire early."

Catherine was alarmed at her words. "I am so sorry," she said. "I got carried away looking at all the plants in the conservatory. I had never thought to see such plants outside the pages of a book."

"I enjoyed myself," Lady Overlea said. "So much so that I forgot I am not as young as I once was."

After his grandmother took her leave, Nicholas turned to Catherine. "That leaves me with the honor of partnering you."

Catherine smiled broadly and led the way to the card table.

Under normal circumstances, Louisa would have enjoyed the game. Catherine was in high spirits, and Lord Kerrick flirted shamelessly with the two of them. Nicholas actually made an effort to join in the conversation, but it was obvious to everyone that his heart wasn't in the match.

In the end, she and Lord Kerrick won. He made a point of commenting on what a good team they made and smiled at her broadly. She returned the smile but couldn't help darting a glance at her husband. He was not amused.

Louisa stood. "I think I, too, will retire now," she said.

She could feel her sister's eyes on her as she bid everyone goodnight and fled to her room, breathing a sigh of relief when she reached it. She was far from tired and picked up a book to read, but found she was too keyed up to follow the story. Instead, she paced back and forth in front of the fireplace, allowing the warmth of the fire to envelop her. All she could think about was her realization that she loved Nicholas. And with that discovery, she found herself thinking more and more about his death.

A soft rap at her bedroom door startled her out of her reverie. She turned in time to see a folded piece of paper being slid under her door, which was followed by the sound of retreating footsteps.

She crossed the room and bent to pick up the note. She paused when she heard footsteps come back down the hall and held her breath when they stopped outside her door. She couldn't keep from hoping it was Nicholas. When the footsteps continued she released her breath in a rush of disappointment.

She glanced down at the note in her hand where her name was written. She unfolded the piece of paper and read the brief message.

Meet me in the library in thirty minutes.
~K

The next half hour dragged by as she wondered what Lord Kerrick wanted to tell her that they hadn't already discussed earlier. Finally, when the appointed time arrived, she made her way downstairs. Relieved when she reached the library without having seen anyone, she opened the door and slipped inside.

The candles were still lit, but there was no fire in the hearth. The room was empty and she found herself waiting yet again. She turned when she finally heard the library door open and was shocked to find not Lord Kerrick, but her husband standing there.

His expression told her he was angry.

"Were you expecting someone else?"

She swallowed hard when he closed the door and moved into the room, his steps measured. Menacing. The odd glint in his eyes sent a shiver of awareness down her spine.

"I take it the two of you have decided to go along with my plan?"

She didn't reply. What could she say? She wouldn't lie to him, yet it was vital that he believe what he was accusing her of.

He stopped before her and she barely resisted the urge to take a step back.

"It would have been nice if the two of you had decided to act with a little more discretion. It will be a miracle if the staff isn't already gossiping about the two of you belowstairs."

Unnerved by the heat in Nicholas's eyes, she looked away.

"Tell me," he said, his voice soft with menace, "have the two of you kissed yet? Surely you haven't already gone to his bed."

Her temper flared at the condemnation in his tone. What was wrong with him? He was the one who wanted her to conceive a child with his best friend, and now he was treating her as if she were a strumpet.

She tilted her chin upward and met his gaze evenly, not bothering to hide her own anger. "It is what you desired, is it not?"

She knew he would take that as confirmation. A muscle twitched along his jaw and he took a step closer.

"Did you enjoy it?"

She looked away. Nicholas's mood was unpredictable and she no longer knew what he wanted from her. "I will not discuss this with you."

She jumped when he grasped her upper arms.

"Answer me."

She remained silent. He lowered his head until their eyes were level and she had no choice but to meet his gaze. She could see the turmoil there.

"Nicholas," she said softly, her anger evaporating in that instant.

His eyes closed and she held her breath. His grip loosened as if he meant to release her, but then he swore and dragged her against his body. The very air seemed to spark around them. Louisa was frozen, afraid to do or say anything that might cause him to turn away from her.

He swore again and lowered his mouth to hers. The kiss was hard at first, punishing in its intensity. She welcomed it, though. Welcomed kissing him and being held against him. She had craved his touch, fearing she would never receive it again.

Her lips parted and his tongue surged into her mouth. She met his urgency with her own. He released her arms and she raised them to encircle his neck, desperate to get closer. His hands streaked down her back and cupped her bottom, and he brought her firmly against him as he continued his assault on her mouth. She could feel the hardness of his arousal and her breath caught with anticipation. She made a low sound deep in her throat and tried to bring her body even more firmly against his. Her desire was a living thing.

Almost as quickly as it started, it was over. He tore his mouth from hers and stared at her, his breath coming in audible rasps. Her own breathing was equally shaky.

He released her, took a step back and looked away.

"Go to bed," he said, his voice uneven.

She placed a hand on his arm. "I want to stay."

Silence stretched between them. She waited as he stood stock-still, his posture unbearably straight. Finally, without another word, he turned and left the room.

She could only stare at his retreating figure, despair sweeping through her. She'd thought the situation bad before when she'd believed he didn't want her, but this

SUZANNA MEDEIROS

was so much worse. Even if he didn't love her, it was clear that he did desire her. It was equally clear, however, that he would fight his attraction for her to the end.

CHAPTER TWELVE

The following morning she was waylaid by Lord Kerrick on her way down to breakfast.

"Did it work?" he asked.

Her lips tightened as her suspicions about last night's encounter with Nicholas were confirmed. "You planned that."

He nodded. "I left another note partway under your door for him to find. I figured if he was annoyed enough he wouldn't be suspicious about my being so careless. I can just imagine the expression on his face when he saw that it was you, not I, waiting in the library."

"You could have warned me about your plans."

He shook his head. "It was better this way so your surprise would be genuine when he entered."

She made an attempt to rein in her annoyance. It was not Kerrick's fault, after all, that Nicholas remained adamant they follow through with his absurd plan.

"He was very angry," she said after a moment.

"Didn't I tell you as much? Despite what he says, he

doesn't wish to see the two of us together." He stopped when he noticed her mood. "Are you all right? What happened?"

She hesitated, but only for a moment. Kerrick was the only person in whom she could confide.

"He wanted to know if we had agreed to his proposal."

"And what did you say?"

"I didn't reply."

He nodded at that. "He would have taken that as a yes."

"He did, and then he…"

"And then he what?"

"He kissed me."

Kerrick released his breath in a low whistle. "I knew it! I knew he cared for you." His expression turned sober. "I don't mean to pry, but I do need to know how things now stand between the two of you. The last thing I want to do is continue to make Nicholas believe I am pursuing you. Not if he has decided he no longer wants me to."

"He left," she said, her voice hitching slightly before she continued. "It was obvious he regretted his actions. I do not think he will kiss me again."

Kerrick swore. "Damn his stubborn hide. That man will go to his grave making himself and everyone around him miserable."

"Yes, well, be that as it may, I have decided that I will not give up. He may have given up on our marriage before it has even begun, but I have not."

Kerrick smiled. "Good girl."

They made their way to the breakfast room. Lady Overlea and Catherine were already seated, but the somber expressions on their faces when they turned to her caused a knot of worry to form in the pit of her stomach.

"What is the matter?"

"It's Nicholas," Lady Overlea said. "A maid found him this morning in his study. He has had an attack."

From the look on the older woman's face, Louisa feared the worst. "How is he?" she asked around the lump in her throat.

"The doctor is with him now, but the attack is severe. He isn't sure…"

Catherine had been silent until that moment, but when Lady Overlea couldn't continue, she stepped in. "They're not sure if Nicholas will survive the day."

Louisa gasped. Her legs threatened to give way and Kerrick braced an arm around her waist to steady her. No, she refused to believe it. She'd seen Nicholas last night and he'd looked so healthy.

"Where is he now?"

"He was moved to his bedroom," Catherine said.

Louisa spun around and hurried back upstairs. Kerrick followed in silence, something for which she was grateful. All she could think about in that moment was her husband. When she reached his rooms she didn't bother to knock and the scene that met her on the other side of the door almost made her heart stop.

Nicholas lay still in his bed, his skin pale as death. The bed sheets were turned down to his waist and leeches had been administered to his torso, dark blots that stood out in stark relief against his too-white skin. Her gaze flew to the doctor, who had paused at her interruption. She couldn't tell if he were applying yet another leech or removing the ones that had already started to fall off, glutted on her husband's blood.

"How is he?" She was almost afraid to ask the question.

The doctor, a small man with graying hair, turned away from her and placed another leech on Nicholas's body.

"Not well. You shouldn't be here."

She watched as he reached into a jar and removed yet another worm. Anger rose within her. Nicholas looked to be on the point of death and this doctor was doing his best to drain him of his remaining blood.

"That will be enough," she said.

He didn't stop. "You shouldn't be here. Women are always squeamish at this sight." He placed the leech on her husband's chest.

Louisa saw red. Without a word, she marched up to the doctor and removed the jar of leeches from his hands. Surprised, he could only stare at her in stunned silence.

"I said that will be enough."

The man sputtered for a moment before drawing himself up. "And who are you to give me orders?"

Louisa met his outraged gaze squarely.

"I am the Marchioness of Overlea. Since my husband is too ill to speak, I will do it for him. You are dismissed."

She held out the jar of leeches for him to take. He stared at her, his face red with indignation, but when she didn't back down he jerked the jar away from her and secured the lid. Without another word or glance in her direction, he dropped the jar into his black physician's bag and stalked out of the room. It was only then that Louisa noticed Kerrick and her sister had followed her into Nicholas's bedroom and witnessed the entire scene.

"Are you sure about this?" Kerrick asked.

"Yes. I've seen him through two such episodes and he recovered both times with his blood intact."

"But the doctor—"

"Lord Kerrick," she said, interrupting him, "I am familiar with doctors. I saw them bleed my father almost to death during his illness. He never improved. All the bleedings did was weaken him further. Nicholas cannot afford to have the same thing happen to him. Not if he is going to fight this illness."

She turned back to the bed. Gorged on blood, a few more leeches had fallen away. She was more concerned, however, about the ones that were still attached, slowly draining her husband.

Kerrick moved to stand on the other side of the bed. "I've heard salt will make them fall off."

Louisa shook her head. "They will, but before they fall off they regurgitate back into the wound."

Kerrick raised a brow. "How do you know that?"

"I tried it with my father and the wounds festered. I did, though, watch to see how the doctor removed them before they fell off on their own." She turned to Catherine. "Fetch me the washbasin," she said, her tone brisk.

When Catherine returned with it, she placed it on his bedside table.

"A seal is created when the sucker attaches to the body. You must break that seal from both ends of the leech before you remove it."

She flicked her finger along the small side of the leech, using her nail to break the seal, then sweeping aside the sucker. She did the same on the larger side of the leech and gave a low sound of triumph when the leech came away cleanly. She dropped the leech into the washbasin and moved on to the next one.

Kerrick copied her actions, the two working quickly to

remove the rest of the creatures. When the last one was removed, Louisa stared down at her husband. He was so pale, his breathing so shallow, she couldn't be sure he still lived. Suddenly afraid, she leaned over him, her face turned so her cheek hovered over his mouth. She exhaled with relief when she felt his soft exhalation.

"I need to clean him," she said. Catherine left to fetch another washbasin from Louisa's bedroom. When she returned, Louisa made quick work of cleaning the trail of blood smears from her husband's torso. The task soothed her, made her feel that she was actually helping him rather than just standing by, powerless. A few of the wounds made by the leeches continued to trickle blood. Fortunately, Catherine had anticipated the need for bandages and had called for some to be brought up while Louisa washed Nicholas.

When the last of the blood had been washed away and the small wounds bandaged, Louisa looked up and met Kerrick's gaze across the bed.

"I'll stay with him in case he needs anything. Can you see what you can do to soothe Lady Overlea?"

"What happens now?" Kerrick asked. She could see his genuine concern in the grim set of his jaw.

"Now we wait and hope that he has enough strength to pull through. I don't know how much blood he lost." She looked down at her husband. "Nicholas is a strong man, and despite these episodes, he is healthy in every other way. He will pull though."

Kerrick nodded.

"Is there anything I can do?" Catherine asked.

Louisa shook her head. "Stay with Lady Overlea. Try to put her mind at rest. She has already lost a son and a grandson. I imagine she is beside herself with worry."

Catherine gave her a quick hug before leaving with Kerrick. After they were gone, Louisa pulled a chair to Nicholas's bedside and settled in to wait.

He was afraid. This was no doubt the end and he had left a botched affair behind him. Edward would be the next Marquess of Overlea.

He thought about Louisa. Tried to hold onto her face, to remember the feel of her in his arms, but it was all starting to fade away.

Time passed and he wondered if he was already dead and just unaware of it. He seemed to be floating in a dark void, his strength slowing ebbing from him. At one point he heard voices, but they were hushed and he could not make out what was being said. Small stings jabbed at him everywhere and he knew this was the end. He was in hell. He gave himself over completely. He had so little strength left.

He was confused at first when the sensation of many small mouths drawing from his body started to fade. Perhaps it was only a momentary respite before the pain worsened. His confusion increased when the cool touch of a washcloth swept over his body. And then he could smell her. Louisa. He breathed in deeply, taking comfort from the thought she was near. And then that, too, was gone.

Bereft, he drifted further.

He didn't know how long he faded in and out before he began to realize he wasn't dead. Opening his eyes, he blinked a few times to bring his sight into focus and exhaled a sigh of relief when he realized he was in his room. In his bed.

He wasn't alone. He turned his head to the right and his eyesight swam again momentarily.

Louisa.

She was sleeping upright in an armchair by his bedside. He stared at her, relishing the opportunity to take her in. Normally he tried to avoid looking at her or thinking about her.

The chair was winged and she'd settled into one of the corners. Her pale gold hair had started to escape its pins and several long tendrils framed the pale oval of her face. Her cheeks were flushed with sleep, her lips parted.

He remembered all too well the feel of her mouth under his. He'd been angry when he discovered the note Kerrick had left for her. It was a stupid emotion and one he didn't fully understand. It had been his idea, after all, to have Kerrick father his future heir. He had promoted the idea to both parties and been anxious for their agreement. Why, then, had it infuriated him to discover the two of them had arranged to meet after everyone else had gone to bed? He should have been relieved.

At the time, however, it had seemed like a betrayal. He told himself that if they had come to him and revealed they'd agreed to his proposal he wouldn't have felt so deceived. The fact that neither of them would speak to him about their acceptance and that they were trying to arrange secret meetings behind his back had him wondering if there was more to the meetings than the practical arrangement he had proposed.

Watching the two of them laughing over dinner, Kerrick flirting openly with his wife, he'd realized it would probably be very easy for Louisa to fall in love with his friend. And why shouldn't she? Her husband had been a cold, unfeeling bastard to her. It would only make sense for her to seek solace from the one man who seemed only too eager to offer it.

When he'd discovered the note, he'd thought Kerrick was trying to steal his wife away from him. He was aware of the absurdity of the situation and that it was all of his own making. Well, not all of it. Most of it stemmed from the cursed illness he had inherited from his father. The one that had caused him to drive his carriage off the road, killing both himself and Nicholas's mother.

Watching Louisa now, seemingly at peace as she slept, Nicholas was painfully aware of just how much he wanted her for himself. The thought of her and Kerrick together had grown hateful to him.

Nicholas made a sound of disgust at his melancholy meanderings and shifted so he could get out of bed. He supposed he shouldn't have been surprised to find that he couldn't manage it on his own.

"Nicholas!" Louisa exclaimed, coming fully awake and bending over his prostrate form. "You're awake."

The enormous smile that crossed her face dazzled him for a moment and he found that he had to look away to clear his thoughts.

"Of course I'm awake," he said. "Why the hell can't I sit up?" He struggled to raise himself onto his elbows.

Louisa's smile dimmed a little and he regretted his curt tone.

"You've been abed for two days and you were bled by your doctor. Your body needs time to regain its strength."

He ceased his struggle to sit up and sank back down onto the bed. Two days? He'd never had an episode last that long.

177

She must have seen his concern, for she hastened to add, "I fear your doctor was overzealous in performing his duty and I sent him away when I saw what he was doing."

Surprised, he could only stare at her for several moments before finding his voice. "You sent him away?"

"He was bleeding you," she said, a note of anger creeping into her voice.

"That is what all doctors do when they don't know what else to do."

"I know. I watched them do it time and again to my father. And each time he grew weaker. I should have stopped them sooner. In the end, he didn't have enough strength left to fight to live." Her eyes blazed with passionate indignation as her gaze met his. "I will not allow them to do that to you. To drain you until you, too, no longer have the strength to fight your illness."

He remembered then his certainty that he'd been in hell. Remembered the feeling of tiny creatures attaching to his body and drinking from him. He also remembered their abrupt removal and the feel of her hands on his body as she'd cleaned him afterward. Her scent when she'd leaned over him again and again, no doubt checking to see whether he was still alive. He also remembered that she'd spoken to him throughout his ordeal, though he couldn't remember now what she'd said.

He gazed at her in wonder, the passionate intensity of her gaze striking a chord deep within him. He realized then that he was already lost. He was in love with her.

He looked away, hating his weakness. She'd seen him like this far too many times for his own liking. And now the episodes were worsening. He wondered how much longer it would be before they killed him. The irony of his situation was not lost on him. He'd never wanted to be heir and had always been grateful he was born a second son. He'd also never wanted to marry, and he certainly had never thought himself such a romantic fool as to fall in love. Now here he was, the Marquess of Overlea, and in love with his wife. And he would never live long enough to enjoy either one.

"You need to eat. I'll send for something light." She moved to the bellpull to summon a servant.

He spoke without looking at her.

"Thank you for everything you have done. However, you are clearly fatigued. You have to take care of yourself as well. If you summon Harrison, I'm sure he'll be able to arrange for everything I need."

He would be safer with his valet. The last thing he wanted was to ask for his wife's assistance in sitting up. He knew he wasn't at risk of pulling her down into the bed with him, not in his current condition. Having Louisa continue to care for him, however, especially in light of his recent discovery about his feelings for her, would add a level of intimacy to their relationship that would be hard to back away from. Much as he hated the very thought of it, this latest episode meant it was imperative that they follow through with his original plan for Louisa to conceive an heir with Kerrick.

She was silent and Nicholas made the mistake of looking at her. Her whole demeanor had stiffened and he knew he'd hurt her. Again. Gone was the warm, sleepy, and happy woman that had just woken. In her place was a woman who was becoming all too adept at holding herself aloof from him.

* * *

Kerrick was relieved to overhear one of the maids telling a footman that Lord Overlea was feeling better. He'd actually feared Nicholas would die. When he ran into Louisa in the breakfast room, however, that relief quickly turned to annoyance. She wouldn't tell him what had happened, but it was clear she was upset.

Not bothering to inquire whether his friend was disposed to receive visitors, he headed straight to Nicholas's bedroom after breakfast, knocked curtly, and entered. Nicholas was, indeed, looking better. His skin no longer had that horrible ashen complexion and he was sitting up, the remains of his breakfast tray resting on the bed beside him.

Nicholas put down the newspaper he was reading and raised a brow in question.

"It would seem that in the last two days people have grown accustomed to entering my bedroom whenever the whim strikes."

Kerrick smiled. Despite the fact that Nicholas was a damned stubborn fool, Kerrick was comforted to see him looking well.

"You had a close one," he said.

"So I hear."

"I hope you realize you may very well owe your life to your wife."

Nicholas frowned. "So everyone keeps telling me."

"Everyone?"

"Grandmother was also here," he said with an exaggerated sigh. "She actually wants me to agree not to move about unsupervised. Not even in my own house. Can you imagine? Me with a nursemaid, at my age?"

It was obvious that he was trying to lighten the mood,

but Kerrick wasn't in the frame of mind to joke about the situation. He went to the chair where Louisa had remained during her husband's illness and sank into the seat.

"What happened, Nicholas?"

His friend blew out a harsh breath and leaned back in his chair. "You know what happened," he said, the corners of his mouth turning downward. "I had an attack. A maid found me and the doctor was called. You would know better than I since I was unconscious for most of it."

Kerrick watched his friend intently. He could always tell when Nicholas was lying or holding something back and his instincts were telling him that he was hiding something now.

"You might as well tell me. I won't go away until you do."

"I could have you thrown out."

"You could, but you won't."

Nicholas didn't bother to deny it. "I need to speak to you about Louisa," he said.

This is it, Kerrick thought. *He's going to tell me he's reconsidered his asinine request that I father a child whom he would claim as his heir.* He was careful to keep his expression neutral as he waited for his friend to continue.

"It appeared to me before this last attack that the two of you had or were about to come to an understanding about my proposition."

He didn't reply. He wanted to know what his friend was thinking first.

"For God's sake, Kerrick, will you answer me?"

"I'm sorry, was that a question? It sounded more like a statement."

Nicholas scowled. "You're damned lucky I'm too weak

to get out of this chair right now."

Kerrick decided now might not be the best time to test his friend's patience. He had no doubt Louisa would strangle him with her bare hands if his baiting caused her husband to suffer a relapse.

"If you must know," he said, "she hasn't told me yet if she's willing to do this. And you already know I won't press her."

"So you decided that the best course of action is to woo her openly in my own house?"

"I haven't been wooing her; I've been getting to know her. You can hardly expect her to agree to bed a man she barely knows. Another woman might do that, but not your wife. Even I know that much from the little time I've spent in her company."

"My brain hasn't been addled by this last episode. I've seen you in action and I know when you are wooing a woman."

This was good, he thought. Nicholas was definitely annoyed and that could only be because he wanted Louisa for himself.

"If you prefer, I can always leave. I wouldn't want to overstay my welcome."

The fight seemed to go out of Nicholas at those words. "No," he said. "I don't want that."

"Then what do you want?"

"I want this whole thing over with already. I want Louisa to already be pregnant with your child and then I want to do my damnedest to forget the whole thing."

Kerrick was stunned. "You wish us to continue?"

"I need you to ask her once and for all if she will do this. Surely she knows you well enough by now. And given what has happened, she'll recognize that time is not a luxury we have."

"But you just said…" He couldn't find the words to continue. He couldn't believe Nicholas wished to continue with this nonsense, especially since it was so clear to all involved that he hated every second of it.

"I said that I do not wish the whole world to see you wooing my wife. I do not wish there to be any question about the paternity of Louisa's child."

Although he'd only been in the role a short time, Nicholas had donned his imperious marquess façade. Kerrick hated it when he did that since it forced him to put on his own formal mask. It was tiresome enough having to do that with the rest of the world. He hated when he had to act the part of the Earl of Kerrick with his friends.

"As you wish, Overlea. I shall do my best to seduce your wife, then remove myself from your presence. With any luck, I won't have to return next month, or in nine months if she has a girl." He caught the reflexive clenching of his friend's hands. Good, he thought. "I believe you were going to tell me what it is you are hiding."

When Nicholas remained silent, Kerrick thought he wasn't going to reply. Despite his annoyance at his friend's colossal obstinacy, he had no intention of leaving the room until he learned what Nicholas was hiding.

"You know both my father and my brother also suffered from these attacks."

Kerrick nodded. Nicholas had been very concerned for their health.

"I have also told you that episodes were often triggered or made worse by alcohol consumption."

Kerrick frowned. "Yes, but that wouldn't apply here

because I know you've been careful."

Nicholas's mouth twisted wryly. "Not quite."

Kerrick swore. Unable to sit still any longer, he stood and began to pace. He couldn't believe what he was hearing.

He turned back to face Nicholas. "Let me understand you. Are you actually telling me that you've been drinking? Knowing what happened to your father and your brother?"

"I've had attacks here and there without drinking."

"Yes, but damn it to hell, Nicholas. Why would you be so reckless? Do you wish to die?" A horrible thought occurred to him. "Good Lord, tell me you weren't at death's door these past two days because you'd been drinking."

Nicholas remained silent, which Kerrick took as confirmation. Horror and guilt washed over him when he realized this was his fault. He'd done this to his friend. His little game to try to make Nicholas realize he cared for his wife had driven him too far. Louisa had told him she and her husband had kissed that night in the library. She'd also told him that the kiss had made no difference to her husband. That he'd still been determined to go through with his plan for his heir. That could only mean Nicholas had been drinking to try to put this horrible mess out of his mind. To forget the kiss he'd shared with his wife. A kiss that might never have happened if he hadn't plotted to prick Nicholas's jealousy and bring him and Louisa together by leaving those cursed notes.

CHAPTER THIRTEEN

Louisa tried not to dwell on what had happened that morning. She'd been so relieved when she'd opened her eyes and found Nicholas struggling to get up... for a moment she'd found herself unable to breathe. His curt dismissal of her had hurt. She'd realized then that his feelings, whatever they might be, didn't matter. He may have been jealous, but clearly he was determined to keep an impenetrable wall between them.

After the kiss they'd shared, it was obvious to her that he did desire her physically. The feel of his hands on her body as he'd crushed her to him, the feel of his arousal pressing against her lower belly... she'd wanted that kiss to go on forever. Instead, he'd cast her aside, just as he had that morning.

She didn't expect to see him that day. He hadn't wanted her to see it, but he was weaker than he cared to admit. She knew it would take time for him to recover. One could not come as close to death as he had without feeling the repercussions afterward.

Louisa resisted the urge to check on him after dinner. Relieved that her grandson had survived his attack, Lady Overlea had made a point of looking in on him frequently. Louisa would have to rely on his grandmother for news of her husband's progress.

Nicholas had been correct about one thing. After staying by his bedside for two days she was exhausted. She'd kept herself busy all day, but that night she fell asleep almost before her head hit the pillow. She woke up the next morning refreshed, but then dread settled over her as she considered the long day ahead. Sighing, she got out of bed and rang for her maid to help her dress.

Lord Kerrick joined them for breakfast that morning. After seeing Nicholas the day before, he'd gone out she hadn't had a chance to speak to him. Looking at the man now, she got the distinct impression that he was trying to avoid her. When he rose from the breakfast table to leave, she excused herself and followed him into the hallway. He was headed out again.

"Lord Kerrick," she called out.

He stopped and turned to face her, his movements curiously cautious.

"Lady Overlea," he said with an abbreviated bow.

She frowned. Something was definitely the matter. "Can I speak with you for a moment?" she asked, conscious of the fact they were being observed by the footman.

"I had other plans—"

"I will be brief. It concerns my husband."

She saw the reluctance in his eyes, but he finally nodded his acceptance. She led the way into the library. She wanted to close the doors but knew it wouldn't be proper.

Instead, she made her way to the center of the large room so they wouldn't be overheard before turning to face Kerrick.

"You've changed your mind," she said.

"Partially."

"What does that mean? Why have you been avoiding me?" She almost laughed at the absurdity of the situation in which she found herself. "Everyone is walking on eggshells around me. They all seem to know something is going on, but no one wants to speak of it. I don't know if they're trying to spare my feelings or if they pity me."

"No one wants to hurt you."

"Including you," she said softly.

He nodded.

"Will you tell me what happened? Was it something I said or did?"

"No, absolutely not. You are not to blame. In fact, I fear that I am."

He was making no sense. "I don't understand."

He closed his eyes briefly before opening them again and looking at her squarely.

"Your husband's last episode, the one that nearly killed him… God, I hate to say this. It was my fault."

She could only stare at him. What was he saying?

"I fail to see how you could possibly be to blame for what happened to my husband. He has a medical condition. This is not the first time this illness has caused him to lose consciousness, though I believe it is the most severe attack he has suffered."

He was still for a moment, his gaze averted. When he looked at her again, his entire posture had stiffened as though he were bracing himself. From what, she wondered. Her condemnation?

"I know about Nicholas's episodes. I've even witnessed one before now," Kerrick said.

"Then you know about his medical condition. So, you see, you couldn't possibly be to blame for what happened."

He shook his head. "On the contrary." He exhaled sharply and continued. "Nicholas told me that episodes can be brought on when he drinks. He has seen the same thing happen to his father and brother and has had it happen to him."

"You gave him something to drink?" she asked, frowning.

"Not directly, no. But I am responsible for him drinking. That night, the one on which he collapsed... well, you already know I'd planned to prick Nicholas's jealousy. To have him reveal himself to you. I thought I was being so clever."

"You were," she said. "And I am grateful you did so. That night confirmed to me that he does have feelings for me. At the very least, I know that he does not find me unattractive."

Lord Kerrick smiled at that. "I doubt very much that anyone would find you so."

She colored at the compliment and he continued.

"I fear my maneuverings that night drove him over the edge."

She shook her head. "That is a little extreme. He didn't hurt me. In fact, quite the opposite," she said, her blush deepening.

"Yes, but don't you see? Nicholas admitted to me that he drank that night after he left you. God!" He turned and paced to the far window. Louisa was stunned as the import of his words sank in. "He will never relent. And this latest episode has only strengthened his resolve. The only thing my stupid game accomplished was to drive my best friend to do the very thing that could end up killing him."

"No," she said, seeing how distressed he was. "No. This was not your fault. And remember, I did agree to go along with your plan."

"I drove him to those drinks, Louisa," he said, his voice bleak. "As surely as if I'd taken the bottle and placed it in his hand myself."

Anger sprang within her, a many-headed beast. How dare he! Nicholas knew that drinking was the very last thing he should do and he continued to do it anyway. Was he trying to kill himself? Was being in her presence that difficult for him?

She moved to stand before Kerrick. "*You* are not to blame for this," she said. "He is. He devised this plan. He married me after leading me to believe he wanted me to carry his heir. *His* heir. What a joke," she said with a small, bitter laugh. "Instead, I find that he wants to hand me over to his best friend. Who does he think he is?"

Now it was her turn to pace. The more she thought about it, the angrier she became. She had to do something. She didn't know what exactly, not at first, but then it came to her. She stopped and turned back to Lord Kerrick.

"We will get through this," she said, her voice firm with resolve. "All of us."

She left an open-mouthed Kerrick standing in the library and marched belowstairs to handle the matter.

After spending a day in his rooms, Nicholas decided to

venture downstairs the following afternoon. He'd recovered from his bout of weakness but didn't relish the idea of making a grand appearance at dinner. If his valet's reaction upon seeing him yesterday morning was anything to go by, he knew he'd be the subject of stares and avid curiosity from the household staff. He may as well get it out of the way now. Show everyone he wasn't an invalid.

Not Louisa, though. He would see her at dinner, but for now he would do his best to avoid her. The revelation of the depth of his feelings for her still unsettled him.

He was surprised at how quickly he grew tired again. Sommers, the footmen, and a few maids had already seen him and he knew word would soon spread to the rest of the staff that he was better. After visiting his grandmother, he decided to go to the conservatory to visit his sister-in-law. He couldn't see Louisa just yet, but he was hoping to learn how she was doing.

He found Catherine poring over a few books that lay open on a small table in the conservatory, a small notebook and pencil at her side. It appeared she was very serious about cataloging all the plants in his grandmother's collection. Grandmother loved the colors and scents of the exotic plants she'd acquired over the years, but she'd never bothered to learn more about them.

Catherine beamed when she spotted him, reminding him of her sister when he'd woken yesterday morning, and he felt a pang somewhere in the vicinity of his heart.

"I am so happy to see you up and about, my lord," she said.

He tsked. "Nicholas, remember? We are family now."

"Of course," she said with a smile.

A small dimple appeared in her cheek and it occurred

to him that he didn't know if Louisa had a dimple. She'd rarely had occasion to smile in his presence, and he'd been too addled the previous morning to notice.

Full of bubbling enthusiasm for her task, Catherine jumped to her feet and started to give him a tour. She was excited to share the information she'd discovered about a few of the plants, but after a few minutes he had to pretend that pressing estate matters needed his attention. Aside from feeling a little tired from being on his feet so long, the overpowering smell of all the exotic flowers was beginning to make him feel light-headed. For a horrifying moment he feared he was about to suffer another attack and almost ran to the doors that led out to the garden. Once he escaped the overheated space with its overpowering perfume, he began to breathe a little easier. The crisp autumn air cleared his head and profound relief coursed through him when his dizziness faded completely. Annoyed that he was obviously still feeling the aftereffects of his last attack, he made his way around to the front of the house.

He was able to make his way to his study without running into Louisa, and there he closed the door and leaned against it, eyes closed. He felt more than a little foolish. He was actually skulking about his own home in fear of one small, albeit very beautiful, woman. One whom he knew would never intentionally harm anyone, but who had done more than anyone or anything else to destroy his peace of mind.

If he was going to spend the rest of the day hiding in his study, he might as well try to get some work done. His steward had left him a plan outlining proposed improvements and repairs to several tenants' homes that would need to be completed when spring arrived. That was still several months away, but he couldn't guarantee his health would hold long enough for him to oversee estate business later. Much had gone unattended by the last two marquesses after they'd fallen ill, one shortly after the other, and he didn't want the same thing to happen during his tenure.

He opened his eyes, turned toward his desk, and froze. Seated behind his desk was the one person he'd been avoiding. Louisa.

She looked very different from the woman who'd been in his room the morning before. That woman had been warm, inviting, and far too tempting. The woman before him now was her complete opposite. Her hair was up, not a lock out of place, and her dress was a rich blue that accentuated her paleness and fair hair. It also underscored her icy demeanor.

She leaned back in the chair, her arms crossed and her expression unreadable.

"You wished to discuss something with me?" he asked when she remained silent.

"Actually, yes."

He watched with disbelief as she indicated he should take the guest chair. The very cheek of her. Despite the fact he should be annoyed, he found himself curious about this side of his wife. He'd caught a glimpse of it when she'd defied convention to travel alone to his home in order to ask for his help with his cousin. He hadn't seen it since.

He sat without a word and waited for her to continue.

"I spoke to Lord Kerrick this morning."

Nicholas's hands clenched on the arms of his chair

before he forced himself to relax and remain impassive. Her words, however, fell like a blow to his stomach. It took him a few moments before he could force himself to speak the lie that was necessary.

"I'm glad to hear the two of you have come to an agreement."

She looked at him as though he'd lost his senses. "He told me, Nicholas."

He had no idea what she was talking about. "I've already explained everything to you. What more was there to tell?"

She made a sound of disgust. A flicker of a nameless emotion crossed her face, but she masked it quickly. For some reason, that made him sad. It appeared he had taught her too well to hold herself aloof from him. It was necessary, of course, but he mourned the loss of her former openness.

"Is that all you can think about? Are you really so anxious for me to bed Lord Kerrick that it wouldn't occur to you I might be talking about something else?"

He ignored the jibe. "I wish the matter to be settled."

He'd never spoken truer words. He wanted the ordeal behind them. Wished she was already pregnant with a child who would hopefully be his heir. He didn't think he could go through with this again if she conceived a girl. The thought of her and Kerrick together, sharing the same passionate kisses the two of them had shared, Kerrick's hands on her body, covering her... Thoughts of their coupling plagued him without end.

"He told me that your illness is made worse when you drink. He also informed me you admitted you'd been drinking the night you fell ill." Her calm façade faded as she spoke, to be replaced with a hint of anger "Why, Nicholas? Why would you do such a thing?"

He didn't reply right away. What was he supposed to say? That he'd been drinking because he hated the very idea of her sleeping with Kerrick, or with any other man? That he'd been drinking to block out the knowledge that he had to continue to push for that very thing to happen despite the fact that every fiber in his being screamed at him to make her his once and for all? That she was making him absolutely crazy?

"I wasn't exactly thinking of the consequences at the time."

She could make of that statement what she would. He wasn't going to discuss it. He stood. "If you're finished mothering me now, I have work to do. I plan to meet with the steward tomorrow and I have to go through some of his proposals first."

Her expression changed and Nicholas flinched when he saw the compassion there. The last thing he wanted was her pity. He'd rather have her anger.

"It's too soon, Nicholas. Whatever you need to discuss, I'm sure it can wait at least a few more days." She stood and moved around the desk to stand before him. She placed a hand on his arm and continued. "You look tired. Perhaps you should go rest now."

The heat of her touch burned through the fabric of his coat. For a moment he could only stand there and breathe in her clean scent while he fought the urge to pull her to him. It was true he was a little fatigued, but he was fairly certain he had enough energy to finally tear down the wall that stood between them. A wall entirely of his own making.

In the end, he took a step back and her hand fell.

"If you'll excuse me," he said, moving around her and dropping into the seat she'd abandoned.

He didn't watch as she crossed the room. Before leaving, she turned and waited until he looked up at her.

"I have instructed the staff to clear away any spirits you keep here and in the library. They have also disposed of the bottles in storage."

She left without waiting for his response

Nicholas buried his head in his hands. If his illness didn't do it first, his wife was going to be the death of him.

Dinner was a somber affair. Lady Overlea assumed Nicholas was taking dinner in his room, but Sommers had informed Louisa he'd gone out just before dinner. Louisa kept that information to herself, however. She knew the older woman was still worried about her grandson, but she would worry more if she knew he was away from home. Louisa was concerned enough for the both of them, although her worry was partially allayed by the fact that he had taken the carriage and a driver.

Lord Kerrick had also gone out earlier in the day and had not yet returned home. Louisa wasn't surprised since he now seemed determined to stay away from her so as not to provoke Nicholas further. Catherine had pouted when she learned he would be away again, but she rallied quickly. She kept the conversation going over dinner, sharing what she had learned about some of the more exotic of the plants in the conservatory.

Louisa had never been very interested in gardening, and so her thoughts kept drifting back to her husband. She'd known him for such a short period of time and had spent most of that time separated from him, yet somehow she could not imagine her life without him. His very presence commanded attention. He wasn't a man who could be ignored, and if anything were to happen to him she knew she would feel his loss keenly.

As if by mutual consent, they all drifted off to their rooms after dinner. Once there, Louisa's gaze settled, as it often did, on the door that connected her room to Nicholas's. She knew the door was unlocked, but neither she nor Nicholas had ever used it. Not even when he was ill and she'd spent most of her time in his bedroom. It hadn't seemed right. To use the connecting door was too intimate. Something a true husband and wife would use to join their spouse for the night. She and Nicholas didn't have that type of relationship, so she had used the more formal method of entering his room through the hallway door.

She was sorely tempted to use that connecting door now. She worried what condition her husband would be in when he returned home. Would he be ill again or merely tired after exerting himself so soon after his last attack? And what would he do if he found her waiting for him in his bedroom? She gave a small self-deprecating laugh at her imagination. If he wasn't having another attack when he came home, he'd be annoyed and would send her back to her rooms.

She rang for her maid and prepared for bed. She was too worried to try to fall asleep until she knew Nicholas was home, so instead settled onto her bed to read. She must have fallen asleep at some point, because the next thing she knew a noise had startled her awake. A quick glance at the clock told her it was after midnight.

The noise came again—footsteps in the hallway. She sat up and put away the book that lay open beside her on her bed. She heard the murmur of a voice, then Nicholas's in reply as they moved past her bedroom door. Needing to see for herself that he was well, she went to the door, opened it, and peered out into the hall. Nicholas and his valet stood before the door to his rooms, and as one they turned to look at her. She took a step forward, then froze when she saw the expression on her husband's face.

Guilt.

Fury overwhelmed her and stole her voice. Unable to speak at that moment, she returned to her room and slammed the door.

She paced for some time, her anger growing with each passing minute. She heard the muffled voices of the two men in the next room and wondered just how much Nicholas had imbibed.

The murmuring finally stopped and the muffled sound of a door closing told her that Harrison had left. As the silence from the other side of the door stretched on, worry started to overcome her anger. What if Nicholas suffered another attack and wasn't discovered again until morning? She went to the door that connected their rooms but stopped, undecided, before it. If he wasn't ill, he wouldn't welcome her intrusion.

She was turning away from the door, her shoulders slumped in dejection, when a loud crash sounded. The last remaining vestiges of her anger and uncertainty evaporated as visions of Nicholas collapsing and lying at death's door in the next room flashed through her mind. Without another thought, she flung open the connecting door and stepped through it. Nicholas sat on the edge of the bed, his head cradled in his hands. The source of the crash soon became evident. A chair lay on its side at the base of one plaster wall that now bore markings from the impact of the chair. Concerned more by his posture than the unmistakable sign of his anger, she took several steps into the room. She froze, however, when Nicholas lifted his head and stared at her. His eyes, dark with an unnamed emotion, seemed to see right through her.

Uncertain now as to his mood, she licked her lips in a nervous gesture. His eyes moved briefly to her mouth and his jaw tightened.

"I feared you might be unwell." Though spoken softly, her words seemed almost too loud in the silence that threatened to engulf them both.

He merely sat there, unmoving, his intent stare pinning her where she stood. His gaze swept over her figure and she realized she stood there only in her nightgown. The one made for her wedding night that was sheer and showed far more than she was used to displaying. The intimacy of the situation was almost too much to bear. Nicholas appeared almost angry, and expecting a curt dismissal, she took a step back.

"If you don't need my assistance, I will return to my room now."

CHAPTER FOURTEEN

She turned to leave, but Nicholas wasn't ready for her to go. Moving swiftly, he rose and crossed the space separating them to reach around her and close the door before she could escape. She stood there facing the closed door, but her attention was focused on the nearness of his body mere inches behind hers. His hand remained on the door, and now his other hand came up to also press against it, effectively caging her. She couldn't move. He surrounded her, the heat of his body reaching out to envelop her.

She drew in a shaky breath and turned to face him. She was too close and took a step back, but stopped when her back met the solid wood of the door. She looked up into Nicholas's eyes. They were darker than normal, almost black. And the heat within them... She shivered, but whether from nerves or anticipation she couldn't say.

Her breath caught when he lowered his head. In the last moment, just before his lips met hers, he moved his head to the side and brought his mouth against her ear. The warmth of his breath there had a strange effect on her, making her need to be even closer to him.

"Tell me, Louisa, are you here to mother me?"

She shook her head, unable to reply.

"Then why are you here, and dressed only in *that.*"

Her voice shook when she replied. "I... I heard the chair fall. I wanted to make sure you weren't ill again."

He exhaled softly into her ear, causing shivers to riot down her spine.

"You should have stayed safe in your own bed."

His voice was low with menace, but she knew in that moment the last place she wanted to be was alone in her cold bed. She wanted to be here, with Nicholas. He was mistaken if he thought he was frightening her. Ignoring the small warning voice in her head that told her she risked being rejected yet again, she placed her hands on his chest. He grew unnaturally still. Encouraged, she parted the edges of his dressing gown to reveal he wasn't wearing a shirt. She could see the rise and fall of his upper body now. His breathing had grown as ragged as hers. Fascinated by the sight of him, and unable to stop now, she pushed the edges farther apart and laid her hands on his bare chest. He was so different from her, broader, his muscles solid beneath her touch.

She moved her hands up to his shoulders, then back down, and he was still under her caress. The dressing gown was fully open now and she saw that he still wore his trousers. The fact that he hadn't pushed her away lent her added courage, and she moved lower to trace the well-defined muscles of his abdomen. She wondered how far she would have to go before Nicholas either pushed her away or finally took her to his bed.

Stealing herself for his rebuff, she trailed her hands lower. When she reached the edge of his trousers, he stopped her by taking hold of her wrists. He'd pulled back and was staring down at her, his expression unreadable. She inhaled sharply when she noticed tightness of his jaw and the sheen of sweat on his brow.

"Are you not well?"

It was a moment before he spoke. "No."

She licked her lips and noticed, again, that his gaze was drawn to the small movement.

"Will you allow me to help you? Or would you rather I summon someone else to care for you?"

He continued to stare at her, his body completely still, and she began to wonder if he was going to collapse. When he finally spoke, it took her a moment to realize what he was saying.

"I think this is something only you can help me with."

He brought her arms up to encircle his neck. Unable to believe what was happening, she clung to him when he released his hold. A thrill of anticipation went through her when he cupped her face in his hands.

"I'm not strong enough to send you away again. I need you to be strong enough for the both of us."

She shook her head. "Not tonight, Nicholas. Not ever again."

He groaned and closed his eyes briefly, as though in pain, before bringing his mouth down on hers. She could taste the alcohol on his breath, but no longer cared that he'd been drinking. She was intoxicated herself on the heady knowledge that Nicholas would not be denying her. That he'd actually admitted wanting her.

He was gentle at first. His thumbs stroked along the

line of her cheeks while his lips sipped from hers. Instead of worrying about her husband, she now feared her own legs would give way and she would be the one to collapse. She clung to his neck and pressed herself against him.

His hands left her face and settled on her waist. She sighed at the delicious feel of his hands caressing her there through the thin fabric of her nightgown before moving higher.

"Tell me to stop, Louisa," he said against her mouth.

"No," she said with a sound of denial. "Please. Don't stop."

She found herself pressed against the door, his hands covering her breasts. He cupped their weight and his thumbs drew maddening circles around her nipples. She gasped and his tongue surged into her mouth, deepening their kiss. She made a soft sound of encouragement and pushed herself more firmly into his hands.

His fingers stilled, then his hands moved up to her shoulders. He raised his head to look down at her and she could see the dark desire reflected in his eyes. He took a deep breath, and for a moment she panicked, certain he was going to push her away again. Instead, his fingers caught the edges of her nightgown and he began to trail the garment down her arms. Mesmerized, she could only stare at him as he took in the progress of the near-transparent material sliding down her body. When it moved past her breasts, she saw the tic of a muscle along his jaw. She stood unmoving as he released the material and it fell to the floor with a soft whisper. She was afraid to move, almost afraid to breathe, lest this moment turn out to be a cruel dream from which she would soon waken.

He stood still as well, staring down at her. Then, as though he had finally decided this moment had always been inevitable, he bent and scooped her up in his arms. Feeling more than a little self-conscious, she buried her face in his shoulder as he carried her to the bed, acutely aware of her skin pressed against his bared chest. He lowered her gently onto the bed and stepped back to stare down at her. Lying before him without a stitch of clothing, she felt as though she just might expire from embarrassment.

"Nicholas," she said, a sense of urgency coursing through her.

He must have known what she wanted. She watched in silence as he shrugged out of his dressing gown, his movements reflecting her own sense of urgency. He unbuttoned the fall of his trousers and stepped out them and the smallclothes he wore, and now it was her turn to stare as he stood naked before her.

He was everything she was not. Hard where she was soft, dark where she was light. Her gaze moved quickly over that one part of him where he was most different, but she did see him and wondered if the consummation of their marriage was going to be very painful. She refused to dwell on that thought, however. This was something she had wanted for what seemed like forever.

He lowered himself onto the bed, his body over hers, but not yet touching. His head dipped and his mouth covered hers. Relief and desire sweeping through her, she brought her hands to his shoulders and clung to him, returning his kiss with an increasing fervor of her own. He closed the space between their bodies, and she gasped at the feel of his warm skin on hers. His muscled chest

pressed against her breasts and that most intimate part of
him brushed against her thigh. Nothing had ever felt so
wonderful.

His mouth left hers and he trailed a line of kisses down
her throat. He continued downward until his lips covered
her breast. He drew on her nipple, and she could feel the
pull of his mouth straight down to her core.

One hand covered her breast, and the other began a
slow, agonizing movement up the inside of her thigh. She
squirmed below him, the riot of sensations almost too
much to bear.

His mouth moved back to her throat while his hand
continued its inexorable movement. She tensed for a
moment, then opened her legs as his hand reached the
juncture of her thighs. Shock froze her when he touched
her there. He parted her with his fingers and started a slow
back-and-forth movement that soon made her forget her
embarrassment. He lifted his head to look down at her as
he slid a finger deep inside her.

She wanted to reassure him, to tell him she was fine,
but in truth she wasn't. She shifted restlessly below him
while he continued, first one, then two fingers moving
inside her while his thumb circled a point of almost-painful
sensitivity outside.

She moaned and brought his head back down to kiss
him.

"Come for me, Louisa," he said against her mouth,
increasing the pace of his stroking.

And then everything flew apart for her. She gasped in
surprise, but he caught the sound with his mouth. His
hand left her then and she made a soft sound of
disappointment. He clasped her knees and widened her

legs farther so he could settle himself between them.

"I can't wait," he said, his voice tight with the strain of holding back.

She laid a hand on his cheek. "I want this, too."

His arousal nudged her swollen sex and instinctively she moved her hips so she could feel him more fully. There was nothing in the world but Nicholas as he started to push inside her. Her body opened to accept him. She had forgotten she was supposed to fear her first time with a man, but the sharp stab of pain reminded her.

She stiffened, her fingers sinking into the muscles of his upper arms as he seated himself fully within her. Seeing her discomfort, he stopped.

"I'm sorry," she said, fearing she'd disappointed him.

"It's fine, Louisa. Here, let me…"

He brought his hand between them and began, again, to stroke that sensitive point just above where their bodies were joined. His mouth captured hers in a heated kiss that made her forget the pain as her blood began to heat anew.

She made a soft sound of distress when he removed his hand again and began to pull out of her, afraid that he would stop now out of concern for her. When he surged back into her, however, she could have wept with joy. The pain had lessened to a dull ache, and that, too, became a distant memory as she delighted in the glorious sensation of being filled by him over and over. She moved with him, matching his thrusts, and he murmured his assent.

"Louisa." He lifted his head and looked down at her again, his eyes reflecting the depth of his passion.

The pace of his thrusts quickened, and feeling as though she were spinning out of control, she wrapped her legs and arms around him. She had never imagined such pleasure was possible.

This time when she reached her peak, she called out his name and took him with her.

Louisa woke the next morning with a smile on her face. Murmuring her husband's name, she rolled toward him. She frowned when she realized she was back in her bedroom. It took her a moment before she remembered waking at one point during the night to find herself in her husband's arms as he carried her back to her room. But he hadn't left her there. He'd joined her in her bed and, despite the fact she'd felt a little tender, they'd made love again.

She stood and reached for her dressing gown to cover her, remembering that her nightgown was still in Nicholas's room. She crossed to the door that connected her room to his, briefly wondering if it was a bad sign that the door was closed. Pushing aside her doubts, she opened the door and entered his bedroom. She blushed when her gaze caught that of the maid who was changing the sheets on her husband's bed. The telltale stain of her blood on the sheets caught her eye and it was all she could do to hide her embarrassment. Soon the whole household staff would know that she and Nicholas had not made love until last night.

"Did Lord Overlea go down to breakfast?"

"No, my lady," the maid said with a curtsey. "He went out to the stables."

She thanked the young woman and went back to her room. She wondered if Nicholas had decided to go back to ignoring her. If he had, he was going to have to fight her every step of the way because she would no longer allow him to push her away.

Nicholas's head ached from having consumed too much brandy the night before, but the pain was nothing when compared to what he experienced during one of his attacks from his illness. He made his way to the stables where one of the grooms approached immediately, but Nicholas waved him off, telling him he would saddle Zeus himself. He needed to keep busy. To try not to think about the horrendous error in judgment he had made the previous night.

He tried to focus on the task at hand. As he brushed the horse, however, his thoughts drifted to memories of running his hands over Louisa's delectable body. He gritted his teeth and firmly pushed the thoughts away. He made quick work of saddling Zeus and securing his bridle, forcing himself to concentrate on the task at hand.

Once he mounted Zeus, however, his thoughts were free to wander, and wander they did. Right back to his wife.

He urged his mount into a gallop, ignoring the pounding in his head. By some miracle he hadn't suffered an attack last night. He couldn't say why, but he vowed not to take such reckless chances in the future. His drinking had, however, erased his resolve to stay away from Louisa. He laughed out loud at that thought, recognizing there was no point in lying to himself. He'd known full well what he was doing the whole time he was with her. He'd known he should have stopped, but he hadn't wanted to. Like the weak, selfish bastard he was, he'd taken what she offered, and now he had to deal with the knowledge that his actions could very well have resulted in Louisa conceiving an heir who was doomed to inherit his family's illness.

He was tempted to keep riding all the way back to London, but he couldn't do that to Louisa. After returning Zeus to the stables and walking around to the front of the house, he was surprised to see his cousin's carriage driving away and quickened his pace. It was far too early for a social call. He didn't think Edward was foolish enough to harass his wife or his sister-in-law in their own home, but he couldn't be certain. Not in light of the fact that his cousin had threatened vengeance the last time they'd spoken.

He breathed easier when the footman informed him that Miss Mary Manning had been there with her maid. Mary was annoying, but she was also harmless. He headed for the stairs, intending to bathe and change, when he overheard Catherine's voice coming from the breakfast room.

"I was surprised to find them together."

For a moment he feared she was referring to Louisa and Kerrick, but recognized the fear was a foolish one. Still, curiosity had him changing direction and heading for the breakfast room.

He found Catherine and Louisa alone, the remains of their breakfast on the table before them. Louisa turned her head and his stomach clenched as their eyes met and held. She was lovely, as ever. Her hair was pinned up in a modest arrangement, her clothing demure, but all he saw when he looked at her was the woman he'd made love to last night. Color crept into her cheeks and he knew she, too, was remembering. He wanted to take her hand and spirit her upstairs. It would be far more enjoyable to have her, rather than his valet, help him in his bath. His body tightened in response to the thought.

He realized he was acting like a lovesick schoolboy around her. If he wasn't careful, he'd soon find himself penning love sonnets to her.

Since neither he nor Louisa seemed capable of speech at that moment, it was Catherine who spoke first.

"You look well this morning. Did your ride agree with you?"

He replied, but he was looking at Louisa when he did so. "It was most enjoyable."

Her eyes widened slightly when she realized the double meaning behind his words and she looked away. Nicholas tore his gaze from her and looked at Catherine, who was sporting a large smile. She must have sensed that his and Louisa's relationship had changed, and it was clear she approved.

He had to force his thoughts back to their visitor. "I saw my cousin leaving. Why was she here?"

It was Louisa who replied. "She invited us to dinner this weekend."

He frowned. "Was there a reason why she extended the invitation in person?"

"She didn't say, but perhaps your aunt believes we'd be more likely to accept if Mary delivered the invitation. It was most curious, especially when her maid disappeared for a few minutes."

He raised a brow. "Disappeared?"

"You won't believe it," Catherine said, leaning forward and warming to the subject. "Mary's maid was alone with your valet."

"Harrison?" Nicholas couldn't have been more surprised. "Are you certain?"

"Oh, yes. They were at the back of the house and didn't realize I was in the conservatory." Her voice lowered as she continued. "She gave him something. I think it was a love letter."

Nicholas couldn't say why, but he was concerned about what his sister-in-law had just told him. Harrison had been behaving strangely of late. His valet knew there was no love lost between Nicholas and his aunt and cousins, however, so it would make sense that he would hide the fact he was having a relationship with one of their servants. Nicholas didn't make a habit of meddling in the affairs of his staff, though, and tried to shrug off his unease at Catherine's news.

"It is a beautiful morning today, is it not?"

He turned to find Kerrick standing in the doorway. To Nicholas's great annoyance, Kerrick walked up to Louisa and took her hand.

"You look even lovelier than usual this morning," he said, bowing over her hand.

Louisa blushed and Nicholas's palms itched with the desire to remove the smile from his friend's face. He watched in silence as Kerrick greeted Catherine in a similar manner before turning back to Louisa.

"Despite Nicholas's desire to bury himself in work, I have had a wonderful stay. I hope it hasn't been too inconvenient that my stay has been a long one?"

Louisa smiled with fondness at him, and Nicholas's annoyance grew.

"Of course not," she said. "As a friend of my husband's, you are always welcome."

Nicholas had to put an end to this once and for all. Things had changed and it was time Kerrick learned that.

Before he ended up killing him.

"I need to speak with you," he said, cutting Kerrick off before he could say anything else.

He turned and stalked from the room, but not before he caught the glance that passed between his wife and his friend. Catherine also caught it, and the expression on her face mirrored Nicholas's own annoyance.

He didn't stop until he'd reached his study. Kerrick followed without a word.

"Close the door," Nicholas said.

His friend complied with a sigh. "You should know that I have grown very fond of your wife. Perhaps one day, after your death—"

Nicholas moved swiftly until he was toe-to-toe with his friend, his anger barely restrained. "If you value your life, you will not finish that sentence."

Kerrick took a step back and tsked.

"We'll be discreet, old boy. Enough time will pass that no one will suspect your heir is really my son."

"Kerrick," he said through clenched teeth, "you need to stop talking."

He was a hairsbreadth away from punching his friend. He turned away and drew in a lungful of air while he tried to control his anger. Even though he knew the previous night was a mistake, he couldn't wish it undone. And he most definitely did not want Kerrick going anywhere near Louisa. He knew that once he was gone Louisa would be a very desirable catch and she would easily find another husband. The possessive side of him, the one that wanted to hoard her away only for himself, didn't want to even consider that future.

Wisely, his friend remained silent. Without his further

taunts, Nicholas was able to bring his burgeoning anger under control. When he turned to face him again, Kerrick raised a brow in question.

Nicholas struggled with what he needed to say, aware that he would look like a fool. Not for telling Kerrick to stay away from his wife, but for ever having made his proposition in the first place.

"There was something you wanted to discuss with me?" Kerrick asked when he didn't speak.

"Yes, damn it. You're going to make me say it, aren't you?"

"You'd better believe it."

"Fine," Nicholas said. "I was an idiot to have suggested you father my heir."

Instead of gloating as he'd expected, Kerrick frowned and crossed his arms. "Not good enough."

"Excuse me?"

"I want to know why you changed your mind."

Nicholas weighed what to tell him. "I decided it was too risky. I didn't want the possibility of a scandal to attach itself to the future marquess."

Kerrick made a sound of disgust. "You can't admit it, can you?"

Nicholas fell back on the icy demeanor he had mastered so well since his brother's death and the announcement that he was now the Marquess of Overlea.

"I have already admitted I made an error in judgment. Let us leave it at that. And don't think to provoke me by continuing your absurd courtship of my wife."

Kerrick laughed. "You're a fool, Nicholas. You know, at first I thought it was just that you found your wife attractive and wanted to bed her yourself. And who would blame you? I am sure most men would feel the same way."

Nicholas scowled.

"Not me," Kerrick said, taking a step back and holding up his hands in innocence. "But seeing you now? Hearing you try so very hard to deny what has become increasingly clear to me?"

"I don't have the patience to play these games with you today," Nicholas said, brushing past his friend and heading for the door.

"Have you even had the courage to admit it to yourself?"

Nicholas wouldn't stand and be called a coward. He stopped and turned to face Kerrick, his face a mask of imperious disdain.

"You're in love with your wife, Nicholas." Kerrick laughed. "I never thought I would live to see the day."

He would be damned before he'd stand there and allow Kerrick to laugh at his feelings. "Are you through amusing yourself at my expense?"

Kerrick sobered instantly. "Between you or your wife, I don't know who to pity more. Are you going to bother telling her?"

Nicholas shrugged casually. "There's nothing to say."

"I see," Kerrick said. "Can I stay the remainder of the week?"

"Do what you like."

He caught the passing expression of resignation on his friend's face before he turned and strode from the room.

Yes, he was indeed in a sad, sorry state. Hopelessly in love with his wife but unable to tell her. First because of how dishonorably he'd treated her since meeting her, and second because he knew his admission would cause her more pain when he died.

CHAPTER FIFTEEN

For the first time since coming to live at Overlea Manor, Louisa was happy. She couldn't believe Nicholas had made that remark about riding in front of Catherine, but it boded well for their marriage that he was no longer avoiding her.

After he left with Kerrick, she didn't see him again until dinner. She was busy with household matters for most of the morning, and Nicholas had met with his steward that afternoon for some time. The way he kept looking at her throughout dinner, his eyes promising a world of sensual delight later that evening, made it difficult for her to follow what everyone was saying. More than once she had to ask someone to repeat themselves when they directed a comment at her. Nicholas grinned in amusement at her state of distraction, which in turn only made it worse. She still couldn't believe how different he was and half feared he would revert to his former distant self.

Later that night after dismissing her maid, Louisa waited for Nicholas. She wore the same nightgown she'd

215

donned the night before, remembering how it had inflamed him, and her hair tumbled loosely down her back.

She'd retired first and it was a little while before she heard the sound of her husband and his valet's voices through the door that joined their rooms. She frowned when she thought about what Catherine had revealed that morning. Harrison was a serious-minded, meticulous man, and while she wouldn't call him old, he was no longer young. She had a hard time believing he would take up with Mary's maid, who was quite a bit younger than him. She acknowledged, though, that her perception might be colored by the fact that he was always very distant with her and she'd never seen a glimpse of his real personality. His formality wasn't the same deference she received from the rest of the household staff. He always seemed very careful to avoid looking at her, which made her uncomfortable in his presence.

She shook her head and laughed at herself for being oversensitive. Harrison was merely loyal to her husband and worried about their marriage. Before last night it had been painfully obvious to all that Nicholas avoided her whenever possible. As his valet, Harrison would have noticed their strained relationship, and it would have colored his dealings with her.

She heard the door close and waited for what seemed an eternity, trying to summon the courage to go to Nicholas's room. It was one thing to rush in there when she was afraid he'd fallen ill again and quite another to enter brazenly.

She stood and took a deep breath. If nothing else, they at least needed to talk. She needed to know once and for all what he expected with respect to their relationship. She took a step toward the door but stopped when a soft knock sounded. She wondered if she had imagined it. She took the last few steps with her heart hammering in her chest and opened the door.

Her husband never failed to steal her breath. He stood on the threshold, wearing his dressing robe over trousers and looking deliciously sinful. His dark eyes roved over her body, barely concealed beneath the sheer fabric of her nightgown.

"I can't seem to stay away from you."

She closed the space between them, throwing herself into his arms, and he gathered her against him and held her close. Relief and joy washed over her. They stood like that for a long time, simply taking in the feel of being in each other's arms.

"I'm a selfish bastard," he said, his breath ruffling her hair. "I should be thinking about the future. God knows, I tried to do the noble thing."

She drew back and looked up at him. "I think I prefer you when you are not noble."

Heat entered his eyes. "Then you're going to like me a whole lot for whatever time we have left together."

She took a moment to examine him closely before replying. Needing to make sure this was what he really wanted, she asked, "Have you been drinking?"

A rueful smile crossed his face. "No excuses, Louisa. This is me. And despite what you might have feared, last night was as well."

She could feel a corresponding smile forming on her own face. Whatever happened in the future, they had each other. Nicholas might not love her, but he did want her. That was enough for now.

He dipped his head and took her mouth. The kiss was gentle, but full of promise. She brought her hands up around his neck and held him to her, afraid to let go while they explored each other. When Nicholas lifted his head, his dark eyes smoldered with intensity. He took her by the hand and led her to his bed. As she lay down with him following her, she caught sight of what was on the nightstand. Anger sweeping through her, she placed her hands on his chest to push him back and scrambled to sit up.

A hint of wariness crept into Nicholas's expression. "Is something wrong?"

She couldn't believe he was going to act innocent. "Is something wrong?" She buried her hands in her hair and shook her head. "What is wrong with you, Nicholas? Are you trying to kill yourself?"

She didn't have to tell him what had brought on her dismay. His eyes traveled to the decanter of brandy and the glass that rested on his nightstand. "I didn't ask for that. Harrison brought it up on his own, thinking I'd want it."

She scoffed. "Is that your favorite brandy? The one I asked the staff to dispose of? And you went out last night to drink. Why? Why would you do that?"

To her horror, she started to cry. Nicholas gathered her to him while she sobbed out all her fears. Almost seeing him die had brought home to her just how little time she could very well have with him and she was furious that he was taking such chances with his life. Furious and terrified.

When her sobs subsided, Nicholas drew back and looked down at her. "I was drinking last night because of you."

She laughed at that, but it ended on a choked sob. He

shook her slightly. "I wanted you so damn much… I was trying so hard to do the right thing, but the thought of you and Kerrick together…" He looked away. "It was killing me."

Seeing the stark pain on his face, her anger began to ebb away, to be replaced with a need to reassure him. She raised a hand to his cheek. He nuzzled against it but kept his eyes lowered.

"Nicholas, look at me."

He lifted his gaze and the anguish in his eyes almost made her gasp.

"I like Kerrick," she said. He started to turn his head away, but she raised her other hand to his face to hold him still. "I like him very much, but only as a friend. I could never be with him. My feelings for you would never allow it."

There were no words after that. He took her in his arms and together they fell back into the pillows. Unlike the night before, their lovemaking was more urgent this time. She had lost her inhibitions and ran eager hands over every part of him she could reach. It was clear from his reaction when she did something he liked, and it gave her the confidence she needed to explore him as he did the same to her. They had not even shed all their clothing when she found herself beneath him, her nightgown drawn up to her waist. He opened his trousers and she shivered with anticipation at the touch of his hard member against her hip. She opened her legs to welcome him inside her, but he surprised her by rolling over and draping her over him.

"Like this," he said, arranging her so that she was straddling him, positioned right over his hard shaft.

She didn't know what she was supposed to do. "I can't—" she started, but he interrupted her.

"Shh," he said, dragging her down for a kiss.

He lined up their bodies again and then showed her how to take him inside her. She eased down over him, loving the way he filled her. She stopped when she hit bottom. He placed his hands on her hips and drew her up along his length, then back down with more force than the first time. She found her rhythm then, and he allowed her to set the pace while his hands moved to her breasts, his strong fingers hefting their weight and stroking the hardened tips through her nightgown. She luxuriated in the feel of him hard inside her as she reached for her own climax. She should have been embarrassed at the sounds she was making, almost panting as she moved over him, but his corresponding groans told her that he was enjoying their lovemaking as much as she.

Impatient, he quickened their movements, thrusting up into her as she slid down. His hands coursed over her body, trailing fire wherever he touched her. Dazed, she stared down at him, at his beautiful face, as she continued to move. The way he was looking at her, his eyes burning through hers, she could almost make herself believe that he loved her.

"Nicholas," she said on a moan, the steady rhythm threatening to tear her apart. His hands settled on her hips and he held her while he pushed into her again and again. She exploded, and he followed moments later.

She collapsed on top of him. He held her to him, one hand buried in her hair and the other laying possessively on her backside, just above where they were still joined. Slowly, their heartbeats steadied and their breathing slowed.

"Can I stay here tonight?" she asked.

For a moment she thought he was going to say no. He rolled them over until they were on their side, facing each other, and she let out a breath when he slipped out of her. He brought her mouth to his and kissed her thoroughly. "I expect you'll be staying here most nights," he said, his expression as satisfied as what she imagined hers to be.

Content, she snuggled against him and fell asleep.

The discovery that his valet might be in some sort of relationship with his cousin's maid unsettled Nicholas. He hadn't paid the man much attention before now because his valet had never been very friendly, but now that he was watching him closely it seemed as though Harrison had the demeanor of someone trying to hide his guilt. Surely Harrison wasn't afraid of suffering repercussions because of his relationship. Nicholas wasn't so unfeeling that he expected his staff to eschew personal relationships.

Nicholas turned the situation over and over in his mind, but still couldn't believe even the most foolish of women would send a love note to his valet. In the end, he decided to speak to Catherine again before approaching Harrison. Perhaps she'd misinterpreted the scene since his valet didn't have the appearance of a man in love. Lord knew Nicholas was intimately acquainted with those very symptoms. Of course, it was also possible Harrison was simply engaging in a romantic tryst and that his emotions weren't involved at all.

"My Lord," Catherine exclaimed when he entered the conservatory. "This is a surprise."

"Catherine," he said with a fond smile, "how many

times do I have to ask you to call me Nicholas?"

"Quite a few, it would seem."

Nicholas chuckled in reply. He enjoyed Catherine's youthful enthusiasm. It reminded him of his own carefree youth. Those days seemed so long ago now.

"I have to show you these two plants I've just identified."

She disappeared down the row of greenery that lined the wall of glass along one side of the conservatory. Nicholas sighed and followed while she rattled off the Latin names for two of the tropical plants. He idly fingered a large white bloom while she exclaimed over the flower, feigning an interest he was far from feeling.

"I wanted to thank you for giving me a Season next spring," she said, reclaiming his attention. "I am looking forward to it very much." She paused for a moment before continuing, heat creeping into her face. "Lord Kerrick has promised to waltz with me at Almack's."

That innocent statement set off alarm bells in his mind and he made a mental note to speak to Kerrick about his sister-in-law. His friend wasn't the type of person to trifle with a young girl's affections, but it was clear Catherine had developed a *tendre* for him.

Nicholas gave a shudder of mock horror. "As always, I will leave the planning of such amusements to Grandmother and your sister."

Catherine exhaled dramatically. "I cannot wait for spring to arrive. I am trying to be patient, but it is so hard."

Nicholas turned the subject to the true reason for his visit. The stuffy atmosphere of the conservatory was starting to affect him.

"I wanted to speak to you about what you told us yesterday. About the meeting between my valet and Mary's maid."

Her enthusiasm dimmed. "I shouldn't have said anything. Will they be in trouble now?"

Nicholas rushed to reassure her. "Not at all. As long as the staff continues to do their jobs, I care not a whit whom they see privately. However, that is the point of my visit. I simply cannot imagine Harrison engaging in such behavior. Are you sure what you witnessed was a romantic rendezvous?"

Catherine frowned in concentration. "Why else they would meet? And he did accept a letter from her."

A dull ache began behind his temple, which he massaged absently. He couldn't explain his sense of urgency, but he needed more information without further arousing Catherine's curiosity.

"Perhaps he was accepting the letter for someone else. I want to reassure Harrison that his position here is secure, but I don't want to say anything if he was merely acting as an intermediary."

She gave him a wide smile that reminded him of her sister. "You are very kind. John didn't think so, but I knew Louisa made the right decision when she accepted your proposal."

He felt a stab of guilt for lying to the girl and more than a little unworthy of her compliment. Her brow furled in thought and he waited, ignoring the increasing warmth of the conservatory.

"It is true that they did not appear overly affectionate with one another. I was so surprised at what I had seen that I didn't consider their demeanor. Now that I think about it, however, they were quite serious."

"Love can be a serious business, especially when one is trying to conceal it," he said, thinking of his own messy situation.

Catherine's brow cleared. "Of course, that must be it."

Nicholas's vision momentarily blurred and dread settled in his belly. Not again. Without a word, he started for the doorway leading outside. He supposed he should head into the house, not outside, but at the moment he was desperate for fresh air.

"My Lord… Nicholas," Catherine said as she followed him, her concern evident.

He fumbled with the door handle, unable to open it. Catherine reached around him and opened the door for him. He stumbled through, his head beginning to swim in earnest now. Teetering, on the verge of falling, he took a few steps along the side of the conservatory in an effort to escape the stifling air coming through the door before stopping to lean against the outer wall. He took in great lungfuls of air.

Catherine had followed him, anxiety stamped on her features. To be honest, Nicholas was more than a little worried himself. All he could think about at that moment was Louisa and how much he didn't want to lose her. Not when he'd just found her.

"I'll go fetch Sommers," Catherine said.

Nicholas shook his head. He was unable to speak coherently, but he could tell this episode was different from the others. His head was already starting to clear. In a matter of minutes, his swimming vision had cleared and his breathing was no longer constricted.

"Do you want me to help you back into the house? The

conservatory is the quickest route—"

"No!" In his panic he'd spoken louder than he intended. He attempted a smile of reassurance. "It is most strange, but I am feeling better now."

Cautiously, he pushed away from the wall. He braced himself for the inevitable stumble and was baffled when it didn't come.

He turned to face Catherine. "You know about my condition?" At her nod, he winced inwardly. Soon everyone would know. The thought made him grim. "I thought I was having an attack, but it appears I was mistaken."

"Has that ever happened before?"

"No, never. I have never had an attack just stop suddenly."

Catherine's brow wrinkled. "What were you feeling?"

He supposed he shouldn't have been taken aback by the forthrightness of her question. He hadn't known his sister-in-law long, but he already knew it was in her nature to be inquisitive.

"Light-headed, for the most part. I also found it difficult to breathe."

"And you broke out in a sweat."

He raised a brow.

"I think I know what caused it. Some of the plants in the conservatory are highly poisonous. Of course, most would only cause symptoms if ingested. Some can leave oils on your skin if you touch them... and you were rubbing your eyes."

"I was?"

"Yes," she said. "You were rubbing your temples, here." She gestured to her own face. "Then you briefly rubbed your eyes." Sadness crept into her expression. "I'm afraid you should avoid the conservatory. It appears that given your illness, you may be more sensitive to the plants in there."

His head was swimming again, but this time with the import of her words. Was it possible...? He hated to even consider such a thing, but was it possible that his family's illness was not due to an inherited condition at all? Was it possible that all the men in his family had suffered because they were sensitive to one of his grandmother's plants? Even more horrifying was the suspicion that their exposure to that plant hadn't been accidental.

He hadn't realized he'd started to pace. He stopped and turned back to face Catherine.

"I think perhaps you are correct. Do you think it would be possible to provide me with a list of the plants that are the most likely culprit?"

She was about to ask why, but he didn't want her to know about his suspicions until he had some proof. Anyone who had already murdered two people and was attempting to kill a third would no doubt stop at nothing to keep their secret.

"We'll need to make sure the maids don't bring any of those flowers into the house," he added.

Her brow cleared. "Oh, that would be terrible! I've already identified many of the plants Lady Overlea didn't know, but I'm still searching for information on a few..."

Her voice trailed off and she turned and headed back into the conservatory, intent on her task. He, too, was lost in thought. His whole world had just shifted off-balance, but for the first time in what seemed like forever he began to hope.

CHAPTER SIXTEEN

Louisa wasn't sure she'd ever get used to running such a large house. After going over her new duties, Lady Overlea had handed over the job of looking after all the day-to-day details of running Overlea Manor, telling her that the best way to adapt was to jump in with both feet. Louisa knew she could rely on the dowager marchioness's help if she had questions, but she threw herself into the task with the hope she wouldn't prove to be a disappointment. Lady Overlea had accepted her and Catherine into the family with open arms, and Louisa had grown fond of the older woman in the short time she had known her.

She had just finished meeting with the housekeeper to go over the menus for the week and was about to ascend the stairs to return to her room when she found herself dragged back against a very male figure. She closed her eyes and smiled as a wicked urge to provoke her husband came over her.

"Kerrick…"

She was spun around so quickly she almost lost her

balance. When she saw the look of outrage on her husband's face, she couldn't hold back her laughter. Nicholas was still very sensitive about that ridiculous proposal he'd made to her and his friend, and it was so easy to tease him about it.

It took her a few moments to notice Lord Kerrick standing a few feet away, a look of horror on his face.

"Good God," he said, "do you want your husband to call me out? Don't even jest about such a thing."

She laughed again. "Well, you both deserve it."

"I was as innocent as you. None of that was my idea."

Nicholas watched their exchange in silence but finally broke into their light banter. "I need to speak to my wife for a moment."

His friend seemed only too willing to oblige. With a quick bow, he turned and headed down the hall, leaving them alone.

Louisa wondered why Nicholas wanted to see her. He took her by the hand and led her to the library, closing the door behind them. She didn't like the somber expression on his face. It reminded her too much of the way he was when they were first married. Wanting desperately to see him smile again, she moved closer and brought his head down for a kiss.

There was a tenderness to the way he moved his mouth against hers that made her catch her breath. When he pulled away, he cupped her cheek and ran his thumb over her lower lip. He stared at her intently.

"What is the matter?" she asked, beginning to worry.

"I would like you to decline the invitation to dine at my aunt's house."

Knowing his feelings about his aunt and cousins, his

request didn't surprise her. "Your grandmother is looking forward to it. She hopes it will help to heal the rift in the family."

"I don't believe one dinner is going to accomplish that. There is too much history there. The two branches of the family have never gotten along."

His words made her feel a pang of guilt. His brother's marriage to Mary would have healed that rift. They hadn't yet been formally betrothed, but she knew there had been an understanding. Everyone had expected Nicholas to fulfill that understanding when James died.

"Your aunt doesn't like me. She believes I ensnared you and somehow tricked you into marrying me."

He scowled and dropped his hand. "You can't know that with certainty."

"I do," she said, remembering that horrible meeting shortly after they'd been married. "She made a point of telling me directly."

His temper flared at that revelation. "Then there can be no question of our attendance."

"It is too late. I have already accepted the invitation."

"Louisa, I cannot allow her to insult you to your face and pretend all is well."

She laid a hand on his arm, hoping to soothe his anger. "It means so much to your grandmother. Not that your Aunt Elizabeth accept me, I don't believe Lady Overlea likes her any better than you or I do, but she does want you to be reconciled with your cousins."

Nicholas made a short, dismissive sound. "After what Edward tried to do to you? That is already two out of three members of their family who have insulted you. Should I stand back and allow Mary to do so as well?"

He was correct, of course. She would give anything not to have to attend that dinner. She knew it would be a painful affair and expected there would be much antagonism directed at her. It meant so much to Lady Overlea, however, that Louisa had to try for her sake.

"I don't think Mary is capable of such hateful behavior. She seems very mild mannered."

"She is meek, yes. Not at all," he said, pulling her body flush against his, "like my wife."

He leaned down and nuzzled her neck. He trailed a line of kisses to her ear, sending shivers down her spine.

"Perhaps," he said softly, his tongue tracing the shell of her ear, "we can send everyone without us and stay behind. We'll have dinner brought up to our room and have a little mini-honeymoon."

Louisa was tempted. Her husband knew far too well how to touch her and make her forget everything else.

"We can't," she said, her voice breathy from the desire he was stirring in her. "What will we say? That we are both feeling unwell? Everyone will know we are lying."

His hand cupped her breast and she arched into the caress. He dragged his mouth down to the edge of her bodice and rained kisses over the exposed skin. "We're still on our honeymoon. And frankly, I don't care if my aunt and cousins don't understand that."

She pulled back from his grasp, struggling to right her breathing. "Nicholas, we can't."

His expression held more than a hint of steel. "I say we can."

She would have to try a different approach. "Can you imagine the expression on Edward's face when he is forced to play host to us?"

Nicholas's eyes lit up at that. "It might be amusing to see him squirm." He considered a moment before continuing. "Fine. We'll go, but you must promise to remain at my side."

"Nothing can happen there, Nicholas. Not with a house full of people."

He had an odd expression on his face when he replied. "You'd be surprised what can be done right under one's nose."

It was obvious he was thinking of something in particular. She was about to question him, but he changed the subject.

"I want to take you riding."

A thrill of anticipation went through her. Her first trip to Overlea Manor, when she'd ridden there to ask for Nicholas's help, had been the first time in years that she'd been on a horse. Her love of riding had been reawakened, but she'd been too preoccupied with her dilemma at the time to enjoy it.

"I don't think I packed my habit." She'd been in a daze during the days leading up to the wedding and after all the fittings Lady Overlea had arranged for her with a small army of seamstresses, she'd decided to leave behind most of her out-of-fashion clothing.

"Grandmother is usually quite thorough. I'd be very surprised if she didn't arrange for at least one new riding habit when she was having your trousseau made."

Of course, she thought, her excitement growing. "I'll ask my maid. She seems to know my wardrobe better than I do."

He seemed quite pleased with her enthusiasm. "I'll meet you at the stables."

Louisa reached up to give him a quick kiss, but he caught her before she could pull away and deepened it.

"Perhaps we should postpone the riding," he said, his breath mingling with hers. "I can think of a few things we could do instead that would probably be more fun."

Louisa pulled away, laughing. "Oh no, you offered and got my hopes up. I'm not going to let you change your mind."

He released her with obvious reluctance and she hurried to her rooms to change. Nicholas was right, of course. Her maid pulled a beautiful riding habit of deep red and black from her wardrobe and helped her to dress.

She hurried, but by the time she reached the stables Nicholas was already waiting for her. He smiled when he saw her and pushed away from the wall he'd been leaning against.

"I knew Grandmother wouldn't fail us."

She smoothed her hand over the rich wool fabric of her skirt. "It is lovely."

Nicholas reached for her hand and led her into the stables. She was surprised to see just how many horses the building contained but then shook her head at her own folly. Of course the Marquess of Overlea would have a large stable. As well as horses for riding, they also needed horses for their carriages.

A groom was saddling Nicholas's horse for their ride, but her eyes were drawn to the pure white mare that stood off to the side, already tacked up.

"Oh, she's lovely," she said, dropping her husband's hand and approaching the mare. "You're beautiful, aren't you," she murmured softly to the mare as she ran a hand along her muzzle. "What is her name?"

"Athena," Nicholas said.

"She is as beautiful as a goddess." She turned her head to look at Nicholas, who was watching her with a satisfied smile.

"I'm glad you like her. She's yours."

"Oh no," she protested. "You don't have to do that. I'd be content to visit her and ride her from time to time."

He shook his head in disbelief. "You don't have to be so practical all the time, Louisa. And you no longer have to share everything. Besides, I bought her for you."

Her eyes widened at that. "You bought her for me? When?"

He shrugged, the movement casual. "Before the wedding. I saw her when I was in London and thought of you."

A glow of happiness spread through her. Even while he was concocting his idiotic plan to throw her and Lord Kerrick together, he'd been thinking of her and had bought her a present.

"Thank you," she said, overcome with emotion.

Their eyes locked and they shared a moment of silent understanding. One corner of his mouth turned up as though in acknowledgement of how nonsensical his behavior had been.

He gave her a cursory bow. "Shall we?"

She nodded and together they led their mounts from the stable. Once outside, he helped her onto her horse before mounting Zeus. He turned toward the village and Louisa followed.

"Where are we going?"

"I thought I would introduce you to some of my tenants."

"I already know most of them."

"Yes, but they know you as Louisa Evans. They would have heard about our marriage and I'm sure they are very curious to see you in your role as the Marchioness of Overlea."

She winced. "I'm not sure I can be more than Louisa Evans. I don't know how a marchioness should behave and I fear that if I tried, I would appear ridiculous."

They were riding abreast and Nicholas leaned close to her when he replied. "I'll share a little secret with you. I don't feel comfortable acting as the marquess. I never paid much attention to the lectures to which Father subjected James and me. I was supposed to, of course, since I was the spare, but I never imagined I would one day become the marquess."

"We are quite the pair, are we not?" she said, aiming for a note of levity to lighten the suddenly somber mood.

"We shall have to define our own roles. In the end, no one will dare criticize us. Not to our faces, at any rate. Besides, I am sure you will keep me grounded if I start to think too highly of myself."

She laughed. "I will consider it my first priority."

They rode in silence the rest of the way. There were only a few tenants she didn't already know, and she was nervous about how they would view her in her new role as marchioness. She needn't have worried, however. Aside from a few curious glances at her midsection from some who wondered if the marquess had married her to avoid a scandal, everyone seemed genuinely happy for them. It would appear that despite her husband's reputation as a rake, the people on his estate genuinely liked him. If anything, they seemed relieved he had finally settled down.

That sentiment increased when they learned of his plans to make improvements to many of their cottages in the spring.

It was a long afternoon. Louisa had never before visited so many people in one day and she was drained when it was time to return home. She was glad, however, that she'd gone out with Nicholas. It had given her the opportunity to see a new side of him. He took his responsibility to his tenants seriously and wanted to make sure they were well cared for. His genuine concern made her realize he would be a great father. That thought was followed by a wave of sadness when she thought that he might not be around to see a child of his grow.

She laid a hand on her abdomen, wondering if she could be carrying his child even now. It was still too early to tell, but she hoped that she was.

She had lagged behind him. Nicholas stopped and waited for her to catch up. He frowned when he saw her sadness.

"What is the matter?"

She attempted a smile, not wanting to bring up the subject of his illness. She knew it was a weak attempt at best.

"I'm just tired," she said. "It has been a long afternoon and it has been many years since I have ridden such a distance. It does not help that you kept me up half the night."

A wolfish grin crossed his face. "You had better take a nap when we return, then, for I feel you might be in for another sleepless night."

The way his gaze ran over her body made her blush.

"You seem tired as well. Perhaps you would like to join

me for a rest?"

She spurred her horse forward, not waiting to see his reaction. She had no doubt that Zeus could easily overtake her mount, so Nicholas must have held him back. She didn't mind. The sun was setting earlier these days, but there was only a slight nip in the autumn air. The feel of the breeze on her face and of the powerful animal beneath her was exhilarating. She hadn't realized how much she missed riding.

She had just turned onto the road that approached the manor house when she realized something was wrong. Her saddle slipped ever so slightly, setting off warning bells in her mind. She pulled back on the reins, but the sideways motion didn't stop. The saddle slipped even farther and she found herself falling from the mare's back. Spooked, her horse picked up speed instead of coming to a stop. She closed her eyes in horror and tried to brace herself for the impact, but nothing could prepare her for the feel of her body slamming into the hard ground. She'd had the presence of mind to remove her foot from the stirrup and release her hold on the reins and was glad of that fact when she opened her eyes and saw her mare galloping down the road, the saddle hanging at a precarious angle.

"Louisa!"

She could hear the worry in Nicholas's voice, but couldn't catch her breath to reply. He brought Zeus to a halt, leapt from his back, and kneeled beside her. His face came into focus above hers.

"Sweetheart?"

She liked the sound of that. Nicholas had never called her that before.

"Louisa, stay with me."

She realized that her thoughts were drifting. She tried to focus on her husband's face and voice.

"That's right," he said, laying a hand on her cheek. "Keep your attention on me."

He ran his hands over her arms and her legs. It took her several moments to realize he was checking for broken bones. When he asked her to wiggle her fingers and move her legs, she had finally managed to catch her breath and her head was clearing. She didn't think she was hurt, only dazed, but she did what he asked.

"Can you turn your head?"

She turned it to one side, then the other, wincing at the stiffness. Relief crossed his face.

"Can I sit up now?"

He helped her into a sitting position, then dragged her into his lap. He held her like that for some time, just cradling her.

When she pulled back, she saw his anguish.

"I'm not hurt," she said, needing to ease his worry.

"When I saw you fall off that horse…" He shook his head as if to clear the memory from his mind. "My heart almost stopped."

"The saddle," she said, her voice still shaky. "I could feel it slipping."

His jaw hardened. "I'm going to take you home now."

He stood, but instead of helping her to stand as she expected, he lifted her into his arms.

"I can walk," she said.

He ignored her and carried her over to his horse. He released her then to climb into the saddle before pulling her up to sit sideways before him. It was a little uncomfortable, but she felt safe being so close to

Nicholas. She wrapped her hands around his waist and settled against his chest, trying to draw some of his strength into her.

After insisting Louisa rest after her fall, Nicholas returned to the stables to speak to the grooms. They had no explanation for what had happened, but what he discovered when he examined Athena's saddle made the blood freeze in his veins.

Now back in his study, he paced before the fire, trying to come to terms with what he had learned. He wrestled with the urge to have a drink from the bottle of brandy his valet had hidden away for him, but in the end he resisted, knowing he couldn't risk having another episode. He had to keep a clear head and his wits about him now. Both his and Louisa's lives could very well depend on it.

He couldn't keep the memory of watching, helplessly, while she pulled on her mare's reins before sliding off the animal's back from playing over and over again in his mind. He shuddered as he remembered seeing her on the ground, pale and motionless. He'd been struck forcefully by his fear that she was seriously injured.

Kerrick entered the study, not bothering to knock. "What's this I hear about Louisa having an accident?"

Nicholas stopped his pacing and turned to faced him. He was going to need an ally in this and Kerrick was just the man for the job.

"Close the door and sit down," he said.

Kerrick did so before turning back to his friend. "I get nervous when you tell me to do that. The last time you needed to speak to me in private you wanted me to bed your wife."

"You can rest assured we won't be revisiting that subject." He went to his desk and bent to pick up the saddle he'd placed on the floor next to his chair. He dropped it onto the desk with a loud thunk. "This is the saddle from Louisa's horse. Tell me what you think."

Kerrick raised his brows but didn't speak as he examined the saddle. It didn't take him long to discover the problem.

"The billets broke? Both of them? How old is this saddle?"

"I purchased it when I was last in London. It's never been used before today."

Kerrick shook his head in disbelief. "I don't understand. How could they have frayed so soon? And why wouldn't a groom have noticed their condition?"

"Look at the underside of the billets."

Kerrick flipped them over and frowned. "The fray is smoother," he said, running a finger along the edge where the leather had torn.

Nicholas remained silent, waiting to see if Kerrick would confirm what he suspected.

After examining all the edges, Kerrick swore. "These were cut."

Nicholas nodded. "I believe so. Not all the way through. The underside was sliced, but enough of the leather was left intact that it wasn't visible from the right side of the straps. It was a new saddle. The stable master examined it when it was first delivered, but not again since it was only used for the first time today."

"So it looked fine from the surface," Kerrick said. He examined the depth of the cut again. "It would have held for a time, but then start to fray the longer Louisa rode."

Nicholas barely controlled the anger that seethed under his skin, making him desperate to lash out at someone.

"This makes no sense. Why would anyone want to hurt your wife?"

"That isn't all of it."

Nicholas went on to explain what had happened on the night Louisa had destroyed all his brandy. How he'd gone to the village to drink and hadn't fallen ill. He also told Kerrick about how he'd started having symptoms when he was in the conservatory after touching some of the flowers that Catherine had informed him were poisonous.

"It was in the brandy, damn it. I am all but sure of it. Someone has been adding something from one of those plants to make me ill."

Kerrick was clearly stunned. "I've had some of that brandy."

"As have I, and I've not always fallen ill. I suspect whoever's been doing this is acting selectively, making sure I am the only one who drinks from the bottles that have been laced with the poison."

"Do you know what you're implying? Your father and your brother experienced the same illness as you, which means they, too, were poisoned."

"They were murdered."

Kerrick came to the same conclusion as Nicholas. "You believe Edward is behind this."

"Who else has anything to gain? We all know he's an unscrupulous bastard, and with all the men in my family out of the way he stands to inherit."

"But why would he want to hurt Louisa?"

"The household staff has no doubt realized that Louisa and I have consummated our marriage. Word must have reached Edward. He wouldn't want to risk that she might be carrying my child. If she were to fall pregnant with a boy, he wouldn't be as close to inheriting as he believes he now is."

Kerrick was silent for a moment before speaking. "I'm sorry, Nicholas. To learn that your father and brother were murdered…" He shook his head, at a loss for words.

Nicholas's hands clenched into fists. "I want to go over there right now and strangle the bastard."

"We'll have to call in the authorities."

"I know. That's one of the reasons I wanted to speak to you. I believe you have friends who are uniquely qualified to help us." Nicholas had suspected for some time that Kerrick had ties to the government's Home Office. He'd even wondered if some of his friend's mysterious absences could be attributed to him engaging in spy work. He'd never come out and asked him about it, but Kerrick's response now seemed to confirm his suspicions.

"Of course," Kerrick said, not bothering to pretend innocence about his connections. "I know just the man. He'll ferret out Edward's guilt."

Nicholas nodded his thanks.

"I'll leave today and will return as soon as I can. Try to be careful until then. I've grown rather fond of your wife, and much as I'd like to throttle you at times for your stubbornness, I'd rather not return to find you've become another victim of your cousin's greed."

CHAPTER SEVENTEEN

This was the first outright argument they'd had since marrying and Louisa couldn't understand why Nicholas had chosen that moment, when they were expected soon for his aunt's dinner, to dig in his heels. She'd been dismayed to learn he hadn't yet dressed and had finally cornered him in his study, where she now stood facing him across his desk while he reclined in his chair.

"If we cancel now, the rift between you and your cousins will never be mended."

"Good," he said, his scowl deepening. "They can all go to the devil. I care not if I ever see any of them again."

While she agreed wholeheartedly when it came to Edward Manning, she couldn't help but feel Mary didn't deserve such censure from her husband.

"If you won't attend for your grandmother's sake, will you do it for me?"

"I am doing this for you. I don't want you anywhere near my cousin. I don't care how many people are in the room at the time."

She thought they'd already settled this matter and couldn't understand why he was arguing about it yet again. She'd have to give him extra incentive. With careful calculation, she placed her palms on his desk and leaned forward, giving him a tantalizing view of her breasts which now threatened to spill forward. She hid her smile when his eyes dropped.

"Do you remember that thing you wanted to do in bed the other night?"

His scowl lifted and a gleam of interest entered his eyes. "What are you proposing?"

"Do this one thing for your grandmother, one evening at your aunt's house. In exchange, I will agree to try what you suggested."

He frowned. "That's blackmail."

"I'd rather think of it as negotiation."

He rose swiftly and rounded the desk. When she straightened to face him, he cupped the back of her neck with his hand, his thumb stroking along the column of her throat. "Maybe we can try my thing first and then we can go to the dinner."

His voice was low and husky and despite her misgivings, a thrill of anticipation went through her.

She shook her head and spun out of his reach to press her advantage.

"No. You'll have no reason then to keep up your end of the bargain."

His eyes narrowed. "What is my guarantee that after the dinner you won't change your mind?"

"You'll have to trust me."

He stalked toward her. "Not good enough. I think I'll need a small down payment first."

"We've left it too late to cancel, and we don't have time to… you know." She could feel herself blushing.

"I didn't leave it too late. You decided to ignore my wishes about sending our regrets." He captured one of her hands and pulled her to him. "I think, given the circumstances, you owe me some compensation."

Her pulse quickened when he trailed his hand down the outside of her thigh and began to drag her dress up. She buried her head against his shoulder. She knew her protest was weak, but she had to make it.

"We don't have time…"

"Aunt Elizabeth has waited this long to set up her little reconciliation dinner. She can wait a while longer."

She didn't resist when he shifted her around and started to walk her backward. When her bottom bumped against the edge of his desk, he lifted her so she could sit on the edge. He didn't need to tell her what he wanted. Now almost as eager as he, she unbuttoned the fall of his trousers and reached in to wrap her hand around his hardness. His breath hissed out as she squeezed him.

"Vixen," he said, lifting her skirts until she was bared from the waist down.

"I do believe you prefer me this way," she said, drawing her hand up and down along his sizeable length.

"You cannot begin to imagine," he said, spreading her legs apart and moving between them.

She helped to guide him, her body ready, and moaned in appreciation when he thrust into her with one sure stroke. The rhythm that he set was relentless, and she reached her peak twice before he allowed himself his own release.

* * *

In the end they were half an hour late. From the obvious relief on his grandmother's face, Nicholas could tell she'd expected him to send her on alone. He still had major reservations about the wisdom of putting his wife in harm's way. He'd allowed her to sway him, but only because part of him wanted the opportunity to observe his cousin. He prayed Edward wasn't stupid enough to do anything with the whole family there, but he knew desperate men couldn't be counted on to act rationally. The attempt on Louisa's life was proof of that.

He was on edge and didn't bother to try to mask his mood. The tension in the carriage ride over to his aunt's house was palpable. Even Catherine, always willing to fill any silence with bright chatter, remained silent. He caught Louisa examining him a few times. He hated that he couldn't be honest with her, but he didn't want her to worry or have false hope about his illness until he had proof of his suspicions.

When they reached the house, the reservations Louisa had tried to ignore began to surface. Adding to her stress was the fact that this would be the first time she'd stepped foot in her former home since they were kicked out by Henry Manning all those years before. Catherine had been too young to remember their life before their father lost everything, but Louisa remembered all too well. Nicholas squeezed her hand in reassurance and she smiled up at him, grateful to have him at her side. If Lady Overlea had looked less hopeful, she would have changed her mind right then and returned home. However, she couldn't disappoint Nicholas's grandmother. Not after how quickly she had welcomed her and Catherine into the family. She experienced a pang of grief knowing John would also have been made to feel welcome if he had stayed.

Nicholas raised the knocker and rapped twice, the sound almost deafening in the silence that enshrouded them. The door was opened a moment later by a footman and they were shown into the drawing room.

Nicholas leaned toward her and said softly, "Are you sure you want to go through with this? We can still make good our escape."

Before Louisa could admonish him, his grandmother cut in. "Don't listen to him, my dear." She turned back to Nicholas. "You will be on your best behavior tonight."

"Or what, Grandmother? Do you have something else with which to force my hand?"

His question startled Louisa. What made it more unsettling, however, was the quick glance Lady Overlea cast in her direction. She would have to remember to ask him about their exchange later.

Elizabeth Manning entered the room at that moment and Louisa was glad she'd taken extra care with her appearance. The older woman was dressed in a gown of dazzling golden silk and jewels dripped from her throat and arms. Louisa wasn't dressed as elaborately, but she knew no one would find fault with her attire.

She was followed by a sullen Edward and a demure Mary. Nicholas's Aunt Elizabeth appeared to be the only person in the group looking forward to the evening. Even Lady Overlea, while clearly hoping for the best, appeared cautious.

"I am so happy you are all here," Elizabeth exclaimed. "It has been far too long since our two sides of the family have been together."

Nicholas's grandmother accepted the kiss her daughter-in-law placed on her cheek. Louisa couldn't help but notice that her smile was forced.

"You were invited to my grandson's wedding," she said, her voice carefully neutral.

Elizabeth waved her hand in dismissal.

"Given how hurt my poor Mary was at being deceived about her prospects, I'm sure everyone understands why she didn't feel up to attending. And as her mother, it was my place to stay by her side during her time of great disappointment. We have decided, however, that the time has come to put our disagreements behind us. We are, after all, family."

Louisa darted a quick glance at her husband, half expecting him to make a caustic remark about the falseness of his cousin's hope. She was surprised when he remained silent. She was also grateful. The sooner the subject was finished, the sooner they could move on to less controversial subjects.

"I am very glad of this opportunity to get to know everyone better," Louisa said.

She avoided looking at Edward as she spoke, remembering all too clearly that not too long ago he'd hoped to get to know her very well indeed.

Mary interrupted, speaking in her customary soft voice. "Mama, I believe dinner is ready to be served."

"Of course, dear," Elizabeth said. "We seem to be off to a late start this evening."

Louisa could hear the censure in the woman's voice and was surprised, again, when Nicholas said nothing. When she looked at him she could see why. Edward had moved over to the fireplace and was standing there, one foot on the hearth, gazing into the fire. Nicholas was examining him, his eyes narrowed in contemplation. She wasn't surprised at the hint of anger in his expression, and she guessed then that it was either going to be a very long evening or a very short one if he allowed his anger free rein.

Elizabeth moved toward Nicholas, expecting him to take her in to dinner, but he didn't move from Louisa's side. Trying but failing to conceal her annoyance, she went to her son, who reluctantly turned his attention back to their guests. He led her out and the rest followed.

The awkward stiffness of the evening continued throughout the dinner. No doubt sensing that Mary was the most amenable person in the other group, Catherine tried several times to start a conversation. Her efforts, however, were met with stilted half answers. Elizabeth seemed to make an effort, but she couldn't hold back the little jabs for which she was known. And Edward... Louisa had caught him looking at her once, his face openly hostile, and a shiver of unease had gone through her. Her husband's hands, still holding his utensils, stiffened. For a moment she feared he was going to use the knife as a weapon against his cousin. She placed a hand over his and smiled reassuringly when he turned to look at her. A vein throbbed in his cheek. It was at that moment she realized he was right. They shouldn't have come. If the evening ended without Nicholas and his cousin coming to blows, it would be a miracle.

Louisa turned to Mary. "Catherine will be coming out next spring and we'll be going to town for the Season. Will you be there?"

Mary looked at her mother before replying. "We

haven't decided."

"We didn't expect Mary would need a Season," Elizabeth said, her tone cold, "so we haven't made arrangements. Perhaps, given our recent disappointment, we might impose upon my nephew and stay at his townhouse."

"I'm afraid that won't be possible." Nicholas's tone was smooth but firm.

"But cousin," Edward said, his voice oozing with false sincerity, "surely you can do that much for us since our entire family has been so disappointed of late."

His words were accompanied by an unsubtle leer in Catherine's direction and Louisa's stomach turned over with disgust.

Nicholas stood so quickly his chair would have toppled to the floor if a footman hadn't rushed forward to catch it before it fell. "We're leaving," he said.

Louisa froze, but only for a moment. She removed the napkin from her lap and placed it on the table. Catherine didn't know what was going on, but it was clear she had picked up on the undercurrent of Edward's words and was visibly shaken. Louisa reached for her hand and squeezed it and they both stood.

Nicholas turned to Lady Overlea. "Grandmother?"

Lady Overlea's gaze moved from Nicholas's determined face to the gloating one of his cousin. Edward had accomplished what he'd set out to do. It was clear now to everyone that he'd never intended to mend the rift between the two families.

Without a word the dowager stood and headed from the room.

"Go ahead and walk away," Elizabeth shouted after her

retreating figure. "We all know which grandchild you favor. Why pretend otherwise?"

The older woman's footsteps never faltered. She didn't even glance up at Nicholas when she passed him. Louisa and Catherine followed silently with Nicholas last. They waited outside for the carriage to be brought around. The air was cool, but no one said a word. That silence continued as the carriage pulled away from the house. Nicholas stared out the window, his jaw clenched.

Guilt assailed Louisa. "I'm sorry," she said, her voice sounding unnaturally loud in the oppressive atmosphere.

Surprised, Nicholas turned to look at her. "Whatever for?"

"I should have listened to you. We never should have come here tonight."

"No," the dowager marchioness interrupted. "It is my fault. I know you accepted for my sake."

"It is no one's fault but theirs," Nicholas said. Although he tried, he couldn't keep the anger from his voice.

Catherine asked the question Louisa had been wondering herself.

"What happened between the two branches of the family? It must have been very bad to cause such a great rift."

Nicholas laughed, the sound bitter. "One would imagine that to be the case. The fact, however, is that nothing happened. My uncle always hated my father and he passed that hatred on to his wife and children."

"They were twins, were they not?" Louisa asked.

"Yes," he said. "I remember once, as a young child, mistaking my uncle for my father. I ran up to him and tried to hug him. I could only reach his legs at the time."

He paused briefly, but no one said a word, waiting for him to continue. "He kicked me."

Louisa gasped in horror. She could picture all too well the confusion and hurt Nicholas must have felt at the time.

"I was fortunate, however. My uncle reserved most of his hatred for my father and my brother. Since I was unlikely to inherit, he usually ignored me."

Lady Overlea shook her head and sighed. She held herself with dignity, but Louisa could sense her sadness lurking just beneath the surface.

"Henry never got over the fact that he missed out on the title by a mere ten minutes. It certainly didn't help that my husband made no secret of the fact he favored Nicholas's father over him. I tried to make up for it but obviously failed."

Nicholas reached for his grandmother's hand. "None of this is your fault, Grandmother. My uncle may have felt cheated, yes. I suppose I can understand it, though I have to say I never envied James that he was the heir. Given the closeness of their ages, I have no doubt it was a bitter pill for Uncle to swallow. In the end, however, he is the one responsible for his own actions. He didn't have to spend his life wallowing in his bitterness. And to impart that hatred on to his children was unconscionable."

No one spoke for the remainder of the ride home. Once there, Lady Overlea bid everyone goodnight and went up to her rooms. Louisa's heart went out to Nicholas's grandmother as she watched her climb the stairs, disappointment weighing down her small frame.

She turned to Catherine, anxious to comfort her after the unpleasant ending to their evening, but it was her sister who spoke first.

"I'm all right, Louisa," she said. "I must say, however, that your cousin is not even remotely like you, Nicholas."

"Envy can cause a man to do many vile things."

"I find it difficult to believe it is just jealousy. There is an air of unpleasantness about your cousin and I doubt he would behave differently if he were the marquess."

"Yes," Nicholas said, his expression grim. "Well, at least it is now done. You can trust there will be no repeat performance of tonight's farce."

After saying their goodnights, Louisa waited until her sister was out of sight before turning to her husband. "I am so sorry."

Nicholas took her into his arms. "Stop talking nonsense. None of this is your fault. I want you to put such notions out of your head."

Louisa tried to smile, but the stress of the dinner party still weighed heavily on her.

"Well, at least the evening is over."

"Not quite," Nicholas said, a wicked smile forming. "I seem to recall you promised to do something for me…."

As the days passed Louisa tried to push her fear to the back of her mind, but she couldn't stop watching her husband, waiting for his next attack. Nicholas looked so vital, so healthy, and the last thing anyone looking at him would believe was that he was a man with a terrible illness. There were moments, however, when fear for the future overwhelmed her. Usually those moments came after they made love and she was lying sated and content in his arms. Panic would rise unbidden then, taunting her with the knowledge that such moments of sheer happiness could come to an end any day, and it would take her a long time to fall asleep.

When morning arrived, Louisa would busy herself and refuse to allow such morose thoughts to take hold of her. Watching Nicholas that morning across the breakfast table, she was struck anew by how healthy he appeared.

She was so lost in her own thoughts she barely took notice of Catherine's mood. Her husband's words, therefore, surprised her.

"I can almost hear you thinking, Catherine. Have you decided yet whether you want to ask me about what's clearly on your mind?"

Louisa looked at her sister in time to see her blush.

"I heard that you received a letter from Lord Kerrick yesterday," she said, her blush deepening. "I was just wondering how he is. He left so suddenly without even saying goodbye."

Louisa had been so preoccupied with her own concerns, but now that she thought about it she realized Catherine's mood had been solemn of late. In fact, since Lord Kerrick had left.

"I'm afraid it was unavoidable. A situation arose that required his immediate attention. However, there are still a few matters we need to settle and he should be returning tomorrow."

A smile lit Catherine's face. "I am so glad."

Nicholas raised a brow at her enthusiastic response, but didn't comment further. After he excused himself and headed for his study, Louisa stopped Catherine before she could disappear into the conservatory for the day.

"I fear I have neglected you of late, Catherine. I've been preoccupied with other things, but that is no excuse."

"I'm a little old to expect you to babysit me. I'll be out

in society soon." Her mood brightened further. "Is that what you wish to talk to me about?"

"Lady Overlea told me the modiste we used for my wardrobe will visit later this week to measure you for the evening wear you'll need next spring."

Catherine clutched her hand. "Isn't it wonderful, Louisa? When I think of how things were such a short time ago, how dire our circumstances…" She shook her head. "It was most fortunate that Nicholas found his way to our house that night. I know you worry about John, but we must have faith that he is well."

She winced inwardly when she realized she hadn't thought about her younger brother for some time. "That isn't what I wished to speak to you about. I wanted to discuss Lord Kerrick."

"He's only been away for a week, but I do miss him." Catherine's forehead creased as a thought occurred to her. "I imagine when he returns his visit will be a short one."

"Listen to yourself. Lord Kerrick is eleven years your senior."

Catherine stiffened. "I am aware of his age. What does that have to do with anything?"

"It has become apparent to all that you have developed an infatuation for Lord Kerrick."

"Why should I not? Are you annoyed he may no longer pay attention to you? It is most unfair, Louisa. Must you have every man's interest?"

Louisa was shocked at her sister's accusation, especially since the opposite had been true recently. Over the last few years she'd seen the speculative male glances aimed at Catherine. However, given the deception she and Kerrick had played to rouse Nicholas's jealousy, she couldn't blame her sister for believing what she did.

"Lord Kerrick and I are only friends. I have no desire to receive any romantic attention from him."

Her sister's anger deflated. "Really?"

"How could you think otherwise? Is it not clear that I have feelings for my husband? You know I am not a flirt."

Catherine appeared all of her seventeen years, her uncertainty and relief very evident.

"I didn't think you the type, but there were times when I saw the two of you together… I couldn't help but wonder."

Louisa weighed how much to tell her sister. If she'd noticed the game she and Kerrick had played in order to waken her husband's jealously, then how many others had also noticed?

"Lord Kerrick was amusing himself at Nicholas's expense. He found my husband's displays of jealousy amusing."

"I am relieved to hear you say that," Catherine said, but Louisa wasn't sure her sister believed her.

A horrible thought occurred to her. She didn't think Lord Kerrick was the type to take advantage of an innocent, but she had to ask. "Did Lord Kerrick make any inappropriate advances toward you?"

Catherine colored. "Of course not. I am not yet out."

Louisa knew that wouldn't stop many men. She was relieved, however, to know that her faith in Nicholas's friend was not misplaced.

Catherine stood and turned to leave, and Louisa let her go with a silent hope that her sister wouldn't be in for future heartbreak. She knew Kerrick liked Catherine and found her attractive. She'd caught him looking at her enough times to discern his admiration for her beauty. But that didn't mean he intended to court her.

"Oh, I almost forgot," Catherine said. "Before you came downstairs I gave Nicholas the list of plants he wanted."

Louisa frowned. She hadn't thought Nicholas was interested in botany. "What list of plants?"

"The list of poisonous plants he asked me to get for him."

"Why does he need a list of poisonous plants?"

Catherine rolled her eyes as though the answer should have been obvious.

"To keep them out of the house. One of the plants in the conservatory made him dizzy last week."

Catherine turned and left the breakfast room, leaving her dumbstruck. Nicholas had suffered another spell recently and hadn't told her about it? She started toward the study to confront him but stopped short when she realized she was overreacting.

She would have known if he'd suffered an attack. He had been dizzy, though, and Catherine and he both thought one of the plants in the conservatory had caused it. What did that mean? More importantly, why hadn't Nicholas told her about the episode?

Nicholas looked up from the papers he was studying and rubbed his eyes. He'd never realized how much work was involved in being a marquess. As the younger son he'd never had to learn all the details involved in running the estate, and while he'd always held an interest in politics, his opinions had been just that. Opinions. Now that he was expected to sit in Parliament, he took that responsibility seriously. Especially since he now had renewed hope for his future.

His future. He smiled as he thought of Louisa and the life they would have together. But first he had to determine Edward's guilt. Kerrick couldn't get here soon enough. His letter had said he would be accompanied by Lord Brantford. He didn't give further details, but Nicholas knew Kerrick had friends who were involved in intelligence. He'd never imagined the Earl of Brantford was one of those men, however.

He turned his attention back to his reading but was interrupted a few minutes later by a knock at the door. Hoping it was his Louisa, he bade her enter, but instead it was his valet. He was disappointed, but only for a moment. Harrison had been acting strangely and it was time to get to the reason for his evasiveness.

"I beg your pardon, my lord," the valet said with a brief bow.

The man was definitely nervous. Nicholas made a show of looking at the mantel clock before speaking.

"Is this something that couldn't wait until I saw you later?"

"Lady Overlea may interfere later."

It appeared he would not need to draw his valet out after all. He knew the man referred to Louisa and had to tamp down on the urge to reprimand him for speaking against the mistress of the house.

"What is it, then?"

"I was able to acquire some bottles of your favorite brandy. Lady Overlea was quite thorough when she had all the spirits in the house disposed of, and I know she took the last bottle I gave you. I thought it would be more prudent if she did not learn that you have new stock."

New stock? Good lord, how much did the man acquire? He realized it was very likely that his next drink would contain a lethal dose of the poison. Edward must be getting impatient.

He leaned back in his chair, affecting an appearance of resignation. "That won't be necessary, Harrison."

"She has relented?"

He shook his head.

"I'm afraid my wife may have a point. Given the severity of my last attack, I've decided to stop drinking."

Nicholas watched the other man carefully for his reaction.

"Not drink? You mean not drink brandy, my lord? If that is the case I can obtain something else for you."

Nicholas shook his head. "I'm afraid I will have to stop drinking spirits altogether."

The expression on Harrison's face was priceless. "But you've always enjoyed a good drink now and again."

Nicholas sighed. "I'm afraid those days are now behind me. It shall have to be tea and coffee for however long I have left."

"Tea?"

While his valet was off-balance, Nicholas moved in for the kill.

"When were you planning to tell me about your connection to my cousin's household?"

The color drained completely from Harrison's face.

"I beg your pardon, my lord?"

"You were seen, Harrison."

His valet appeared as though he wanted nothing more than to turn around and flee.

"Did you think I would frown on you forming a romantic attachment? I may have been an avowed bachelor before my marriage, but I was hardly a monk. I understand that a man has needs."

The relief on the other man's face was laughably obvious. He hoped Harrison never took up gambling. He would be horrible at it.

"A romantic attachment. Of course. You are referring to…"

"Your meeting with my cousin's maid. She was seen passing you a love note."

Harrison looked away and cleared his throat before continuing. "There was nothing to tell, my lord. I'm afraid the girl has formed a stronger attachment than I'd intended. It was merely a light flirtation."

He stumbled over his words as he spoke. Good, Nicholas thought. He had the man clearly rattled.

"I understand. But if the relationship becomes more serious, you will come to me, I hope. I am not such an ogre that I would expect the two of you to continue to sneak around behind my back."

"No, my lord. Thank you, my lord. I will allow you to get back to your work now…"

Nicholas's mouth firmed into a grim line as he watched the man scurry from the room. It was clear that Harrison was involved in the poisoning. Nicholas had every confidence he would fold quickly under questioning.

He stood and began to pace. He wanted nothing more than to follow his valet and wring the man's neck. To ferret out the details of the plot that very moment. When he thought about how Edward had killed his father and brother… His fists clenched and he had to take several deep breaths before he could relax. Nothing would be gained by rushing in now. He only hoped that his impulsive questioning hadn't tipped his hand. It was vital that his cousin believe he would be successful in killing the current marquess.

He made his way back to his desk and tried to refocus his attention on his reading. All he could do now was wait.

CHAPTER EIGHTEEN

From the way Louisa kept looking at him over dinner, Nicholas could tell she wanted to speak to him. Since Catherine had given him the list he'd requested that morning, he guessed she may have told her sister what had happened in the conservatory. He'd wrestled with how much to tell her about that incident and his increasing conviction that the men in his family had been, and were continuing to be, poisoned. He didn't want to lie to her, but it was paramount that he keep her safe. She'd already been on the receiving end of one deliberate attempt to hurt her. Would knowing the truth allow her to be extra cautious, or would it place a larger target on her if she started behaving differently after learning the truth?

Thank God Kerrick and Lord Brantford were due to arrive tomorrow. He wanted this whole mess finished. There was no telling what Edward would do next.

Louisa retired after dinner, claiming a headache. The look she gave him before she headed upstairs, however, made it clear that she wanted him to follow. He smiled as he contemplated all the things he would do to try to distract her from the questions she wanted to ask. He'd leave her with no doubt that he was at the peak of health.

Grinning, he entered his rooms a quarter of an hour later. He'd expected to find Louisa awake, so the sight of her asleep on his bed, atop the coverlet, gave him pause. Perhaps she really was suffering from a headache.

He closed the door softly before approaching the bed and looking down at his wife. His heart turned over with the depth of his feelings for her. He couldn't wait for this ordeal to be over so he could tell her he loved her. While his life was in danger, however, he didn't want to add to her loss if something were to happen to him. He guessed she felt the same way about him. At least, he hoped she did. He suffered a moment of doubt as he wondered if she was only worried about him because it was in her nature to take care of others. She had, after all, been in charge of her family's household for some years, taking care of her younger siblings and nursing her father during the illness that finally took his life. He frowned as doubts crowded his mind.

His breath froze when he noticed she was flushed. That wasn't a normal symptom of a headache. He placed a slightly shaking hand on her forehead and swore silently when he discovered how hot she was to the touch. This was more than just a headache.

It was only then that he noticed the teacup peeking out from under a fold of her dress. His gaze moved to the night table, upon which rested a tray with teapot and another cup. He'd been so preoccupied he hadn't noticed it and his heart clenched as he realized what must have happened.

He cursed himself for his stupidity when he'd baited Harrison that afternoon, telling him that he would only be drinking tea from that point forward. It never occurred to him that Louisa might consume a poison that was meant for him. No, not only for him. There were two cups. Sweat broke out on his own brow. Had Harrison, in an act of desperation, decided to take matters into his own hands, or had he been ordered to do so?

He strode to the bellpull and tugged on it before returning to the bed. He placed the empty cup with its mate on the tea tray and with exaggerated care lowered himself onto the bed beside his wife. He brought a hand up to cradle her cheek and spoke softly.

"Louisa? Can you hear me?"

Nothing.

He shook her gently. "Louisa? Please, sweetheart, open your eyes. Let me know you are all right."

To his relief her eyelids fluttered open, but they closed again almost immediately. Her mouth moved, forming his name, but no sound escaped.

There was a soft knock at the door before one of the house maids entered. Nicholas wasn't surprised. After such a desperate act, Harrison was probably long gone.

He ordered the maid to send one of the footmen up and to send for the doctor. Panic clouded his brain and his stomach clenched as he looked down at Louisa, lying motionless on the bed. Her breathing was shallow, but he thanked God that she was still breathing.

He rose when the footman entered. Nicholas didn't know the man personally, but he did know his family. The Tates had been tenants of the estate for many generations and from everything he'd heard they were a good, solid family. There was nothing else for it. He'd have to hope that the man could be trusted.

"Nancy told me that Lady Overlea has taken ill," the servant said, his gaze going to Louisa before returning to Nicholas. "Whatever I can do to help, my lord, I will do it gladly."

Nicholas nodded grimly at the man's words. He knew Louisa was well liked among the staff. "I need your help, William. Can I count on you to keep quiet about what I tell you?"

The footman straightened at the question. "Upon my word, my lord, I will tell no one."

"Good man," Nicholas said. "First, I need to know if Harrison is belowstairs."

The footman shook his head. "I'm not sure, my lord. I saw him about an hour ago but haven't seen him since. It is a big house."

"I think you'll find that Harrison is gone."

Tate's eyes widened as the import of Nicholas's words struck him and his gaze moved again to Louisa. "You don't believe…"

"I fear he may have given Lady Overlea something that made her fall ill."

William's fists curled. "The cur. I will find him myself and make him sorry."

Nicholas agreed wholeheartedly with the sentiment. He wanted nothing more than to chase the man down, but he couldn't leave Louisa's side. Not while her life was in danger.

"I need you to see if you can find him. If he isn't in the house, then ask at the stables. See if you can find out what direction he may have traveled. And please, don't tell anyone about my suspicions."

He watched as the footman, his fists still clenched, turned and hurried from the room. If Nicholas was any judge of character, William Tate wasn't involved in this scheme. He'd seemed genuinely surprised and angry at what he'd learned.

Nicholas ran his hands through his hair. He wished Kerrick was already there. It killed him to know Harrison was likely escaping at that very moment. But as long as the maid remained in his cousin's employ, and it was unlikely his valet had taken the time to send word to her, they had someone who could testify as to Edward's guilt. It was Harrison who had administered the poison, though, and Nicholas would make sure he hanged for it.

The door had just closed when it swung open again and a fair-haired whirlwind flew into the room.

"I heard that Louisa was ill."

Catherine rushed to her sister's side and took in her flushed face and still form before turning to face him. "What happened? She said she had a headache, but this is like no headache I've ever seen."

Catherine. If he'd been thinking clearly, he would have sent for her first. She'd been studying the plants in the conservatory. She knew some were poisonous, and it was possible she'd know what needed to be done now.

He closed the bedroom door and turned to her before removing from his pocket the list she'd given him that morning. Holding it out to her, he asked, "Which of these plants might cause your sister to fall ill in this manner?"

Her face turned white with shock. It took her several moments before she found her voice. "What are you saying?" She took the list with trembling fingers but didn't look at it.

"I realize this is a lot to take in, but I need you to think, Catherine. That reaction I had the other day in the conservatory... I believe it was caused by a sensitivity I have to a certain plant. A plant someone has been administering to me without my knowledge for some time now."

"But why?"

"Why does not matter for now. Suffice it to say I've come to believe that my illness was in fact a result of being poisoned. It makes sense that the source of the poison is the plant that caused me to react. In all likelihood, it's also the poison that Louisa drank."

Catherine gasped at the news and stared, distraught, at her sister.

"I need you to concentrate," Nicholas said, his voice urgent. "Which plant could cause this, and more importantly, what can we do to counteract its effects?"

Catherine shook her head as she stared down at the list. "I don't know. It could be several. It would all depend on how much was given..." She looked up at Nicholas, despair in her eyes. "Some of these are fatal if ingested in any quantity."

Nicholas closed his eyes briefly, concentrating on holding back his own panic before replying. "We have to assume she was given the same poison I was given. That would eliminate the plants that are immediately fatal."

Catherine nodded and looked down at the list again. "Some of these will make one very ill but are not fatal unless administered in a large quantity." Her eyes were hopeful when she looked up at Nicholas again.

He thought back over the course of what he'd thought

was his illness. "I believe we are looking for a plant that can be administered in small quantities to produce changes in perception. It would cause dizziness, forgetfulness, and bring about a fever. And yes, it would also cause death with a large dose," he said, thinking about his brother.

Catherine swallowed visibly. "Do you think Louisa…"

"I hope not," he said, sending up a silent, fervent prayer.

Her hands shook, but she reviewed the list again carefully. "I'm not certain. It could be the *Datura*, but I am not sure of all the symptoms."

Nicholas took a deep breath before asking the next question. "Is there anything we can do? Louisa was only upstairs fifteen minutes before I found her."

The little color that remained in Catherine's face seemed to drain before his eyes.

"For it to have this effect, the dose must have been a large one."

Nicholas's mind spun with the implications. He looked down at his wife again. Her color was high and her breathing still shallow. He'd become well acquainted with feeling helpless over the past months as his own illness progressed, but this was so much worse.

Catherine broke into his misery with a sound of exclamation. "The poison hasn't been in her system long. We may be able to flush the rest of it before it is fully absorbed."

Nicholas turned to her, momentarily confused.

"How…?"

Catherine was the picture of efficiency now. She reminded him of her sister, which made his heart hurt.

"If she only drank the poison a little while ago, it will

still be in her stomach. We can induce her to empty its contents—"

"Which would lessen the size of the dose she received," he finished for her. Of course. He should have thought of that.

He moved swiftly to the washstand and returned with the basin.

"Would you like me to do it?" Catherine asked.

"I'll do it. Go and fetch some water from the kitchen. Bring up a large pitcher and a glass. After I finish here, making her drink water may help to dilute what has been absorbed into her system." He shook his head. "I don't know if it will be useful at all, but there's nothing else we can do, so we must try."

Catherine turned to leave, but he stopped her, adding, "Make sure you do the pouring yourself. We have no way of knowing who else may be involved in this plot."

Catherine nodded and without a word fled from the room.

Nicholas turned toward his wife and squared his shoulders.

"Time to wake up, Louisa," he said, the time for gentleness past. "We need to get this damned stuff out of you."

It was a long night, but at some point in the early hours of the morning Louisa opened her eyes and looked at him. "Was I imagining things, or did you...?"

She brought a hand to her mouth and mimed the motion.

Relief more powerful than anything he'd ever experienced swept through Nicholas.

Louisa frowned. "And why are you not in bed with me?"

He climbed onto the bed beside her, dragged her into his arms, and just held her. It was a full minute before he could find his voice.

"You scared me to death last night."

Louisa struggled to sit up. "What happened? Why am I still in my clothes?"

"Do you remember what happened last night after dinner?"

She stared at him blankly. "After dinner? Nothing happened."

"You told everyone you had a headache and came upstairs."

She brought a hand to her head.

"My head does hurt." Her frown deepened. "But it didn't hurt last night. I only said that because I wanted to speak with you privately." She dropped her hand. "Speaking of which—"

He cut in. "Before we get to that, tell me what happened when you reached my room."

"I already told you, nothing happened. I came in here to wait for you."

Nicholas had to know if Harrison had laid a hand on Louisa. If he'd forced her to drink the tea.

"Was my valet here?"

"Harrison? No, the room was empty." She looked up at him, her expression curious. "Since when have you started having tea before bed? I found a freshly brewed pot of tea and two cups on your nightstand."

"And you had a cup?"

"It was a little cool, but I thought it would calm my

nerves while I waited. I was most put out with you. Catherine told me you'd had a brief episode in the conservatory. Have there been other episodes you've kept from me?"

The time for shielding his wife was now over. With Harrison gone it was likely they were safe from any immediate danger, but Nicholas couldn't take that chance. Until this matter was at an end and everyone involved apprehended, they were both going to have to be careful about everything they consumed.

He told her what he knew and about his suspicion that his cousin was poisoning him. He'd expected her reaction to be similar to Catherine's the night before—shock and disbelief at first. What he didn't expect was the sudden understanding and compassion that lit her eyes.

"Oh, Nicholas," she said, reaching for his hands. "It goes far beyond just you, does it not?"

He should have known that her first concern wouldn't be for herself, but for him. A lump formed in his throat. He'd been trying not to think about his parents and his brother. He'd felt their loss keenly, but had managed to maintain a façade of composure whenever he spoke of them. And after learning about the poisoning, the emotion he'd been predominantly experiencing whenever he thought of them was anger. Anger for the person who had caused their early deaths—his cousin Edward—and an almost overwhelming need to avenge them. Faced now with Louisa's compassion, however, that anger receded.

He buried his face in his wife's neck and clung to her as a wave of grief swept over him. He couldn't say how long they remained that way. What he did know, however, was that God had given him a gift when his path had crossed with that of Louisa Evans. He'd almost bungled their relationship with his absurd scheme to have her beget an heir with another man, but somehow he hadn't succeeded in pushing her away. He vowed that he would do whatever it took to keep her safe, even if it meant killing Edward himself.

CHAPTER NINTEEN

The Earls of Kerrick and Brantford arrived shortly after breakfast. Nicholas had them shown into his study where he joined them after tearing himself away from his wife's side.

As he entered the dark-paneled room, Nicholas wondered, again, at Kerrick's choice of person to call in to help them investigate the poisonings. Brantford was a few years older than he and Kerrick, but the fair-haired, blue-eyed man seemed younger. There was an air of serene calmness about him, and Nicholas couldn't help speculating now about how much of that was a façade.

He filled in the two men on everything that had happened, ending with the previous evening's events. William Tate had learned that Harrison had, indeed, left the house while the family was at dinner and was last seen traveling north. Instead of returning to give Nicholas that information, however, the footman had sent him a sealed note and had ridden out after Harrison himself.

"Does the man have any experience in situations such

as this one?" Kerrick asked.

Nicholas shook his head. "Not that I'm aware of. He does know the area very well, though. Better than Harrison, who grew up in London. That should give him an advantage."

"Let us hope that Tate thought to bring along a weapon," Brantford said, his expression grim. "Desperate men are, as a rule, dangerous when confronted."

"I want to confront my cousin as soon as possible," Nicholas said. "After all the commotion of the past day, it won't be long before word of Harrison's flight reaches Edward. He'll realize we know about the poisoning when he hears that the lady of the house is personally overseeing the preparation of all meals."

Brantford nodded. "I think it best for Kerrick to go after Tate and assist him in tracking down your valet. I will keep a watch on your cousin's house to make sure he doesn't leave. We need to gather as much information as we can from your man before we confront Edward Manning. After all, we have no evidence he is involved. A confession from Harrison, along with an examination of the tea you had the foresight to keep, should go a long way toward proving his guilt."

"There is a maid in my cousin's household who is also involved," Nicholas said. "We could question her right now."

Brantford considered that possibility before finally shaking his head. "Not yet. You said that she passed a note to Harrison. If it was sealed, the maid may not even be aware of what it contained. No, it would be better if we had Harrison first. He administered the poison, so we know he has the information we need."

273

Nicholas ground his teeth together in frustration.

Kerrick clapped a hand on his shoulder. "Brantford knows what he's about. And with Tate already in pursuit, we have a head start in tracking him down. It's a good thing he thought to send word back. From the sound of it, I wouldn't be surprised if he is already on his way back with the bastard as we speak."

Nicholas nodded, his mood bleak. This whole ordeal could not be over soon enough. He was right at the edge of his patience and he wasn't sure how much longer he'd be able to sit back and do nothing.

Louisa looked up from her embroidery and stared at her husband, who was sitting behind his desk reading more reports. Her heart expanded as she took in his dark good looks. Lines of fatigue bracketed his mouth, the only evidence that he'd stayed up all night watching over her, but he'd refused her suggestion that he rest. She knew she'd be able to tempt him into bed if she promised to join him, but she was still enduring the aftereffects of her recent poisoning. Her head throbbed and her entire body was leaden. She shuddered again as she thought about how close she may have come to dying. After all those weeks she'd spent worrying about Nicholas's health, it would have been the height of irony if she'd been the one to succumb to his supposed illness.

She smiled when Nicholas looked up from his reading and met her gaze.

"You should rest," he said, concern etched on his face.

"I was just thinking the same of you."

He pushed his chair back from the desk, stood, and walked over to where she sat.

"Fine, you win," he said, holding out his hand to her. "We will ask Catherine to oversee the preparation of dinner and retire for an afternoon nap."

She narrowed her eyes in suspicion. "You're going to wait until I fall asleep and come back downstairs."

He placed a hand over his heart and widened his eyes, appearing very much like a contrite child. "You wound me with your distrust."

Louisa couldn't stop the laugh that bubbled out of her. The day had been a difficult one, and not only because of the lasting physical effects from the night before. The knowledge that someone, Nicholas's own cousin no less, had tried to hurt the two of them—had, in fact, succeeded in killing Nicholas's parents and his brother—hung like a dark cloud over everything. She found it almost impossible to believe. Nicholas smiled at her and her breath hitched. Even if he didn't return her love, she told herself they were good together. If they could stop the poisonings, it was possible the two of them could have a long, happy life together. She had to cling to that hope.

She placed her hand in his and allowed him to help her up. Nicholas opened the study door but stopped, his head tilted to one side.

"What is the matter?" she asked.

She heard it then. The sound of several angry voices carrying from the front of the house. Their eyes met.

"Do you think…?"

"I intend to find out."

Nicholas strode from the room. She was only a step behind him.

Her first impression was one of chaos. The front hall was filled with people, and several voices vied to be heard above the others. Edward Manning was cursing profusely, his face red with rage. His mother's voice, shrill with indignation, matched his in volume. Mary was the sole member of that family who remained quiet. She hung back from the crowd, her face serene. The group included Nicholas's grandmother, the Earl of Brantford, and Kerrick.

Silence descended when the group noticed Nicholas and Louisa's entrance, but only for a moment.

"What are you playing at, Cousin?" Edward asked.

"I demand an apology," Elizabeth Manning screeched. "How dare you have my son dragged here like a common criminal—"

"Enough."

Nicholas's voice was barely raised, but the command in his tone brought instant obedience. Looking at him now, Louisa found it hard to believe he hadn't been raised from the cradle to be the next Marquess of Overlea. The silence was absolute as all eyes fixed on Nicholas, who stood tall and unyielding, his demeanor that of someone who would brook no defiance.

Nicholas turned to face Brantford. "What happened?"

Elizabeth took a step forward and interrupted before the other man could reply.

"This… this *person* accosted your cousin—"

Her voice died when Nicholas turned the full brunt of his icy anger on her.

"When I am ready to hear you speak, madam, I will ask for your version of events."

His aunt took a breath to reply, but she changed her mind and wisely chose to remain silent. Given her husband's current mood, Louisa wouldn't have been surprised if Nicholas locked her away in one of the manor's many rooms to keep her silent.

The Earl of Brantford had been leaning against a wall, an expression of extreme boredom on his face. He straightened when Nicholas turned his attention back to him. Louisa was surprised to see that he was almost as tall as her husband. That, however, was where the similarity between the two men ended. Whereas Nicholas had dark hair and dark eyes, Brantford was fair. Light to her husband's darkness. His hair was cut fashionably short and his eyes were the palest of blue. Louisa had no doubt that those eyes could cut right through a person.

"Your cousin's residence was quiet until noon, at which time I observed the servants carrying trunks from the house. As there were two carriages prepared, one for the family and one for the luggage that was being stowed for travel. I could only surmise that a very long absence was planned. When your cousin and his family entered their carriage I had them brought here instead."

Nicholas raised a brow at that, but Brantford replied before he could ask the question.

"I had a pleasant discussion with the coachman and he agreed to let me drive the coach."

Nicholas nodded.

Edward had remained silent long enough. "Now see here, Overlea," he began, his face still red with rage. "This is taking our family disagreement a little far. We do not have to beg for your approval to move about."

Nicholas's voice was unnaturally calm when he replied, and Louisa knew he was keeping his anger tightly in check. "Where were you going?"

Edward sputtered. "I don't have to answer to you—"

Her husband moved so quickly Edward did not have a chance to evade him. Nicholas was nose to nose with his cousin, his arms grabbing the edges of the other man's coat to hold him in place.

"My patience with you is at an end," he said, his voice a low growl.

Aunt Elizabeth broke in. "If you must know, we were going to town," she said, disdain lacing each word. "Edward has been bored here and we must start making arrangements for a new wardrobe for Mary's Season next spring."

It was several moments before Nicholas released his cousin and took a step back.

"I thought you had no place to stay while in town."

"We are not totally without connections," his aunt replied.

"Would you care to explain why you were having our house watched by this *ruffian*?" Edward asked.

The man in question took a step forward. "The Earl of Brantford," he said, bowing with a flourish. "I am pleased to make your acquaintance.

Edward's eyes bulged slightly, which made Louisa very curious. Whereas before he'd been the picture of indignant anger, he now seemed clearly uneasy.

"Why have you decided that we be kept a prisoner here in Kent?" Edward asked.

Nicholas ignored him and turned, instead, to Lord Kerrick. "I didn't expect to see you back so soon."

"Indeed," Kerrick said. "I wouldn't be here now if not for your footman. By the time I'd managed to track him down, Tate was already on his way back with Harrison."

Louisa's eyes were on Edward as Lord Kerrick spoke,

but if Nicholas's cousin was worried about that piece of news he betrayed nothing by his expression. If anything, he seemed completely confused.

"And?" Nicholas prodded.

"And the man was most cooperative. After telling us everything, Tate took him to the local magistrate." Kerrick paused only briefly before continuing. "You were right, Nicholas, about the poisoning."

Louisa sucked in her breath. Intellectually, after what had happened to her, she'd known her husband was correct in his suspicions, but to have them confirmed… A part of her hadn't wanted to believe it was true. To know without a doubt that such evil and jealousy existed in the world.

She hadn't realized that Catherine had come into the hallway until that moment. Her sister came to her side and squeezed her hand. Louisa could see that she was also very troubled by what she was witnessing.

"Damn it all," Edward said. "Will someone tell me what in blazes is going on?"

Nicholas turned back to Edward. The corners of his mouth curved up, but there was no satisfaction on his face, only grim determination. Louisa wanted so much to go to him, but she held back, knowing he had to do this on his own.

"Game over, Cousin," he said, his voice almost weary. "We know about the poison. You'll hang for this. You've murdered not one, but two marquesses and attempted to kill a third."

The color drained from Elizabeth Manning's face, but Edward continued to protest his innocence. "You are insane," he said, the first hint of fear touching his eyes.

SUZANNA MEDEIROS

"You can't possibly hope to make people believe I poisoned anyone, and especially not my own uncle and cousins."

"We have proof that Nicholas was being poisoned," Kerrick said. "We have the poison itself. Harrison, being the fool that he is, still had it on him. He was hoping to dispose of it once he left Kent. And he confessed that he was paid handsomely to add a small quantity to Nicholas's brandy so that everyone would believe he was ill. His eventual death would, therefore, be attributed to that mysterious illness."

Edward's gaze swung wildly between Kerrick and Nicholas.

"You are both mad. I didn't poison anyone."

"Actually," Kerrick said, "I already know that."

Now it was Nicholas and Louisa's turn to stare at him in confusion.

"You just said that Harrison confessed," Nicholas said.

"He did, but he wasn't being paid by Edward."

At that explosive piece of news all eyes turned to Elizabeth Manning. The woman's anger flared higher still and she made no pretense of hiding her hatred.

"I had nothing to do with any poisonings. If this person hopes to pin the blame for his own actions on me, he is sadly mistaken."

Kerrick shook his head. "No, not you. I know you are innocent. Your daughter, however, is not."

"Mary? That is preposterous!"

Mary had been standing silently in the background, taking in the whole scene as though she was merely a spectator. Now that she was thrust into the spotlight, however, her entire bearing changed. Louisa could only

280

stare in horrified fascination as the formerly meek woman transformed right before their eyes. She took a step forward and stood with her head held high. Her voice rang out in a volume they had never before heard from her.

"I obviously dallied much too long. I should have finished you off months ago," she said, hatred and something else blazing in her eyes.

It took few seconds for Louisa to recognize it. Madness. From the expressions on the faces of Mary's mother and brother, it was clear they were equally shocked.

"What are you saying, Mary?" Elizabeth's voice was unsteady. "Stop this nonsense at once."

Mary laughed and the sound caused a frisson of disquiet to race down Louisa's spine.

"Nonsense? You didn't think bartering me off to a hated cousin, then attempting to do the same with a second one, was nonsense. Oh no, I'm the meek, mild Mary. I'm supposed to stand back and allow you to sell me off so you can have more spending money."

"Mary!"

Edward was stunned at his sister's words. She turned to face him, her composure back in place.

"You should thank me, brother dear. With this family out of the way, you were next in line to inherit. We'd both have been free then. You to do whatever you wish without monetary restraint and me from being forced to marry."

"You did this horrible thing for me? Murder? What the hell were you thinking?"

"Don't be stupid, Edward, I did it for me. Don't look at me that way, Mother. When Nicholas slipped out of your grasp and married someone else, we both know you were intending to marry me off to the next highest bidder once we hit town. No doubt some old goat who would maul me."

After her stunning outburst, Mary turned to leave, but Brantford had moved behind her while she spoke and now barred her exit.

"I'm going to have to insist that you accompany me to the magistrate," he said. His tone was even, but even in her madness Mary could see that he was not a man to be crossed. She said nothing further as the earl led her from the house. Louisa couldn't tell if she failed to recognize the consequences that lay ahead for her or if she simply didn't care.

Nicholas turned to Louisa and took hold of her hands, squeezing them lightly. She could tell from his expression that the revelation it was mild-mannered Mary who'd been behind the poisonings had shaken him.

"Kerrick and I need to go with them," he said.

Louisa nodded. Of course. The magistrate would need to know everything Nicholas had experienced over the past months and what had led to his suspicions he was being poisoned. And there were also the two attempts on her life.

"I'll be back as soon as I can. Try to get some rest while I am gone. I know you're still not feeling well."

He dropped a quick kiss on her lips before releasing her, and Louisa watched him leave without a word. She'd thought she would be relieved when the danger they faced was over, but she wasn't. New doubts flooded her mind and her heart. Now that Nicholas knew he was healthy, would he regret his hasty decision to marry her? Her mood sank as she contemplated that possibility.

* * *

So much had happened over the past few months that it was almost impossible for Louisa to take it all in. After Mary's dramatic confession and exit, Edward and Elizabeth had left without another word. Along with the now-deceased Henry Manning, their family had resented Nicholas's branch of the family with a hatred that went beyond reason. It was clear, however, that no one had imagined their hatred would infect Mary, the most fragile member of the family, in such a manner.

When Nicholas returned, he told Louisa that Mary had confessed to everything. How she'd learned of the poisonous qualities of the flower she liked so much from a friend's casual remark shortly before the two sides of the Manning family finalized the agreement for Mary and Nicholas's brother, James, to marry. What they hadn't known was that Mary had fallen in love with the youngest son of an impoverished baronet during her first Season, but her mother had forbidden the match. She had watched, brokenhearted, as he courted and then wed another.

The seeds of her madness had been planted and they grew rapidly. She'd attempted to kill herself by consuming a tea brewed from the leaves of the plant. Instead of dying, however, she had merely fallen ill. She then conceived the idea of giving the poison to her uncle, hoping that his resulting illness would cause the Overleas to postpone her wedding to James.

She hadn't intended to kill him, but the effects from ingesting the plant weren't instantaneous if only a small amount was used. When Nicholas's father suffered a delayed attack while driving into the village, he lost control of the carriage, killing him and his wife instantly. Instead of feeling guilt, however, Mary had been relieved. Her betrothal to James had not yet been officially announced, and she hoped that he would change his mind during the mourning period.

She'd been disappointed when she learned he intended to go through with their union after the period of mourning was over and had moved forward with a more aggressive timetable for James, not caring that she was playing an active role in another's death. In her desperation, he was given much larger doses and his swift death from the poison had been inevitable. She was so deep into it at that point that she couldn't stop. She'd decided that she would only be free from her mother's matchmaking schemes by ensuring her brother became the Marquess of Overlea.

They were preparing for bed when Louisa told Nicholas that she felt sorry for Mary.

Nicholas scoffed at her softheartedness. "That 'poor girl' killed my family and almost succeeded in killing me. And lest you forget, she did the same to you. Not once, but twice. The first when she ordered Harrison to sabotage your saddle so you'd fall from your horse."

Louisa gasped. "She caused my accident? When did you learn that?"

"I knew your saddle had been tampered with almost immediately."

"And you never said anything?"

"I didn't wish to frighten you." Nicholas reached for her and pulled her into his arms. "I already suspected the poisoning but didn't suspect you'd also be in danger. I believe by that time Mary wasn't thinking clearly at all."

"I don't believe she was ever thinking clearly," Louisa said, shaking her head. "What will happen to her?"

"It's likely she'll be committed to an asylum."

Louisa shuddered at the thought. Death would be more merciful.

"I don't understand Harrison's part in all this. You said Mary's maid didn't know what she was delivering to him, but Harrison clearly knew exactly what he was doing."

"He did it for the money," Nicholas said. She frowned in disbelief and he continued. "Apparently he fathered a son in his youth. When the boy reached his majority he developed a liking for cards, but he had no affinity for it and quickly amassed a rather large amount of gaming debts. Of course, he made his situation worse by borrowing money from the wrong people." Nicholas paused as he struggled to keep his voice even. "If Harrison had gone to my father instead of accepting payment from Mary to poison him, I'm sure he would have helped him."

He pulled her into a tight hug, and she hoped he found as much comfort in the embrace as she did.

"Thank God he was found," she said, drawing back a little to look up at Nicholas. "If he'd managed to get away, we never would have known Mary was behind everything and she might have found someone else to finish the task."

"Yes, thank God and William Tate," Nicholas said. "He remembered that Harrison had spoken about having family in London. When the groom told him Harrison had headed north, he played a hunch and headed toward town."

"We must think of a way to thank him."

"I already have. Since I am now in need of a new valet and I could think of no one more deserving, I offered him the position. I'm sure we'll both muddle through until he learns the ropes."

She returned his smile with one she was far from feeling. She'd been trying, unsuccessfully, to shake off the sense of melancholy that had settled over her when she realized what she needed to do. Nicholas had married her thinking he was on the verge of death. It was true that their relationship had grown from the one he'd initially envisioned, but she loved him enough not to force him to spend the rest of his life with someone he didn't love in return. He had already lost so much in his life. His parents, his brother. He deserved the chance to have someone in his life he could love. If that wasn't her, she would step aside so he could find that person. It would likely kill her, but she would do that for him.

Nicholas had grown to know her well in the little time they'd been together, and she couldn't hide her mood from him.

"Something is the matter," he said lightly, tilting her face up to meet his gaze. He ran his thumb along her lower lip. "You are unhappy."

Louisa shuddered at his touch. She wouldn't be able to do this if he was touching her. Taking a deep breath, she stepped out of his arms.

"You are completely healthy," she said.

"I'll have the doctor look me over, but I hope to learn that I have suffered no lasting ill effects from the poison." He examined her, trying to read her intent. "I hope the fact that you are now stuck with me indefinitely is not causing you distress."

He spoke lightly, the words an attempt to elicit a smile from her, but they had the opposite effect.

"Actually, that is what I wanted to speak to you about," she said. "Now that you are no longer ill, you have no pressing need for an heir."

His eyes narrowed. "I still need an heir."

She soldiered on, her words coming out in a rush.

"Yes, but you do not require one from me." He started to respond, but she held up a hand to stop him. "I have to say this now, while I can. When you asked me to marry you it was a matter of convenience. I required your help and you needed something from me. But that is no longer the case."

An odd expression crossed his face. His voice was gentle when he spoke. "I still need you, Louisa."

She waved her hand at him and pressed on. "You need me in the same way you did the mistresses you no doubt had before me, but you do not have to be tied down to me."

A hint of wariness entered his eyes. "What exactly are you saying?"

This was it. Would he be relieved when she told she was giving him back his freedom?

"The circumstances surrounding our marriage were extraordinary ones, and at the time you were under a misapprehension about your health. We both know that under normal circumstances you would never have married me." She had to take another deep breath before continuing. "I would understand if you wanted to separate. It is done all the time and no one would talk."

A long, uncomfortable silence stretched between them when she finished.

"And what about you," he said finally. "Do you really think I would just cast you aside as so much garbage and go back to living like a bachelor in town?"

She winced at his words and turned away, unable to face him. She didn't hear him move and was surprised when he spun her around to face him again, his hands gripping her upper arms. He was angry with her.

"Do you think so little of me that you believe I would do that to you?"

She reached up and placed a hand against his cheek. He was so handsome and could still take her breath away. But she loved him enough not to bind him to her if he didn't share her feelings.

"Ours was not a love match. You deserve that, Nicholas."

He reacted as though she had slapped him. He released her and took a step back.

"Let us speak plainly here, Louisa. I know you are used to caring for others. Catherine, John, your father. Me. Was that all I was to you? Another cause? Someone for you to nurse, and now that you know I am fine you find the notion of spending the rest of your life with me unbearable?"

She gasped at the bitterness in his tone.

"No—"

He laughed, but the sound was not a happy one. "Well, that is too bad. I will not agree to a separation."

They stood there for what seemed an eternity. He was so very angry with her. His hands were balled at his sides, his breathing harsh.

"We seem to be at an impasse," he said finally.

Louisa could feel all the energy draining from her body at his words, to be replaced by defeat. She had ruined everything. She'd wanted only to make him happy, but instead all she had accomplished was to ruin what little happiness the two of them had managed to wring from the situation in which they'd found themselves.

She turned and headed for the door that connected their rooms. He was angry with her and she couldn't be around him when he was like this. Like the cold, remote stranger she had married. It hurt too much. Perhaps, over time, they could get back to the easy camaraderie they'd recently developed. It might be enough that she loved him and he did seem to like her. Or at least he had before this evening.

She reached the door and turned the knob, but Nicholas came up behind her and reached around her to hold it closed. They stood there like that for several heartbeats, she facing the door, Nicholas looming large and powerful behind her, caging her between his two arms. Her thoughts went back to that other night when she'd found herself in the same position. The night the two of them had made love for the first time.

She was afraid to say anything that might make him angrier. She'd thought only to give him the freedom he deserved, and instead he had taken it as an insult. She should have realized he wasn't the kind of man who would abandon his responsibilities.

"Is this truly what you want?" he asked, his voice strained. "To leave?"

She closed her eyes as grief washed over her. That was the very last thing she wanted to do.

His mouth dropped to the curve of her neck and he kissed her there. She relaxed into him and released the breath she'd been holding.

"I don't want to go."

He turned her then, but didn't step back. She brought her hands to his chest and met his dark, intent gaze.

"Good, because I'm not letting you go that easily."

His mouth met hers in a tender kiss that stole her breath. She made a sound of relief and brought her hands up to tangle them in his hair, holding him to her. His hands glided down her back and brought her fully against him.

"Tell me what you do want," he said, his mouth hovering over hers.

She swept her tongue over his lips and he groaned in response.

"I want you. I know I shouldn't. You deserve to be happy, Nicholas, not bound to me, a woman you married only out of necessity."

He lifted his head and stared down at her, clearly baffled.

"I *am* happy, Louisa. Our marriage may have taken place for all the wrong reasons, but you are the woman I want. The woman I love."

Happiness unfurled in her chest. "You love me?"

"I would have thought it obvious. I've been acting like a lovesick fool since I met you, although it did take me a while to realize it."

She threw her arms around him and clung to him.

"Does this mean I'll hear no more nonsense about ending our marriage?"

"I love you, too, Nicholas," she said, almost afraid to let go of him, lest she find she was only dreaming.

He exhaled with relief and buried his head in her neck. "Thank God."

EPILOGUE

If Louisa had thought the activity surrounding the preparation of her wedding trousseau was impressive, the modiste and small army of seamstresses that descended upon Overlea Manor in late winter put that experience to shame. Nicholas's grandmother had clearly spared no expense in making sure Louisa and Catherine would be dressed in only the most current fashion for the upcoming Season.

Under the discerning eye of one of London's most sought-after modistes, the sisters had shifted through a seemingly endless variety of fabrics and designs. When that stage of planning their new wardrobes was complete, the never-ending fittings began. Louisa was certain they would never need so many different outfits, but she took joy from seeing how the activity lifted Catherine's spirits. Her sister's normal cheerfulness had faded when Kerrick left shortly after the discovery of Mary Manning's crimes, but her mood had improved with this concrete sign that the start of the Season was almost upon them. Louisa only hoped Catherine would find someone to distract her from thoughts of the man for whom she was so clearly pining.

With only a week left before their departure for London, they were once again in Catherine's bedroom trying on the last of the new outfits. Two seamstresses were helping Catherine into a new gown while another was on her knees before Louisa, pinning up the hem of her dress. The modiste looked on, her mouth a moue of displeasure as she took in the awkward fit of Louisa's dress.

Louisa's thoughts drifted. On the surface, the day was like many others they'd experienced over the last month, but it was one she would never forget. Nicholas had left that morning to deal with estate matters and she was counting the minutes until his return.

"What do you think, Louisa?"

She looked up to see her sister examining herself in the cheval mirror. The pale yellow gown perfectly complemented her sister's fair coloring and the low neckline was guaranteed to draw attention.

"You will have every man present eating out of your hand," she said, knowing it wouldn't be an exaggeration.

They turned at the sound of raised voices in the hallway.

"You can't go in there—"

The door to the room burst open and Nicholas stood there, his grandmother beside him.

"Thank heavens you are both dressed," the dowager marchioness said.

Louisa's heart stuttered, then sped up at the grim expression on her husband's face. She'd seen that look many times during the beginning of their marriage and had hoped never to see it again.

"What is the matter?" she asked, hurrying to his side.

His gaze swept over the room but before he could reply, Catherine stepped forward.

"I think I would like to take some refreshment. You can all return later to finish the fitting," she said in dismissal to the modiste and seamstresses.

Nicholas moved into the room as its former occupants filed out. Louisa's thoughts were centered, though, on what could have happened to upset her husband and paid them no heed. For one heart-stopping moment, she'd almost thought he was having another attack. It seemed she was still not over her concern for his health, despite the fact there had been no further episodes since Mary's guilt had been exposed.

When the last person had left, Nicholas closed the door and just stood there staring at her. The haunted expression in his eyes had her imagining all sorts of horrible things.

"Has something happened? Nicholas, you're worrying me."

He gave a small, abbreviated shake of his head and swallowed hard. "The doctor was here to see you."

She frowned. "Yes. But why are you so upset?"

He grasped her upper arms. "Why was he here?" His eyes ran over her before returning to her face. "If you are ill…"

Understanding dawned. After having experienced so much death and having had to face the possibility of his own impending demise as well as her own not that long ago, it was only natural that he'd jump to the worst conclusions after hearing about the visit from the physician.

She rushed to reassure him. "Everything is fine. I am well." When he didn't release her, she said, "You're hurting me."

He dropped his hands and took a step back, but her words hadn't comforted him.

"You've been tired lately," he said. "And yesterday morning you were ill. You must tell me—"

"No, Nicholas, listen to me. I am not sick." She took his face between her hands and smiled. "I am with child."

It was several moments before her words sank in.

"You're not sick?"

She shook her head. "Well, not exactly. I do feel a little queasy in the mornings, but I am told that is to be expected."

He drew her hands from his face and clutched them in his own. He closed his eyes and Louisa waited.

"When Grandmother told me you'd sent for the doctor, I was so afraid. I had to see you for myself. Make sure…"

He didn't have to finish. She knew he'd needed to make sure he wasn't about to lose her, as well, just as he'd lost his brother and his parents. He crushed her against him and she squeezed her arms around his waist, hoping to impart as much comfort as she could with that simple gesture.

"Nothing is going to come between us. You are well and truly stuck with me."

"Thank God," he said, drawing back to look down at her. "You've given me everything. A family, a reason to live. And now a baby."

The look on his face was one of wonder and Louisa felt her heart squeeze. She loved him so much—more than she had ever imagined possible.

His gaze dipped and his expression changed. "What on earth are you wearing?"

She followed the direction of his stare and felt heat creep over her skin at the way her breasts were threatening to spill over the top of the bodice.

"Madame Bonlieu is quite displeased with me. I appear to be increasing in *every* way."

Nicholas's grin could only be described as wolfish. "I heartily approve. Here, let me help you out of your dress."

"We are in Catherine's room—"

He didn't give her a chance to finish before sweeping her into his arms. He opened the door with ridiculous ease and carried her into the hallway, which was mercifully empty. She wouldn't have survived the embarrassment of having witnesses to her husband's amorous attentions.

It was not long, however, before Louisa's thoughts became focused solely on her husband and the lavish attention he was bestowing on her.

AUTHOR'S NOTE

Thank you for reading *Loving the Marquess*. If you enjoyed this book, please consider sharing it with a friend. All honest reviews are welcome and appreciated.

I had a lot of fun writing this book. I will admit, however, that I had some difficulty finding the perfect poison that would cause the effects experienced by Nicholas during the course of this story. I settled on the Datura flower as being closest to what I needed, but I will admit that I took some liberties with the symptoms. For that reason, it is never stated outright which plant was used by Mary Manning and Harrison.

I will also admit to a special fondness for the waltz, which in 1806 was still several years from being accepted by British society. I have taken creative liberties by including it here. As always, any mistakes or inaccuracies in the story are my own.

If you'd like to learn more about my books, please visit my website at http://www.suzannamedeiros.com. To learn when I have a new release coming, you can sign up for my newsletter at http://eepurl.com/nmliD.

Suzanna

Beguiling the Earl—book 2 in the Landing a Lord series—will be released in summer 2013.

Turn the page to read a preview of *Lady Hathaway's Indecent Proposal*—book 1 in the Hathaway Heirs series—which will be released in spring 2013.

Lady Hathaway's Indecent Proposal—EXCERPT

Andrew Osborne, the Earl of Sanderson, thought he'd gotten Miranda Hathaway out of his blood years ago. Yet here he was, following her butler into the drawing room of her London townhouse.

He told himself it was only curiosity that had led him to accept her request for a meeting. They hadn't seen one another in twelve years, so why on earth would she ask to see him now?

He took in the room's luxurious furnishings as the butler bowed and left to fetch his mistress. Viscount Hathaway had always made a point of displaying his vast wealth at every opportunity, as was evidenced by the amount of gilt in the room. He wondered if Miranda approved of the decor, or if she, too, found it lacking in taste. The old Miranda would have believed the latter. Or so he'd thought at the time, but that was before she'd broken it off with him to marry the much wealthier older man.

Unease settled in the pit of his stomach, and annoyed at

the sign of weakness, he moved to the window and looked out onto the fashionable Mayfair street. It was early for a social call and the road was quiet. No doubt, most of Miranda's neighbors were still abed, recovering from whatever entertainments had kept them up the evening before. He would have been sleeping as well if Miranda's message hadn't arrived last night before he'd left for his club.

He resisted the urge to turn around and leave, just as she had done that last time they'd seen one another. Once again, he was at a disadvantage with her. In her house, at her summoning, no knowledge of what this meeting was about. He was not, however, the same untried youth he'd been back then. If Miranda assumed so, she would be surprised.

He sensed her approach and turned in time to see her enter the room. He couldn't help but notice that she still moved with the same grace she'd possessed as a young woman, setting the Ton ablaze during her first Season with her beauty and unaffected charm. It had been inevitable that she'd captured his interest as well.

That was a lifetime ago.

"My lord," she said, executing a fluid curtsey. Her expression gave away no hint as to why she had sent for him.

He inclined his head in acknowledgement and watched in silence as she sat on one end of the ornate settee. A chair was positioned at an angle from her and it was clear she expected him to use it.

A need to ruffle her impassive bearing had him remaining silent and ignoring the chair. He moved past her and sat, instead, beside her on the settee. He left a respectable distance between them, but the way she stiffened told him she hadn't expected him to sit so close. It was self-indulgent, but he felt a small measure of triumph at her discomfort.

He watched, more than a little surprised, as she collected herself, smoothing away all signs of discomfort. Her body relaxed, her expression becoming one of polite cordiality as she held herself with an almost unnatural stillness. It appeared that Miranda Hathaway had learned to control the youthful exuberance she'd once possessed. He wasn't sure whether to applaud her for her newfound reserve, or mourn the loss of that vibrant, impetuous young woman.

Silence stretched between them for several seconds before she turned to face him. He was struck once again, as he had been all those years ago, by her beauty. Her dark brown hair and the unrelieved black of her dress called attention to her pale coloring, making it seem as though she were carved from ivory. Her grey eyes were larger than he remembered, but she was also much thinner than when he'd known her. Almost painfully so. He wanted to ask if she was well, but resisted the impulse. He had no desire to hear about how much she mourned the loss of her husband, whose funeral had been held only the week before.

The only things about her that were still full were the curve of her breasts and her unfashionably plump mouth. His eyes flickered downward and he remembered with unexpected vividness just how those full lips had felt under his. He'd been with many other women over the years, but he'd never enjoyed kissing anyone as much as Miranda. Thoughts of how she could put that mouth to another use sent a wave of unwelcome heat through him.

He'd miscalculated. He'd wanted to set Miranda off balance, but being this close to her was having an unwanted effect on him.

"Thank you for accepting my invitation," she said, cutting through the uncomfortable silence. "I know it is early, but I can ring for tea if you haven't yet eaten."

His wayward thoughts under control, he met her impassive gaze with one of his own. "I think we can dispense with the niceties. We both know this isn't a social call."

Those luscious lips tilted ever so slightly at the corners. "I see you are still as direct as always."

"And I can see you've taken to hiding behind social conventions. You were never one to dance around a subject. You asked me to visit, and despite my reservations I came. You clearly have something you wish to discuss with me."

He was surprised when she stood.

"This was a mistake," she said, taking a step toward the doorway. "Forgive me for inconveniencing you."

After a brief moment of hesitation, he rose from the settee and moved to block her path. She stopped, but kept her eyes down.

"Miranda."

She didn't move. Against his better judgment, he placed a hand under her chin and tilted her face up to his. They stood that way for several long moments during which he was painfully aware of the small woman before him. The woman who, he now knew, still had the power to cause him discomfort.

He dropped his hand and kept his voice low, sensing

she was a hairsbreadth away from bolting from the room. "Why did you wish to see me?"

ABOUT THE AUTHOR

Suzanna Medeiros was born and raised in Toronto, Canada. Her love for the written word led her to pursue a degree in English Literature from the University of Toronto. She went on to earn a Bachelor of Education degree, but graduated at a time when no teaching jobs were available. After working at a number of interesting places, including a federal inquiry, a youth probation office, and the Office of the Fire Marshal of Ontario, she decided to pursue her first love—writing.

Suzanna is married to her personal hero and is the proud mother of twin daughters. She is an avowed romantic who enjoys spending her days writing love stories.

She would like to thank her parents for showing her that love at first sight and happily ever after really do exist.

Made in the USA
Coppell, TX
03 April 2023